THE WORKHOUSE CHRISTMAS ANGEL

ANNIE SHIELDS

PROLOGUE

She knew death.
She'd seen it many times in her life.

Lilac irises stared up at her from the foot of the stairs. Staring into the abyss that many feared, yet one that she knew there was no escape from when the time came. No more sparkle. The light that once filled them was gone forever.

Death could be many things.

Painful. Peaceful.

A release. A pity.

It was always final.

Addy didn't cry. She knew it was pointless. The dead couldn't console your tears. They didn't know the pain that their loss left behind.

The scent of lavender perfume lingered in the air. Behind her, the tall grandfather clock chimed the late hour. The stained-glass panel in the tall window scattered a kaleidoscope of colours across the parquet floor of the foyer, illuminated by the soft light of the muted winter's day.

She crouched down and laid her hand gently along the woman's cheek.

Cold to the touch. Yet still soft as a feather.

Addy sighed. "I'm sorry," she whispered, even though she knew that the dead couldn't hear her.

She knew that life would carry on, long after you died.

It was just the way it went.

Addy heard the clunk of the salon door closing down the hallway, followed by the click of approaching footsteps. She turned in time to see the flicker of surprise give way to one of horror. How her mouth parted as though she couldn't quite believe her eyes.

Addy tried to think of something to say, something appropriate that would ease the burden of loss. Words that she'd never heard when she'd stared death in the face the first time.

But the shock of silence broke when the mouth opened and screamed. The scream wasn't one of loss.

It was terror. Fury.

The accusing finger pointed at Addy. Addy shook her head, raising her hands to explain.

Panic spread through her as the accusation rang clear:

"Murderer! Call the constable! Addy Hill is a murderer!

CHAPTER 1

Archie Hill softly closed the book and ran his hand over the leather-bound cover of *The Labors of Heracles*. "Well, what did you think of that one?"

Addy scrunched up her nose, wide green eyes fixed on her father as she considered his question.

"I think," she began slowly, her brow furrowed, "I think I should never fall in love."

Her father chuckled and set the book on the small table beside her bed. He removed his spectacles, amusement shining in his eyes as he folded them and held them loosely in his hand. "My darling girl," he leaned forward, elbows on his knees, "why would you not want to fall in love? I love your mother very deeply. And if it wasn't for your mama and I loving each other, we wouldn't have you now, would we?"

"Because," she said, "all the stories we read end in tragedy. Orpheus descended into the Underworld to retrieve Eurydice. It was his love that made him look back, and he lost her forever. Ariadne was abandoned by Theseus. Even that other poor girl loved the Minotaur. And now, Hercules has lost his family. Love leads to heartbreak, Papa. Heartbreak leads to sadness. If I never fall in love, then I will never be sad."

"Addy, sometimes I think you are too clever for your own good," His gentle sigh was more amused than frustrated. He held the edge of her blanket, and Addy snuggled deeper into her bed, burrowing into the warmth as he pulled the woollen blanket up around her shoulders. "I want you to read these stories because they are classics. I told you that education is very important. It has brought many opportunities to my life, and I always promised myself that if I was ever blessed with any children, then I would ensure that they had every chance at one, too."

"I know, Papa," Addy nodded quickly. She had seen the young girls and boys who scrambled over the clattering cotton looms up at Whitehurst Mill each day, their small hands busy with the work their families depended on. She knew their parents couldn't afford the luxury of education beyond what little they picked up during the few hours at Sunday School. Meanwhile, Marjorie Lowther, whose father owned the land her father managed, had a Governess to teach her French, music, and the art of proper deportment.

"My darling, your wonderful mind works in the most mysterious ways. But if these tales are upsetting you, perhaps we should leave them until you are a little older?"

Addy elbowed up off her bed, dislodging the blankets. Ignoring the chilled air stealing over her nightgown, she grabbed his hand imploringly, "Please, Papa. I don't want you to stop."

He placed his spectacles on top of the heavy-bound

book and reached across to brush her auburn hair from her forehead. "Love is not always a tragedy. Hercules was given a series of challenges, yes, but he met each one. He overcame them. Each of these stories can be taken as a lesson, my darling.

"Life can be challenging, and very often, things come our way that we are not always prepared for. These trials teach you to find your way through them. Hercules met each of his with strength... and cunning... He had resilience."

Addy rolled the unfamiliar word around in her mouth, sounding it out carefully. She tucked the word away, safe in the vault of her mind where all the new words her father taught her lived.

His smile softened as he kissed her cheek. "One must always be strong when life gets hard. We cannot give up, even when things seem dark and difficult. And love takes courage, more often than not.

"Sometimes, love can feel scary, but it can also be the best feeling in the world," he stroked her cheek, an indulgent smile moving over his mouth. "I love you," he said.

"Of course, you do," Addy shrugged with confidence and conviction. "You are my Papa, and you have to love me."

Her father chuckled then, the sound rolling around in his deep chest. The laughter rumbled into a cough. Amusement danced in his eyes even as he stifled the cough into the crook of his elbow.

Addy knew her Mama worried about this cough, too. She'd heard the two of them speaking when they thought she was distracted with her books. His cough followed him daily and always grew worse when the weather grew cold.

Addy was warm in her bed, yet she could see where the winter's breath had spun icy patterns across her bedroom window like delicate lace. Last winter, her father had taken to his bed for three days with a cough, too sick to work.

Her father wiped his mouth on his handkerchief, folding the cotton into his hand as he offered a smile. "You have such a worried look in your eye, little one."

"Because the winter is coming, and Mama says that it always goes straight to your chest. You've been coughing a lot for days now, Papa."

"I'm fine, darling."

Addy shook her head. "Do you have to go to work?"

"It's just a cough, Addy," he told her reassuringly. He tucked her back in. "And Mr Lowther is a kind employer. I have a fuel allowance and a stove in my office. It will be just as toasty in my office tomorrow as it is in this bedroom."

Addy wasn't entirely convinced. Her father, serving as the land agent for the enormous Lowther estate, was responsible for overseeing the extensive acreage and sprawling farm buildings and the full management of the estate. This included the hiring and dismissal of workers, resolving disputes among tenant farmers who worked the lands, supervising the harvest and livestock, collecting rents, and maintaining the estate's financial records.

A splendid job indeed but it meant he was often outdoors, administering everything in all seasons, sometimes for hours on end. Whenever she accompanied him on his rounds, she was always bundled tightly into her red woollen coat and a thick muffler, the cold biting at her cheeks. But no matter how frigid the air or how long the day, she knew how much her father loved his work.

He took pride in his role, and Addy loved to see the gleam of satisfaction in his eyes when he told her the stories about how he'd started his working life. In the early days, he was a junior copyist in a factory office in the bustling city of Liverpool. From there, he had worked tirelessly, earning the trust of Mr Chester Lowther, who first employed him as a clerk and accountant. Now, overseeing the grand estate felt like a reward for his years of dedication to the Lowther family.

"It's bedtime now." The candlelight flickered as her father collected up the candleholder, the flame casting shadows around the soft cream walls of her bedroom.

Her father pressed a kiss to her temple. "Sleep, my beautiful girl. Tomorrow is another day full of possibilities."

"Good night, papa," she whispered. She listened to her father's footsteps retreating along the corridor and down the stairs.

She could see where the silver moon hung in the sky from her bed, casting its soft silver light across the bedroom floor. Nights like this meant that the frost would be hard. Soon, the promised snow would bring along winter and its cruel grip.

Many children looked forward to the snow. They could ice skate on the river and sledge down the many hillocks in the surrounding countryside. But for Addy, she dreaded it. Her father always struggled with the cold.

Addy closed her eyes and prayed that winter would pass by quickly.

CHAPTER 2

The Hill residence, named Lowther House, was situated at the edge of the village of Whitehurst. The charming Georgian home had a symmetrical façade and tall sash windows, the stone and stucco exterior softened by ivy that climbed gracefully along its clean lines. Though not as imposing as the grand Lowther Manor, the house still carried an air of understated sophistication.

Nestled near the edge of a thicket, the Lowther House boasted a small brook that meandered through the walled garden. It was far enough away from the cotton mill that, unless the wind was blowing in the right direction, you couldn't hear the thundering of the looms that hammered day and night.

A gravel path wound through a stone arch to the understated entrance. Inside, the house reflected the Hill family's modest prosperity. High ceilings crowned wide, airy rooms, and gilt-framed paintings depicting pastoral scenes dotted the foyer walls. A grand oak staircase with polished twisted balusters flowed elegantly to the first-floor landing, where the family's bedrooms were situated. Higher still, on the attic floor, was the servant's quarters.

The house often hosted lively gatherings. The dining room would be filled with tenant farmers, mill managers, and occasionally even Mr Lowther himself, who would sit around the long mahogany dining table, talking all things business. Addy loved those evenings when the house was alive, and extra servants were drafted in to help keep the elaborate feasts running smoothly.

The household was made up of a small but efficient staff. The cook ruled the kitchen with an iron hand and prepared everything from simple suppers to lavish banquets. Two maids helped manage the household chores. The newly appointed maid, Mary, had just begun her duties and was steadily finding her feet under the watchful eye of Mrs Kemp, the housekeeper. The other maid, Millie, assisted her mother with dressing and daily duties. There was also a manservant, a stern-faced man named Dover, who attended to her father's needs, travelling with him when needed. Outside, a gardener tended to the grounds as part of the Lowther estate. He kept the flowerbeds neat and the lawns immaculate throughout the seasons.

Most days, Addy was left to occupy herself. She would read or complete the lessons set out by her father. These never took her long to do.

She liked Sunday's best, mostly because her father stayed home. After church, they would all play card games or read in the parlour. The house seemed brighter on days her father was there.

Addy disliked days like this when the rain cascaded down in sheets. On days like this, her mother strictly forbade her from leaving the house. Perhaps Mary had taken pity on her, but whatever the reason, Addy was thrilled when the young maid finally relented and accepted her offer to help.

Addy concentrated very hard on following Mary's instructions to the letter. As carefully as she could, she scooped up the ashes and transferred them into the scuttle bucket on the edge of the hearth. Slowly, she tipped the small fireplace shovel so that the ashes poured into the bucket, making a small, grey puff as they dropped to the bottom. She beamed up at Mary, who carefully watched her.

At thirteen years old, Mary was only two years older than Addy was, yet she seemed much more worldly. Addy was already in awe of her. "Did I do it right?" Addy asked her hopefully.

Mary gave her a quick nod and glanced nervously over her shoulder. "You did, but I ought to finish it now. It is my job, after all. Your Ma won't like it."

Addy shook her head quickly and plunged the tiny shovel back into the hearth, scooping up another heap of chalky ashes. "I don't mind helping you. As my papa always says, many hands make light work."

Addy was aware of Mary fidgeting at her shoulder. She shovelled another load of ashes into the scuttle bucket and smiled up at their new maid. "You can carry on with what else you were meant to do. The quicker you are done in here, the quicker you can rest."

With a half-shrug, Mary picked up the small duster and cloth by her feet and swiped the duster across the dark wooden sideboard. "Not much chance of a rest,

THE WORKHOUSE CHRISTMAS ANGEL

Miss. I still have to do upstairs. Cook needs a hand washing the pots, too."

Mary had started her working life as a scullery maid in a grand house. Addy had listened, fascinated, as Mary had told her how she had been part of a large staff, complete with maids and footmen, hall boys and boot boys, all overseen by a very stern butler. Now, in this small household, she was expected to perform all the tasks she once shared with many others. Addy got the feeling that Mary didn't like having to do so much work by herself.

Her father had left managing the household staff to her mother. Her mother had given Mary the job because she'd arrived with excellent references and knew the area. Addy hoped that Mary liked working here because she liked having another young girl in the house.

She began sweeping the hearth with a short, stubby brush, taking great care not to drop anything on the carpet. She wanted to do a very good job. With her tongue clamped between her teeth, she was just adding the last remnants of the previous night's fire to the scuttle bucket when her mother burst into the sitting room.

"Adelaide!"

Addy jolted, then emitted a small gasp of alarm when ash shot over the hearth and onto the oriental rug in front of the fire.

"What on earth are you doing?" her mother demanded, furious. "Get out of that hearth this instant!"

Addy looked in dismay at the mess she'd made. Even her dress was covered. She tried to sweep it away but smeared it, making more of a mess.

Her mother turned to Mary, demanding, "Is this what I'm paying you for, girl? To make my daughter do your job?"

"I'm s-sorry, Mrs Hill," Mary began.

"It's not Mary's fault!" Addy tried to defend the blushing maid, but her mother's iron grip closed around her arm, hauling her upright with a force that took Addy by surprise.

"You are *not* a servant," Mrs Hill snapped. "You are a young lady from a respectable house. You do not belong on your knees, grubbing around in the ashes like some muckmiser!"

"P–please, Miss," Mary stammered, "I didn't—"

But Mrs Hill cut her off with a dismissive wave, her sharp gaze fixed on Addy as she marched her daughter across the floor.

Addy winced as her mother's grip tightened. "Mama, I was only trying to help," Addy explained as she glanced back at Mary. "She's been working so hard today, and with your lunch guests arriving soon—"

Her mother was in no mood for excuses. She glared at Mary from the threshold, her voice as cold as the rain that lashed the windows. "Get on with your duties! And stop trying to shirk your tasks by using my daughter as an excuse. I won't tolerate laziness in this house."

Mary's eyes dropped to the floor, her cheeks burning with humiliation. Addy wished Mary would look up to see the apology on her face, but the young girl whirled, her hands moving quickly as if trying to make up for lost time.

The door closed and her mother marched her up the staircase to her bedroom.

"You are not to involve yourself in the work of the servants. How many more times must I tell you?"

"Yes, Mama," Addy whispered, though her heart rebelled against the words. She didn't understand—she didn't see why it was so wrong to help, to be kind.

She stood in the centre of her bedroom as her mother flung open her wardrobe doors and quickly began to flick through the array of pretty dresses.

"Take that dress off at once, Addy."

Addy knew better than to argue with her mother. She adored her mother, truly, but she had learned that when her father was absent, her mother's temper could flare without warning.

Miserably, Addy did as she was told. Her dress was ruined. Her carelessness had caused more work for Mary, and now the maid was upset with her, too. Her bedroom was cold. Poor Mary had not yet reached the upper floors to stoke the fires.

Gooseflesh raced over her skin as her mother berated her. "I don't have time for this nonsense, Addy. Why do you always insist on interacting with these people?"

She tried to stem the shivering. Complaining about the cold room would be pointless and only cause more trouble for Mary.

"Helping the maid is not your place," her mother remarked as she pulled out a green dress and shook it, inspecting it. "You'll have to wear this one. The ladies have seen you in it before and now, they'll think there's something wrong with us."

Addy kept her head down, compliant as her mother instructed her into the dress. Her mother tightened the satin bow a little too tightly, but Addy remained stoic.

Her mother turned her, levelling her eyes with Addy's. "What were you thinking? Are you determined to have people think less of us?"

Addy blinked against the tears that stung the back of her eyes. "No, mama," she whispered. "I just thought that perhaps I should know how to do these things in case I ever have to do them."

"Stuff and nonsense," her mother retorted, lips pressed into a thin line, disapproval radiating from every inch of her. "You are not to do the work of a servant."

Her mother guided her to the chair next to the miniature dressing table and positioned her just so. Addy sat still as her mother brushed her hair roughly, weaving a green ribbon that matched the colour of her dress into her auburn curls. Addy looked away from her tearful reflection in the mirror.

Henrietta Hill sighed. "Addy, look at me."

Addy complied. In the large wooden-framed mirror, their reflections were side by side—so alike, yet different in many ways. Same rich auburn hair, though Addy's eyes were green like her father's.

Her mother's expression softened slightly. "One day, you'll marry a good man. He'll be handsome and wealthy. You'll oversee a magnificent house of your own, I've no doubt. Your husband will keep you so there really is no need for you to learn household tasks, other than ensuring the housekeeper isn't ripping you off." She speared her daughter's reflection with a look. "You must learn to always hold yourself above these people."

Addy knew all too well the future her mother envisioned for her.

It was a life of fine dresses, social calls, and securing a good marriage—one that would raise their family's status. One where she would never have to lift a finger in toil. But often, Addy felt that she didn't quite fit into the world her mother carefully planned for her.

Addy knew she was better off than many of the families in the village. She'd read the newspapers. She'd listened to the stories spread in the churchyard after the service on a Sunday morning. Her father's position as land steward afforded them a modest but respectable life. She had never known hunger or hardship. Through her father's good work, they were comfortable.

Her father had told her all about the indentured children she saw trudging daily between the mill and the apprentice's house, their clogs clomping against the cobbled lane. But neither did the Hill family enjoy the privileges of the very wealthy, like the Lowther's.

Addy listened rapturously to the stories that Majorie Lowther told. Her father entertained all kinds of people, often from exotic places in far-off lands. Watching her mother, she wondered now if Henrietta Hill resented the life her father worked hard for.

Addy sometimes felt like she was stuck somewhere between the two worlds—one of privilege, where she was expected to live up to her mother's ambitions, and another of woe she could glimpse through the mill windows.

Her mother stepped back and admired her daughter's image, the worst of her temper assuaged as she gave a nod of satisfaction. "That's better. Now, you sit in here and do not move until everyone has arrived."

"Yes, Mama."

Her mother swept from the room, and Addy could hear the strained tone of her voice as she scolded Mary through the floorboards below. Addy sighed, knowing Mary would never allow her to help again.

CHAPTER 3

To stay clean as she waited for her mother's visitors to arrive, Addy sat cross-legged in the window nook, a book spread out in her lap.

The rain had passed, leaving behind a dank, grey day. Mists clung to the trees and puddled in the fields and dips of the rolling land. Across the treetops, she could just about make out the ornate rooftop of Lowther house and, next to it, the tall black chimney stack of the mill before it disappeared into the low cloud.

Addy watched as the shiny carriages began to pull up outside their house. Just as expected, she dutifully walked down the stairs. She sat in the corner, back straight and her hands tucked in her lap, as the conversation moved around her.

Dresses...who was marrying whom...local gossip...

If this was the life her mother envisioned for her, she wasn't sure that she wanted it.

Addy longed for something more, something with

purpose—though what exactly that was, she couldn't yet put into words.

Her mother seemed pleased with her behaviour, and Addy hoped that it meant she was forgiven for her carelessness that morning.

The afternoon stretched on with polite conversation and empty smiles, and as soon as the last of their visitors left, her mother declared that she was going for a lie-down. Addy quickly swapped her shiny shoes for her older boots. She slung her shawl over her shoulders and darted out the back door.

There was a biting chill to the damp afternoon. She took the direct route to the manor house, trotting along the narrow lane that was hemmed in on either side by tall hedgerows. Red and white colours of hawthorn and holly berries popped against the deep green.

The closer she got to the manor house, the louder the rumble of the cotton mill became. The incessant clatter ran for sixteen hours a day, six days a week. At this time of the year, when the river levels ran low, the steam-powered engine pumped water to drive the looms. Mill workers unloaded cotton bales from a dray. She hurried past them.

Through the orchard, ducking under the arbour and weaving her way through the stable yard. Horses crunched on their hay, watching her with interest as she skipped across the yard and under the ivy-covered arch. Thick fog almost swallowed the russet-coloured stone house, but Addy had taken the route so often she could have made it in the dark as sure-footed as a goat on a mountainside.

Without knocking, she opened the door to the

servant's entrance and was immediately enveloped with the warmth of the house. The tantalising smell of roasted meats and fresh bread scented the air.

Addy paused in the kitchen. The room buzzed with efficiency. Kitchen maids and the undercook quick-stepped around each other as the cook barked out her instructions. Steam billowed from the pans on the range. Copper pots and jugs hung from the walls. To Addy, it seemed chaotic, yet there was a synchronicity to it all.

Cook, a rotund woman with rosy cheeks and a permanent frown, beckoned at Addy and pointed to the chair in the corner. She sent the woman a grateful smile when she spotted the plate of biscuits on the tabletop waiting next to a glass of milk.

She clambered up onto the chair, mindful to stay out of the way of everyone as they worked. Cook's tongue was almost as sharp as her mother's.

Down here in the servants' quarters, Addy felt more at ease than she ever did in the grand, echoing rooms above. The house seemed too large to her and was filled with many exotic trinkets from around the world, all collected by Mr Lowther and his relatives.

She bit into the buttery biscuit and washed it down with a gulp of fresh milk. Feet swinging, she was just finishing her snack when Miss Fisher, Marjorie's governess, swept into the kitchen.

"You're early," the woman snapped out, her face pinched in distaste.

"Y-yes, Miss Fisher." Addy had never quite understood why the governess disliked her so, but the woman's icy demeanour always made her skin prickle.

"Miss Marjorie is waiting for you upstairs," the

governess said tersely. Her eyes darted to the biscuit crumbs on the floor, her lips tightening in disapproval. "Mind you don't make any more mess than you already have," she shook a finger at Addy, then pointed down the hall. "And take the back stairs. Quickly, now."

Her words snapped like a whip, and Addy felt the heat rush to her cheeks. She slipped from the chair, head down, and hurried past the glaring woman. Up the narrow steps, past the second footman who gave her a cheery hello, to the second floor.

Marjorie waited for her in her playroom, which had once been a nursery. Expensive toys were scattered across the floor.

Marjorie greeted her friend as soon as she spotted her in the doorway. "Addy, come! Look what Uncle Peter fetched from Africa for me!"

She held aloft a beautiful doll, dressed in the finest silk. Carefully, Addy picked her way across the floor, stepping over wooden toy soldiers and a gleaming train set that had derailed from its brass track.

Addy admired the doll, running her fingers over the surface of its painted cheek.

Marjorie shrugged, the novelty already forgotten as she turned towards the tea set that had been laid out on the carpet for them. "Let's sit and have tea together," she giggled. For Marjorie, these toys were just another part of her life, ordinary and almost expected. Addy wondered if Marjorie ever considered the children who toiled endlessly in her father's factory. But she didn't mention this because Addy didn't have many friends, and she didn't want to upset Marjorie.

The two girls played together. Addy would have much rather explored the library that she knew was downstairs but instead, she pretended to drink tea and eat biscuits.

Before too long, the strict governess was in the doorway, ordering Addy to go home. The time had passed quickly, as it always did.

"Thank you for having me," she said politely to Marjorie.

"Of course," Marjorie replied. "I hope to see you again tomorrow."

The governess shooed her out, closing the door in her face. Addy grinned her thanks at Cook when the woman gave her two more butter biscuits for her walk home.

Daylight waned, chilling the air further. The bell at the mill tolled, signalling the end of another long, gruelling day for the mill workers. It also meant that her father would soon be home, too. Addy stuffed the last chunk of biscuit into her mouth and checked her shawl for telltale crumbs. She didn't want to get into trouble for eating between her meals. Ahead, Lowther House glowed in the darkness, and she ran the last few steps home. She let herself into the kitchen, saddened when Mary turned her back to her.

"The bell has just rung," she said into the room.

Mary ignored her; Cook indicated that she ought to hurry. Sure enough, her mother was waiting upstairs.

"Addy, it's dark," Henrietta looked up from her embroidery.

"Yes, Mama."

"Did that cook feed you again?"

Addy was saved from lying outright when her father called out a jolly hello from the front door. He was handing his scarf and hat to Dover when Addy barrelled into the hallway, straight into her father's waiting arms.

"Ah, there's my girl," Archie scooped her up. "Did you see Marjorie today?"

"Yes," Addy said. "She has a new dolly. Her uncle brought it for her from Africa."

"Golly," he carried her into the dining room, "I bet that was very beautiful."

"I helped Marjorie name her. We chose Dinah."

"Goodness, how unusual," he smiled at Henrietta, "Hello, darling."

"Archie set her down at once," her mother chided. "Not only has she been grubbing about in the fire ashes today, but she was out after dark despite my repeated requests for her to be home on time."

Addy shot a quick look at her father's face and caught the weary expression as he looked down at his daughter. "Henrietta…"

"No, Archie, I am trying to raise a proper lady. You indulge the girl, and she rides roughshod over everyone in this house."

Her father gazed down at Addy.

Addy held the look quietly.

"Why were you in the fire ashes?"

"Helping Mary," Addy admitted.

Archie's tired sigh conveyed just how exhausted he felt. "Henrietta, she meant nothing by it. And she's been up to the manor every day for more than a year. I'm more concerned with whether she completed the schooling I set for her."

Henrietta looked to be working up a full head of steam when Dover opened the door and announced that supper was ready.

Archie gave Addy a quick wink. "Come on. Let's go

one through. You can tell me more about this new dolly and then we should talk about what book we're going to read tonight."

Addy didn't dare look back at her mother. She knew that her father siding with Addy would be met with her mother's wrath away from his eyes. But, for now, that was tomorrow's problem.

CHAPTER 4

Winter had clamped its icy jaws on the land, and the world around the cottage slowed to a crawl. A thick blanket of snow layered the land, muffling every sound and slowing every step.

For Addy, the days dragged. The sun rose later and vanished earlier. Barely any light filtered through the thick frost that clung to the windowpanes. Snow piled high in the lanes, making it nearly impossible for visitors to call. She wasn't allowed to go to the big house, even though she could make the trip with her eyes closed.

It became so that she would almost welcome one of her mother's aloof visitors if only to break up the monotony of the days. Other than reading and practising her letters, Addy had nothing to do. She didn't even have Mary to converse with. The young maid now treated Addy with a coolness that rivalled the white world beyond the front door. Addy had tried to apologise, and the words had been accepted, yet Mary remained distant, barely meeting her eyes.

It wasn't just Mary.

Even her father was irritable and gruff. He coughed long into the night, and Addy would swear he was getting sicklier. Her parents waved off her concerns and sent her to her room.

The long nights were the worst. She lay in bed listening to the harsh, rattling cough that often left him gasping for breath, and even when it subsided, there was still a shallow wheeze whenever he sat quietly. His face, once rosy and jovial, had taken on a pale, sallow hue. Dark shadows circled his eyes, and his dapper suits hung from his frame.

Addy knew something was wrong the day her father didn't go to work.

When it had happened the winter before, they had all rallied around him, fetching hot water and soup to see him through the darkest of the winter days. But this time was different. This time, her mother was worried, the strain in her tone evident as she dispatched Mary to fetch the doctor from the village.

Addy waited in the hallway outside her father's room. "What's wrong with Papa?"

"Not now, Addy," her mother waved her away and hurried down the back stairs to the kitchen. From the upstairs window, Addy spotted Mary wading through the deep snowdrifts, bundled up in a shawl and a bonnet.

The doctor arrived, his neat little spectacles perched on the end of his nose, catching the pale light of the winter morning. He was tall and slender, with a calming manner and a reassuring smile. He fetched tonics meant to soothe the cough. Tinctures to rub on Archie's chest. She heard the comforting assurances he gave. But none of his medicines seemed to make a difference.

However, the haunted look in her mother's eyes deepened Addy's fears.

Addy did everything that was asked of her. She fetched and carried items to the bedrooms. She ate the food that Cook set down on the table. She coaxed her mother to do the same.

She helped her mother tend to her father's every need, but it seemed to Addy that every time she entered the stuffy room where her father lay, he'd worsened.

He lay in the bed, propped up by pillows, his breathing raspy and shallow. His body was bruised with exhaustion. The violent coughing fits wrecked his chest, and to Addy, it sounded as if something was breaking apart inside him. A sickly smell lingered in the air, and Addy knew she would never be able to forget it.

She dipped and wrung the cloth out, laid it across her father's clammy brow. "Mama, will Papa be alright?"

Her mother was sitting in a chair next to the fire. Tears had clumped her lashes into wet spikes around her eyes. Her face was pinched and tense, her fingers ringing tightly in the fabric of her apron. "Addy, you shouldn't be in here. Go downstairs and stay out of the way."

Addy sighed softly, doing as her mother asked.

She left the room, pausing only when she met the doctor walking up the staircase.

His usual calm smile was in place. "Hello, Addy."

Summoning her courage, she interrupted him as he

passed by her. "Please, sir," she asked, her voice choked with emotion, "will my Papa be alright?"

The doctor's tepid smile didn't alter. "Young lady, it isn't for you to worry about such matters."

Addy grabbed hold of his sleeve as he brushed past her, her eyes imploring. "I'm old enough to know. I've read about death. And I have ears, sir. I hear the words that are said around me. Consumption, that's what he has, isn't it?" Her voice trailed off to a harsh whisper.

The doctor patted her head. "He's a strong man, Addy. All you can do is carry on as you are. Do as you're told and pray for him." He continued up the stairs, and Addy watched his progress across the landing.

So, Addy prayed.

Morning, noon and bedtime. She squeezed her eyes tight shut and pleaded with her Heavenly Father that her dearest papa would open his eyes once more, that he would laugh with her, tell her a story, ruffle her hair, and give her a kiss goodnight.

But her father never left his bed. That awful cough filled the house. It permeated the walls in the small hours. The servants grew more and more stilted as the house itself seemed to wait for a miracle.

Then one night, when the moon was full and casting its silvery fingers of pale light far across the frozen land, it seemed that Addy finally had an answer to her question.

She woke to a deep, unsettling quiet.

She slid from her bed, the chilled air nipping at her fingers and toes as she padded along the landing. The door to her father's room was slightly ajar. Through the crack, she could see her mother kneeling at the bedside.

The fire had died down to glowing embers, its strange red glow casting shadows around the walls. Her mother's cheeks shone wet with tears in the low light.

Addy held her breath in the doorway as she listened for the next cough or the familiar shallow wheeze of her father's breathing.

But it didn't come.

There were only her mother's soft snuffles that tore through the stillness. That sound alone ripped her heart from her chest. Heedless, she erupted through the door and flung herself onto her father's bed. She begged, and she pleaded, and she promised to be good, if only her father would cough once more.

There was only silence.

"Addy, stop that at once," her mother used the heels of her hands to wipe her face. She dragged her wailing daughter off the lifeless form of her husband and set the child away from her as she sternly said, "He's gone."

Addy shook her head, refusing to think of such a thing.

Her mother shook her hard, her voice flat and devoid of any emotion. "He's gone. Dead. Do you understand?"

Addy's eyes moved from her father's slack face to her mother's unyielding expression.

As if moving mechanically, her mother draped a black cloth over the mirror on the sideboard. "We are all alone now."

Silent tears streaming down her face, Addy could only stare at her father's still form.

He would never laugh again. He would never read her a story. He would never sweep her up into a hug and dance around the parlour when her mother wasn't looking.

"Come now," her mother started from the room. "I have to wake the servants and send for the doctor."

"But why?" Addy whispered. "Why does he need a doctor? There is no tonic for this."

"Because even in death there are things that we must do, Adelaide. And screaming and raving at the futility of it all will not help."

When Addy didn't move, her mother clamped a hand around her arm and propelled her from the room, closing off the room. "Go to your room, Adelaide. Do not come out from there until it is light." She gave her daughter a little shove along the landing.

Her mother glided down the stairs, ever the socialite, even in her bedcap and nightgown.

The next morning, the house felt strained and quiet, as if all the life had been drained from it. Addy waited, watching as the pink dawn streaked the sky. A fresh layer of snow glistened like diamonds, burnished by the morning light.

It felt cruel that the world could appear so breathtakingly beautiful while she was drowning in despair. The thought of never hearing her father's voice again didn't seem real. For him, there would be no more sunrises.

Church bells tolled, the charming sound rolling across the crisp white landscape. The sound of chatter and movement below her bedroom window drew Addy's curiosity. The lane in front of the house was full, people wading through the snow drifts, their cheeks reddened against the chill. Laughter and joy filled their ruddy faces.

She hadn't seen a soul along here for weeks. For a moment, Addy was confused. *Why today?*

Her bedroom door opened, and Mary stepped

short. The maid's expression showed how uncomfortable she was in the face of Addy's unbridled grief.

"Good morning, miss," Mary said quietly. She avoided her eyes and kept her head down as she carried the scuttle bucket across the floor to set it down on the hearth.

Addy frowned and turned back to the window. "Why is everybody outside today?"

Mary hesitated before she answered. "Because it's Christmas Day, miss."

CHAPTER 5

Addy hadn't noticed as spring tiptoed across the land.

The days seemed to blur into endless silences and bleak moods, interspersed only by her mother's unpredictable rages that occurred almost daily. Not even when the first green shoots of daffodils and snowdrops peeked through the patches of icy snow did her mother's visitors return.

To Addy, life had lost its colour. There was no clatter of dinner parties. No bursts of joyous laughter from her parents. The lively hum of daily life had been reduced to a quiet, oppressive stillness.

Her mother sank into a despair that permeated everything. And when Addy couldn't even summon up the desire to visit Marjorie, she wondered if she had the same affliction. Neither of them had set foot outside of Lowther House since the day of the funeral. Marjorie had sent for her, but Addy couldn't care a fig about new dollies or conversations about her father's latest travel exploits.

Not when she had nothing to smile about. She hadn't wanted to return to where her dear papa had been laid to rest, either.

She woke most nights in tears, the echoes of her father's laughter drifting away in her dreams. Dressed in mourning black, her mother drifted around the house like an apparition.

The land outside seemed eager to shed its winter coat, and before too long, April rolled around. The sun was out, nudging back the winter days with its warmth. A sharp knock echoed through the subdued house, drawing Addy from her listless staring out the window. She exchanged a puzzled look with Mary, where the girl stood by the fireplace, iron poker in hand.

They waited as Dover answered the door, and the deeply resonant voice of Mr Lowther echoed through the foyer. Moments later, the parlour door swung open, and Mr Lowther stood there.

He was a stout man with a florid face and grey whiskers that sprouted from his jawline. His usual good-humoured smile was absent today, replaced by a solemn expression that Addy was used to seeing. Dressed in green tweed, he handed his cap and cane to Dover. He declined the offer of tea. "Is Mrs Hill home?"

The manservant hesitated. "She is, sir. She is resting in her bedchamber."

Mr Lowther considered this and gave a slight nod. "Perhaps you might rouse her. My visit is urgent."

"She... she might be a while, sir. She hasn't been receiving any guests."

"I understand," Mr Lowther said evenly. "And while I wait, I will have a tray of tea brought in, after all."

"Very well, sir," Dover acknowledged and left the

room. The room was silent save for the ticking of the clock. At some point, Mary had managed to slip from the room, too.

Addy wished she'd had the same foresight as Mary, especially when Mr Lowther turned his attention to her.

"Good morning, Addy," he said.

HER HEART THUMPED against her ribcage. She couldn't remember the last time he'd set foot in Lowther House during the day. When he had, her father had always been present. He usually conducted his business with her father up at the mill or the big house. Dread pooled in her stomach as she realised this unusual occurrence could not bode well.

"HELLO, MR LOWTHER," Addy smiled politely.

"Have you read any good stories lately?"

SHE WISHED right there and then that she could just do what she normally did whenever her mother had visitors: sit quietly in the corner while being studiously ignored. But the landowner seemed determined to hold a conversation with her. She tried her best to answer him, but they quickly ran out of banal subjects to discuss. Mary fetched the tea tray in and quickly set it down, then hurried from the room.

MR LOWTHER HAD FINISHED a second cup of tea when her mother finally arrived in the parlour. He was standing at the fireplace warming his hands and glanced back when she swept into the room.

Her mother had put on her black dress, a widow's symbol of mourning. She smiled, though it didn't quite reach her eyes. Even to Addy, she seemed fragile, as if just a stiff breeze would shatter her into a thousand pieces.

"Good day, Mrs Hill," Mr Lowther said politely, turning to face her. "I'm dreadfully sorry to insist upon seeing you. I understand that this has been a very difficult time for you."

Her mother didn't come any further into the room. Her hands were twisted in front of her, and for the first time in her life, Addy realised that her mother was uncertain. "I haven't been up for visitors," she replied thinly

"Perhaps we can talk away from Miss Addy," Mr Lowther inclined his head towards where Addy stood near the window.

Her mother's eyes were glassy with unshed tears. She dismissed Addy from the room. Reluctantly, Addy did as she was asked but then she lingered at the door, pressing her ear to the crack.

. . .

Mr Lowther cleared his throat. "Mrs Hill, there is no easy way to say this, so I shall just come right out and say it. I've been as patient with you as I can. I know how difficult these past few months have been for you all here. Archie was a good man. The best, in fact. He served me well. That's partly why I've been as patient as I have, out of respect for a dear friend. That said, I'm afraid that my estate cannot remain without a steward."

Addy's chest tightened with premonition as she heard her mother's soft gasp.

A new estate steward?

She couldn't imagine anyone else in her father's place, walking the estate and overseeing tenants. The job had been her father's pride and joy, and it was yet another sign that her father was no longer with them.

Mr Lowther cleared his throat. "I know this is an arduous time for you." There was a pause before he continued, "The new agent is set to begin immediately to continue Archie's good work."

Addy could hear the quiet sniffling of her mother and a further apology from Mr Lowther.
"I've tried to give you time, Mrs Hill. Truly, I have. But the estate simply cannot afford any further delays."

. . .

The sound of her mother's forlorn sniffling was heartbreaking. A muffled exchange continued, too muted for Addy to hear. Whatever it was, it broke her mother's fragile composure. A sudden, doleful howl filled the room; whatever he'd said had sent her mother spiralling.

"*No!* You can't! Please, Mr Lowther," her mother's shrill voice rose, drowning out any words that Mr Lowther was saying.

Addy leaned into the door, her breath catching as she strained to hear more over the sounds of her mother's wailing. She had never heard her mother so hysterical.

The parlour door suddenly swung open. Mr Lowther stood in the doorway, his grim face set with regret and frustration. He drew back when he saw Addy standing there, her wide green eyes staring up at him.

"I wish there was another way, Addy," he said softly. "But I've waited long enough."

He stepped around her, leaving her staring at his retreating back. Dover waited in the doorway, almost as if he expected this sudden departure as he handed over the cane and cap. Mr Lowther left the house without a backward glance. In the resounding silence, Addy looked around at the servants, who had gathered in the hallway. Everyone watched her warily.

WITH A KNOT of alarm tightening in her chest, she turned and crept back to the parlour. She peered around the edge of the door; her mother collapsed onto the sofa; her face buried in her hands.

"MAMA?" Addy whispered, stepping hesitantly into the room. "Mama, what's wrong?"

THE ALARM TURNED her blood icy when her mother raised her head; her face was blotchy and etched with misery. "Lowther House... It came as part of your father's job as the land agent. And now that he's gone, Mr Lowther says that we must leave so the new man can move in here."

"LEAVE?" Addy whispered in horror. "But where would we go?"

HENRIETTA HAD no answer except her pitiful sobs that filled the parlour.

CHAPTER 6

They were leaving.

Addy had waited and prayed for a miracle, but everything had changed in a matter of days. Only Mrs Kemp and the cook were to remain at Lowther House. Mary, Millie, and Dover had all found new positions, scattering to various households and farms.

The house had been packed up around her. Their belongings had been placed into trunks and crates, with much of the furniture needing to be sold. The house they were taking up was smaller. The furniture they could keep was being sent ahead of them to a place that Addy had never seen but already despised.

With a hand pressed against the carriage window, Addy watched Lowther House roll past the glass, keeping her eyes on it for as long as she could.

"Stop crying, Adelaide," Henrietta said brusquely. She sat with a straight back on the bench opposite Addy, her gaze fixed straight ahead.

Addy quickly wiped her cheeks; she hadn't even

realised she was crying. She couldn't understand how her mother could be so detached. They were leaving the only home she had ever known. All those cherished memories of where her father had lived and loved them.

Addy kept her hands in her lap, her gaze downwards as she tried to stem the tears that wanted to burst free. But it was no good. It was where her father had read her stories, where she had played in the garden, danced and laughed, and chased butterflies. All now taken from them because her father was no longer there to protect them.

"Really, Adelaide," her mother muttered tightly, frustration evident in the shake of her head. "Your tears won't change anything, so why cry?"

Addy kept her head bowed.

She'd read about grief—the winding path of how a heart feels after great sorrow. She had never truly understood the stories her father had read to her until now. The ancient tales of gods and mortals, love and tragedies. How Electra had been consumed by a desire for vengeance after the death of her father. Except Addy could not assuage her grief through vengeance. Her father had been taken by a disease that did not discriminate.

Living with her mother these past months, with her violent outbursts and despairing melancholy, had been like watching Niobe, who, in her overwhelming grief after the loss of her offspring, had turned to stone.

Some days, her mother was cold and unfeeling, her face a mask of indifference. Almost as though the moments of happiness she'd had with her husband had been her only reason for smiling. On other days, her only display of emotion was abject rage. The unpredictability fed into the storm of emotions that churned within Addy, where everything was uncertain, and there was nothing left for her to hold onto.

The laden carriage rolled through the village of Whitehurst and out into the countryside. The hills gave way to flat, bleak moors. Gnarly trees and grey stone walls crisscrossed the brown grass. Wherever she looked, Addy could see where the country was trying to shake off the last vestiges of winter.

Onward they rolled.

Soon, the countryside shifted, and the occasional farmhouse became clusters of houses. Clusters become streets. The clear day disappeared behind a smoky veil. Streets became constant, and Addy could just about make out the chimneys and rooftops through the thick clouds of smog that hung low over the city skyline.

The roads were busy, with carriages and wagons filling the wide cobblestone streets. Drays stacked with heavy sacks of goods rumbled along the roads, steered by men, their faces obscured by dark hats pulled down low.

Addy pressed her face against the glass, studying the grimy exterior of the tall buildings. Gulls and birds wheeled in the air. In the distance, she could see the spindly spikes and chimney stacks of boats as they bobbed along the inky ribbon of the River Mersey.

Eventually, they turned down a narrow road. Townhouses crowded in along the pavement. Black gas lamps lined the streets. It was unlike anything she had ever seen before. Not a single patch of greenery was visible as they stepped down from the carriage. The air stank, a mix of acrid smoke and something else —putrid and salty.

The facade of the building they stood in front of was sooty and grim, the windows murky. All around her was busy as carts and wagons trundled over the cobblestones in a never-ending stream of traffic.

"Up you go." Henrietta propelled her up the narrow stone steps as the front door swung open. Behind them, several boys streamed out of a different entrance that Addy could see was below road level. They came to help the driver unload their luggage.

Henrietta greeted the woman who opened the door. "Adelaide, this is Mrs Spearing. She is to be our new staff who will help us settle in here on Fletcher Street," her mother briskly stated as she plucked off her gloves and handed them to the woman.

Mrs Spearing didn't appear much older than her mother. She wore a black uniform with a white apron over it, just as Mary and Millie had worn. Addy smiled politely as the woman swept a fleeting glance over them both.

"Hello, Miss Hill." The woman spoke with a thick accent, one that Addy had heard only from the mill workers. "Not all of the furniture has arrived yet, Mrs Hill," she addressed her mother in her no-nonsense attitude as she hung up the coat that her mother held out to her. "And I am given to understand it may be a day or two. Mr Lowther did his best to make sure–"

"You will refrain from mentioning that man's name in this house," Henrietta stated. "He unhoused my daughter and me, casting us out of the only home we'd ever known."

Addy had spent most of the past week with her ear pressed against one door or another, which had been easy to do as the servants were all occupied with packing up the house. Hushed voices with visitors and tradesmen, not to mention her mother's tense conversations with Mr Lowther himself, all fragments of conversations that had allowed Addy to learn what was to happen to them both.

She now understood that her father had left them a small sum of money to live on. Lowther House had accounted for a substantial portion of her father's income, so Archie's insurance policy had been comparatively modest. As such, Mr Lowther had been instrumental in helping them secure this new home. He even arranged for their luggage to be packed, ensured the servants received their wages, and ensured all their local accounts were settled.

But none of that seemed to matter to her mother.

"Of course, Mrs Hill," Mrs Spearing answered.

"I trust everything else is in order?" her mother asked her, gazing around the ordinary hallway.

Through her eavesdropping, Addy also learned that Mrs Spearing was expected to manage their house, including the cooking and cleaning.

"As much as I could manage in such a short time," Mrs Spearing said. "We've had a few deliveries of food. Perhaps you would care to discuss how we will manage the accounts once you're settled."

Her mother flapped her hand and Addy held her breath, waiting for the explosion of temper, though thankfully it seemed Henrietta was too frazzled. "We'll get to it. First, I must lie down. The rumbling and jolting of that carriage have given me the most wretched headache."

"Would you like me to fetch you some tea?"

"You can, but don't disturb me for an hour. I must rest." Her mother climbed the staircase, leaving Addy alone with a stranger.

"And how about you, miss?" Mrs Spearing asked. "Are you hungry?"

Addy gave a small shake of her head, desperately trying to hold back the tears. "Perhaps you could show me to my room, if it's not too much trouble, Mrs Spearing."

The woman's eyebrows bobbed a little, but she indicated the staircase. Addy followed her up the steep staircase to the first floor. Their footsteps echoed through the empty house.

Mrs Spearing opened the door furthest along the landing, and it swung open with a faint creak. She indicated that Addy should precede her into the room. "Your mother has chosen this room for you."

Addy slowly inspected the room. Dust bunnies gathered in the dim corners. Lacy cobwebs swung from the ceiling. The wallpaper peeled in one corner, revealing a dark patch of dampness that had started to creep down the wall from the window. "It's very nice."

"I can light the fire for you if you wish?"

Addy offered a small smile. "Actually, I know how to light the fire. Our cook taught me how just to stop me from pestering me, I think."

The woman's eyebrows flickered, though her face gave nothing away. "Some tea then? Perhaps something to eat?"

"That would be lovely, thank you," Addy said. Mrs Spearing turned and headed for the door, stopping as Addy called out to her. "Do you know if my books have arrived yet?"

"Just the bare essential furniture so far," she pointed at the small bed tucked against the back corner of the room. "There'll be more to come, plus I hired some local lads to fetch in what you brought with you today."

Addy longed for the comforts of having her familiar things around her; she would have to be patient. "Thank you, Mrs Spearing."

Listening to the echoes of the retreating footsteps as the housekeeper made her way back along the corridor and down the stairs, Addy took her first proper look around her new bed chamber. It was much smaller than she was used to. The bare wooden floorboards were stained and bore signs of wear from previous occupants.

Addy crossed the floor to the window. Instead of rolling hills and the familiar line of trees, she looked down onto an alleyway.

The buildings crowded tightly around the back window, blocking any natural light that might have pierced through the thick fog enveloping the industrial city, leaving the bedroom especially dark and gloomy. Addy could almost reach out and touch the neighbour's brick wall from her window.

Lines of washing crisscrossed between the structures. Between the laundry, she could see small children playing below. Their clothing was grey and drab, and from what she could see, not a single one of them wore any shoes.

She looked out across the jagged city skyline of rooftop spires and industry. No matter the direction, she saw a sprawling labyrinth of factories, tenements, and narrow streets. Even from here, she could hear the sounds of the city pulsing through the glass.

A far cry from the rolling hills and quiet lanes that she had known all her life.

"What do you think?"

She hadn't heard her mother enter the room and had to swallow a yelp as spun around. "Mama! You scared me!"

Henrietta slowly circled the room, much as Addy had done not five minutes before. Her mother sighed softly.

"I thought you wanted to rest," Addy murmured.

"It's very noisy," her mother huffed, standing beside her daughter. She peered down through the glass. "And very different from what we're used to, isn't it?"

Addy's gaze drifted back through the glass. "Yes, Mama."

Henrietta's frustrated sigh bloomed on the chilled glass. "I'm sure we'll be able to find something better and far more suited to our standards soon enough, but this was all that wretched miser, Mr Lowther, could deliver to us on such short notice. Had he allowed me a little more time, I know I could have found something more suitable."

Addy held back from reminding her mother that it was only out of respect for Archie Hill that they hadn't been cast out of Lowther House sooner. She didn't want to provoke another outburst.

"We shall just have to make the best of a bad situation, won't we?" Henrietta said brightly. Addy could see the effort it took to force that smile. But it only made the worried niggling at her insides grow that bit more.

"Yes, we will, mama," Addy replied carefully.

Henrietta turned Addy, scrutinising her daughter's face. "You must believe me when I tell you that this isn't forever."

"I do," Addy said quickly. "It's just that..."

"What is it, Adelaide?"

"I'm given to understand that living here is expensive."

Her mother's face pinched white as she glared at her daughter. "Of course, it is. Everything in this life is expensive. Your papa left us a small – *very* small," she amended not too politely, "inheritance. We shall make do until something else comes along."

"How—how can we afford to live here long-term, mama? We don't have jobs. What will happen to us?"

Her mother's smile faltered, her patience fraying visibly. "Adelaide, you mustn't ask such ridiculous questions. I've told you I will take care of it, and take care of it, I will! Mark my words. We will be back in a grand house full of fine dresses fit for royalty before too long."

Addy wanted to reassure her mother that she didn't need the grand house or the fine clothing. She knew her mother liked to keep up appearances, but right now, she could only fear what was next for them.

Her father had always been honest with her because he understood she thrived on the information. He'd explained that women at the mill were paid less than men. Those without the protection of their husbands were forced to take in extra scraps of work to make ends meet.

However, talking about such things with her mother wouldn't do any good. So, she gave her mother her most beautiful smile. "I believe you, Mama."

This time, her mother's sigh was much softer. Rather than anger, her mother's hand reached out to her in comfort. Relieved, Addy stepped into the embrace and wrapped her arms around her mother's slender waist. But she couldn't help but wonder what would happen to them both in this strange new world.

CHAPTER 7

*I*t turned out that life on Fletcher Street wasn't all that different from living in Whitehurst.

Rather than labourers and millworkers, the families living on Fletcher Street were salaried professionals—solicitors, accountants, and merchants. Despite their modest prosperity, they seemed very wary of newcomers. They treated Addy and her mother with quiet suspicion.

The first of the neighbours to thaw was Mrs Warner. She was a widow, though her husband had died many years ago. Her enduring grief was evident in the black dresses she always wore.

As May bloomed, the longer days arrived. They were warmer, although the smoky haze that dwelled upon the city meant that the sunshine rarely broke through.

Under Mrs Warner's guiding hand, Henrietta joined the local chapter of the Girls' Friendly Society, a charitable organisation that sought to provide help, support, and strong moral education to young girls. For Henrietta, it seemed to provide her with a sense of purpose and belonging. She threw herself into the activities with surprising vigour, and before long, Addy was once again seated in the parlour as her mother hosted afternoon tea parties.

Addy's greatest joy was the arrival of the piano. She had begun lessons on it a few months before her father had died, and her mother delighted in the attention it drew from her afternoon visitors. Addy thought it had been sold on, and she couldn't help but wonder if Mr Lowther perhaps still held a little bit of influence over their lives.

Surrounded by her books and reconnecting once more to her music, Addy began to feel a little more at ease on Fletcher Street.

It also reignited her mother's enthusiasm for ensuring that Addy was raised as a proper young lady, destined for a life far beyond the confines of Fletcher Street. This meant participating in many church activities and attending Sunday school.

Henrietta saw to it that Addy also returned to her studies. But without her father's gentle guidance and wry humour, things just weren't the same. Her mother lacked Archie's patience and penchant for storytelling, which had ignited the joy for education within his daughter. Addy was almost relieved on the day that her mother enrolled her in the local girls' school.

The dowdy building was just a short walk from their new home. Addy had grown accustomed to the clatter of carts on cobblestones. The constant rumble of wheels and shifting shades of movement had faded into the background of her mind.

The school itself was small and unremarkable. The

headteacher was austere and implacable. He wielded his cane unconditionally to terrify his pupils into compliance.

Each morning, on her way to school, Addy passed by the skinny children who lived on the road beyond Fletcher Street. They stopped and stared at her with vacant eyes, their families crammed into the overcrowded tenement buildings. Poverty was unmistakable in their threadbare clothes and lean faces.

The city was never quiet.

Even in the dead of night, the rattle of wagon wheels would echo on the damp cobbles. The continuous drone of factory life buzzed through the air. Thick factory smoke blurred the sky.

Most days, she yearned for the quiet and gentle life she had once enjoyed at Lowther House. But with her father gone, she had come to accept that life was now irreversibly different.

Mrs Spearing ran the house efficiently. Henrietta relented and hired a cook, much to Mrs Spearing's relief. The other woman was endlessly patient with her mother, running the small townhouse with the ruthless efficiency that Mrs Kemp would have admired.

Life on Fletcher Street found a new equilibrium.

But that all changed the day her mother met Fred Latchford.

***

THE RAIN CAME DOWN in lines, a relentless downpour that collected in the ruts and pockets at the edges of the streets. Brown rivers gushed along the fog-drenched streets, dragging the detritus and dropping it on corners so that lakes started to form.

The rain didn't wash anything clean. The smoky sky seemed closer, almost oppressive, squashed down by the weather. Rivulets formed along the carriage windows. The inclement weather had been why her mother had indulged in a cab back from the trip to the dressmakers.

Addy hadn't particularly wanted a new dress.

Her mother was cross because Addy had outgrown everything, and she'd protested about the additional expense. But Henrietta had appearances to uphold, and Addy was now the proud owner of a beautiful navy blue dress.

Her mother tsked and sighed as the cab careened around another one of the corners. Bracing herself against the side of the carriage, her mother muttered, "Good heavens, I think we're being driven by a madman."

Addy didn't have time to reply.

The carriage seemed to buck, and both Addy and her mother were flung across the interior, slamming against the velvet-padded walls with a force that stole the breath from her lungs. The carriage shuddered all around them as it pitched this way and that, tossing them both around even more.

The carriage lurched again. The thunderous crack was deafening, followed by the shriek of iron as the cab scraped along the road before coming to a grinding halt.

The dreadful sounds came to a stop.

Then the muffled cursing and shouting started.

CHAPTER 8

"Mama?"

"Addy? Are you hurt?" Henrietta reached across the interior as Addy blinked.

"My arm," Addy replied, squinting through the chaotic interior. Terror licked through her when she saw Henrietta's dishevelled state. "Mama, you're bleeding from your head."

Henrietta pressed her fingers to her temple and sighed, more with exasperation than anything else, when her fingers came away soaked in blood.

"Never mind that," her mother said, "gather up your belongings. We can't stay in here."

On one side, all Addy could see was the road. The door wouldn't budge. The other window was filled with rain clouds. With difficulty, as the carriage was sitting at such an angle, Henrietta stretched up to try and unlatch the door, but to no avail.

"The wheel must've come off," Henrietta muttered as she continued to fiddle at the handle.

The angry male voices were still outside, growing more agitated by the minute.

Pain radiated from Addy's shoulder, and she struggled to hold their purchases. "Are we trapped?"

In response, her mother hammered her closed fist against the side of the glass. "Open this door at once! Do you hear me? Your terrible driving has brought this about. Let me out this instant!"

Her mother had to try shouting again before the door was finally opened. Rain splatted Addy in the face.

A dark-haired man with brown eyes and a warm smile appeared in the opening. "You appear to have gotten yourselves into quite the pickle," he announced, with a small chuckle. "Are you ladies alright?"

"Not really," Henrietta replied primly.

The man barked out several orders. He reached in and lifted her mother clear of the wrecked cab. Then he reached in for the boxes Addy held and disappeared from view again.

Addy had to wait alone for a few moments before she was lifted out by two other people. A quick look around confirmed her mother's suspicions. A shattered wheel lay on the floor; the wreck of the cab had caused complete chaos in the centre of the road. The coachman was in a heated argument with the driver of a coal wagon.

All around them, people had gathered in the downpour to survey the chaos. Frantically, Addy looked around for her mother.

The man who had first appeared in the carriage doorway was chatting to her. Her mother was smiling broadly at him.

"Thank you again, Mr Latchford," she heard her

mother say as Addy got closer. She had a white handkerchief pressed to the injury on her head.

"Please, Mrs Hill," the man replied. "No thanks are needed. I'm only sorry that this has happened to you. But I insist that you let me escort you both to the hospital."

"Oh," Henrietta giggled. "It is but a scratch. I have an ointment at home. I'll be fine."

Addy held onto her arm; eyes narrowed against the deluge.

"If you're sure," the handsome stranger smiled.

"Quite sure, Mr Latchford."

"Then let's get you ladies out of this rain. Let me find you a new carriage and send you on your way."

"I don't want to go in a new carriage," Addy said quickly, her shoulder throbbing. But the two adults ignored her. Mr Latchford indicated his way along the street, a guiding hand at her mother's elbow as he weaved her through the onlookers.

As quick as a flash, he hailed a new cab. He handed her mother into the interior of the cab, then turned and lifted Addy up. Finally, he passed the purchases through the open doorway. "Where shall I tell the driver to take you, Mrs Hill?"

Her mother didn't seem particularly concerned about the gash or the growing knot on her forehead. Indeed, her mother's cheeks were quite flushed, with a blithe smile on her face. "Mr Latchford, you've already been too generous."

"The address, Mrs Hill," Mr Latchford responded as his charming smile grew.

"We live at number twelve, Fletcher Street."

The warm brown gaze lingered upon her mother's form for a fraction of a second longer than was polite.

They watched as Mr Latchford stepped back and shut the door. Through the window, he tipped the brim of his hat towards her mother.

With a flourish, he flipped a coin through the air towards the driver and barked out the street address.

Addy whimpered and gripped the edge of the seat as the carriage jolted forward. She looked at her mother for reassurance that everything was going to be okay, but her mother was leaning at an angle towards the glass, watching the fading figure of Mr Latchford.

The next day, a battered and bruised Addy was sitting in her room when she heard the unusual baritone of a male voice drift through the house. Frowning, she crossed to the bedroom door and tiptoed onto the landing. There, in the hallway and taking in the very modest interior of their home, stood Mr Latchford. She watched as Henrietta hurried out of the parlour.

"Mr Latchford," her mother greeted him buoyantly, "I didn't expect to see... What are you doing here?

He gave her a slight bow by way of greeting. "Mere concern for you and your daughter's welfare. It occurred to me yesterday that I hadn't ensured that you had a safe return home. I've been awake all night worrying about you both."

"Goodness," her mother exclaimed breathlessly, "that's very kind of you."

Addy frowned, her gaze shifting between the two adults as they regarded each other with strange, knowing smiles. Something was unsettling in the way their eyes lingered, a silent exchange passing between them that made her stomach twist with unease.

"Perhaps I could..." Henrietta touched her hair.

Pressed a hand to her midriff. "Golly... Would you like... maybe we should have some tea?"

Her mother was rarely this flustered. Addy's frown deepened.

"If that's not too much trouble," Fred grinned.

"Not at all," Henrietta turned, jerking as though she'd forgotten about the housekeeper standing right behind her. "Mrs Spearing, this is the kind gentleman I told you about. He was instrumental in ensuring that Addy and I escaped from the accident yesterday unharmed."

Unharmed? Her mother had a whacking great knot on her head, and Addy's shoulder was ablaze. If not for Mrs Spearing running her a bath last night, Addy would surely be in a worse state.

"Very good, Miss," the housekeeper nodded.

"We will have a tray of tea for two," Henrietta looked back at her house guest. "Shall we take it in the parlour?"

"Why not?" Mr Latchford gestured through the air and then disappeared out of view as he followed her mother through the house.

~

FRED LATCHFORD'S arrival at the Fletcher Street home signalled a significant change in Henrietta. It was almost like seeing a bright summer's day after the long and dreary winter as she made her way out from under the cloud of grief. She seemed younger somehow and lit up in a way that Addy hadn't seen in her mother since before her father had grown sick. The angry outbursts had all but vanished except when they were alone with Addy's study books spread across the table.

Charming and attentive, Mr Latchford became a regular visitor at the house. Before too long, he began to arrive with small gifts for both Addy and her mother—a first-edition book for Addy and a posy of flowers for Henrietta.

She listened as her mother relayed Mr Latchford's antics to Mrs Warner and their afternoon guests over tea.

"What does this Mr Latchford do for a living?" Mrs Warner, ever the shrewd woman, inquired.

"He's in shipping," her mother replied confidently, swirling hot water in a cup to warm it.

"That's fairly common in this city," the neighbour responded crisply. "Doing *what* in shipping?"

Her mother poured tea through the strainer. "His company has connections around the world. In fact, that's where he is today. He's on his way to a meeting with several important people. Fred tells me that a lot is riding on his new business venture. It sounds very exciting, Mrs Warner. I'm sure you know that Liverpool is the busiest port in the world, bigger than London," her mother added gleefully.

Fred Latchford also became a regular guest for dinner and was always the perfect gentleman.

Addy had heard Mrs Spearing and the cook discussing the fact that Henrietta was still supposed to be in mourning. Mrs Spearing didn't like it, but the cook shrugged it off. "We should all make an effort when he's here. She's happier. Lord knows there isn't much to be happy about in this life."

He showered Addy with attention. He told many stories of his adventures in business, the many interesting people he had met, including one of the princes at a lavish dinner at a palace in Dover.

"Did you hear that, Addy?" Her mother's eyes sparkled with happiness. "A prince."

She had smiled dutifully, finally understanding. Fred Latchford was connected in society and, knowing her mother the way she did, Henrietta saw Fred Latchford as their ticket out of Fletcher Street.

Mark my words. We will be back in a grand house full of fine dresses fit for royalty before too long.

Dread pooled in her stomach as she realised that her mother intended to replace her father. Perhaps that was why Addy was so wary of him.

Summer passed them by. Autumn arrived with its bracing breath, turning the leaves on the trees red and brown. Before too long, the leaves dropped, collecting in the parks and the gutters so that when Addy returned home from school, her black leather boots were sopping.

She let herself into the kitchen and stomped off the leaves, relishing the warmth of the house. The simple pleasure was soon extinguished when she caught the droll look on Mrs Spearing's face.

"Your mother is in the sitting room with Mr Latchford," she told her.

"How long has he been here?" Addy whispered. It was unusual for him to visit during the day.

The housekeeper shrugged as if it was none of her business. "Your mother asked me to send you up as soon as you were home."

Addy climbed the narrow back stairs as Fred's rich baritone of laughter drifted through the house. Addy drew in a breath and pushed open the door. The warmth of the roaring log fire greeted her as she entered, but it was the exuberant faces of her mother and Mr Latchford that snagged her attention.

"Addy!" Her mother beckoned her. "Come in."

Fred's brown eyes sparkled as he toasted her with a champagne saucer. "We're celebrating, you see."

Addy shook her head. "Celebrating what?"

"Your mother and I have gone into business together."

Addy's eyes moved between them both – her mother's giddy demeanour, Fred's sycophantic bearing. "What kind of business?"

Her mother snatched up a piece of paper and held it aloft. "I'm officially in the shipping business. See?"

Addy took the piece of paper. She saw the gold seal at the top, with several signatures from men she'd never heard of scrawled across the bottom. The sum of money was eye-watering.

"I don't understand, Mama," Addy murmured. "We know nothing about shipping."

Fred drained his glass and wiped his mouth with the back of his hand, struggling not to choke on his laughter. "You're right, Ella," he teased her mother playfully. "She is as sharp as a tack, this one."

But her mother didn't seem too amused by her direct question. Her smile dimmed slightly. "Fred has managed to secure a major government contract."

"I'm not sure that you would understand such a thing," Fred shook his head pityingly at Addy.

"Mama... this money..." *Her father's way of looking after them both.* She wasn't sure of the amount left behind but the sum on this contract was dwarfed by it, she was certain.

Her heart popped into her mouth as the familiar rage lit her mother's eyes, but Fred quickly dismissed her worries. "Your mother is a sensible woman. She's made her enquiries and is satisfied. Aren't you, Etta?"

Henrietta nodded once, glaring at her daughter.

Fred continued, "This is a surefire success. I have everything lined up, and now, thanks to your mother's investment, I can sign the final paperwork."

"An investment?" Addy knew better than to talk about money in front of people who weren't members of the family. Instead, she focused on her mother. She wanted to know.

"Addy," Henrietta tutted. "Don't give me that strange look in your eye." She turned to Fred. "Do you see it too?"

Keen to diffuse the situation as mother and daughter drew their battle lines, Fred patted the air between them. "This investment will have tripled your mother's money within months, Addy. This is for both of you. Don't you see? It will bring you security and wealth, which will only elevate you both in society. Your mother wants only the best for you. You can move out of the city, which I know you long to do.

"This is a chance for you and your mother to live the life your father would have wanted for you both."

Addy's eyes narrowed at the mention of her father. If not for his hard work, then none of this would have been possible in the first place.

"It's true, my darling," her mother stepped forward, nodding enthusiastically. "Imagine the possibilities! And... we have more news."

Addy's heart thudded dully as they exchanged another of their silent messages in a shared look. Her mother's heartfelt sigh set alarm racing through her. "You see, Mr Latchford has..."

Fred gathered up her mother's hands and drew

them up towards his chin. Addy could only stare as he brushed his lips across her mother's knuckles. "Your mother has agreed to become my wife."

Much as it had on the day of the carriage accident, her breath left her body in a rush. Blood pounded in her ears as she realised that all her fears had come true.

"Isn't it wonderful?" her mother asked her, although she was staring up into Fred Latchford's handsome face.

"Yes… wonderful," Addy said, though she wasn't too sure if the words were heard. Her mother gazed happily into Fred Latchford's face.

And Addy knew that her life would never be the same.

CHAPTER 9

The long dark table in the parlour was laden with an elaborate spread that would have been the envy of any hostess in Knightsbridge. Egg and cress sandwiches, the crusts removed and cut into thin finger-sized pieces so as not to ruin the gloves of the ladies present. Smoked salmon with lemon slices and chicken with chutney were all arranged on fine porcelain plates. Golden twists of cheese straws stood alongside plum cake, shortbread biscuits, and tart lemon curd tarts that gleamed in the middle of the table. Dainty china cups were filled with steaming Earl Grey and Assam tea.

Addy was in her usual spot in the corner, unnoticed by the occupants as the drizzle rolled down the windowpanes. Outside, mists lingered over the grey October day. She could hear carriage wheels sloshing through the puddles in the street. The atmosphere inside the parlour was as dreary as the day outside.

Not least because several expected guests were missing from the table. They had made their excuses, of course, and the small notes written in flowing script full of apologies had been arriving at the door all morning. Addy was aware of the discontent that lingered around her mother.

The ever-alert Mrs Warner sat at the head of the table. Her back was ramrod straight, her hands tucked neatly in her lap as her sharp eyes took in every detail.

"So, the trip is taking a little longer than usual?" Mrs Warner asked, her questions always as pointed as a needle.

Henrietta took a sip of her tea, deliberately setting the cup back into its saucer before she answered. "Yes, that's right. Mr Latchford tells me he's in The Hague, finalising some very important business matters with his government contacts there."

"You mean to say that you've heard from him then?" Mrs Warner didn't bother to hide the surprise in her voice.

Addy's attention shifted to her mother. Under the direct gaze of Mrs Warner, she was surprised to see Henrietta with a semblance of composure. Henrietta was disinclined to ever show signs of discomfort, especially when she had company, but her movements appeared stiff.

"Yes, of course, I've heard from him," Henrietta replied in a rush.

Addy had to roll her lips inward to keep from gasping over the blatant lie her mother had just told.

Henrietta quickly turned her attention to the other neighbour seated in the armchair opposite Addy. "Won't you care for some more tea, Frances?"

Frances Hawthorne didn't answer. Just like everyone else in the room, she was waiting for the real answer to Mrs Warner's direct questioning, the blatant curiosity written across her face. The silence quickly stretched into awkwardness, and tension filled the room like the fog that lingered outside.

It occurred to Addy at that moment that their guest absences and all the polite notes of apology from them might have nothing to do with the rain and more to do with the discouraging rumours swirling around Henrietta Hill.

Henrietta had sidestepped this question on more than one occasion, leaving Addy to fill in the blanks by herself.

Fred Latchford had left for London more than three weeks ago, claiming he needed to finalise the contract for their steamship venture. He had left her mother excited, promising to return within a few days to discuss further details about their upcoming marriage.

However, he was now overdue by over a fortnight. Initially, her mother was frantic with worry. She had sought assistance from the police, who'd assured her that they would locate him.

Henrietta had paced the floors, making wild assumptions on the whereabouts of her fiancé. She feared the worst. London was a vast and dangerous city. Anything could have befallen a man like Fred—illness, an accident, or perhaps something even more sinister. But there had been no news. Henrietta's anxiety intensified after the police informed her that there was no record of anyone matching Fred's description at the lodgings he purported to stay at in London.

The days rolled passed.

Speculation along Fletcher Street exploded.

Mrs Warner, always quick to voice an opinion, had

never hidden her scepticism about Fred Latchford. After all, she expressed, his company name was obscure and not well known locally. Despite Henrietta's firm assurances of his legitimacy, Mrs Warner remained unconvinced, especially given the number of well-informed merchants residing on their street who also had never heard of Latchford's business dealings.

The afternoon tea lingered awkwardly, with long, uneasy silences broken only by the sharp clink of china and sporadic attempts at forced pleasantries. Her mother struggled to find words, adding to the palpable tension in the air. When, at last, the visitors left, much of the table spread remained untouched. Addy couldn't help but wonder about the cost of putting on such a show for her neighbours, yet her mother remained determined to prove to the naysayers that their worries about Fred were unfounded.

Mrs Spearing returned from the front door, hovering in the doorway. Addy followed the housekeeper's gaze to where her mother sat in the armchair, perfectly still, head bent, shoulders tense.

"Would you like me to clear, Mrs Hill?"

Her mother blinked, almost as if she'd forgotten where she was. "Pardon? Oh, yes, yes please, Mrs Spearing."

"What should I do with the rest of this food?"

Her mother looked as if she was about to cry as she stared at the amount of food left. Dejected, she shook her head. "Throw it over the back wall. I expect those children that dance in the mud at the back will be able to make use of it all."

With that, her mother stood and swept from the room.

"She's worried about Mr Latchford, that's all," Addy offered the housekeeper a tentative smile as the woman began to pick up the plates.

"With good reason, I dare say," Mrs Spearing offered a rare comment on the situation.

Once the housekeeper had finished, Addy remained in the parlour. The regular tick-tock from the mantel was the only sound in the room.

She didn't fully grasp the complexities of what was happening, but she knew the shape of worry—she could see it in her mother's tight smile, in the way her hands had trembled when she'd poured the tea earlier. In the shadows beneath her eyes that darkened with every day that passed without a word from Fred Latchford. Addy knew that her mother was desperately trying to hold onto her dignity, even as their newfound friends on Fletcher Street were slowly pulling away, retreating in the face of a scandal that had begun to swirl about their house.

She stared out at the darkening sky, her heart heavy with apprehension. Mr Latchford was out there somewhere. The soft rain pattered against the windows as the day began to fade into a cold and uncertain evening. She hadn't liked him but seeing her mother smiling once more had been so wonderful. She clung to the fragile hope that he hadn't done what the rumours seemed to hint at—that he hadn't disappeared with the last of her mother's money.

CHAPTER 10

Snow tumbled from the sky in fat, swirling flakes. Back in Whitehurst, the crisp whiteness had always made her eyes ache. Outside the house on Fletcher Street, the snow quickly lost its purity, turning black as it mixed with the ever-present industrial smoke.

The harsh reality of life outside the walls of their Fletcher Street home had finally caught up with Henrietta Hill, too.

Fred Latchford vanished as suddenly as he had appeared in their lives. He had left behind no forwarding address. No letters had been forthcoming with an explanation of his absence.

Worse yet, there had been no return on her mother's investment.

Addy wasn't sure at what point Henrietta had accepted the full reality of the situation, although her anxiety had turned into despair as she had finally faced the truth.

Fred Latchford was a fraud.

His charming nature and empty promises had swallowed up not only the last of her father's meagre life insurance but also sucked her mother of any joy. The determination to make their new life work had gone.

Henrietta's meticulous appearance began to fray as their situation had slowly unravelled over the past two months. Desperation had driven her to ask friends, neighbours, and even acquaintances to borrow small sums of money to cover their basic necessities—coal for the fire and food for the table. Their rent payments fell further and further behind. Local shopkeepers who had once welcomed her business—the grocers, butcher, and seamstress—were all knocking at the front door, making escalating demands for their outstanding accounts to be settled.

News of their precarious finances quickly spread.

Henrietta sought assistance from the parish and the Girls' Friendly Society, but the financial aid they could offer was limited. Without any practical skills, Henrietta had been unable to secure employment, which meant that any sympathy for her position from the church faded quickly.

Not even Mrs Warner visited the house anymore. And even if she had, her mother had sold what little furniture they had brought from Lowther House to try and meet their spiralling debts, so there was nothing for her to sit on.

Addy had learned the meaning of the words 'bailiff' and 'judgement' as her mother was hauled up in the local courts. They avoided the fearsome-looking men who banged heavily on the door.

Her mother had even swallowed her pride and written to Mr Lowther. But, while the landowner had sympathised with their situation, he had been unable to offer any further assistance to them.

Finally, the landlord's patience had run out. Three days ago, he had sent word that they were to vacate the premises. There was a flurry of activity as her mother found a new place for them to live. A cheaper residence and a new landlord to appease.

Mrs Spearing, armed with a glowing reference from her mother, followed them out of the front door of Fletcher Street for the final time.

Addy shivered in the slush-filled street; her head bowed as her mother thanked the housekeeper stiffly for the short period of service she had provided them.

"I do wish you both well," Mrs Spearing replied dutifully. She hesitated as she was about to say more but then turned on her heel and made her way along the street, leaving behind the drama that had unfolded here on Fletcher Street.

Usually, Addy had to trot to keep up with her mother's brisk pace, but today, she found herself stopping and waiting for her mother to catch up. As the fine snowy haze got thicker, Addy glanced sideways at her mother, who trudged along beside her. Addy wished they could flag down one of the cabs that raced along the cobbled streets. Snow had soaked into her clothes, and she longed for the relative warmth of one of those cabs, but that was a luxury far beyond their reach.

Onward, they traipsed, walking along the maze of streets as they headed towards the district of Everton. Around them, the landscape began to change. The pristine facades of the elegant neighbourhoods gave way to row upon row of cramped, redbrick houses that were stacked tightly together. The sharp, briny tang of the sea air grew stronger as they climbed up the long hill.

There was a noticeable shift in the people they passed by, too. There were no leisurely strollers in the twisting labyrinth of terraced houses. No fine clothes or delicate parasols. Instead, the tight streets were filled with hurried figures, heads down, focused on their own existence. Just like the thoroughfare behind Fletcher Street, hollow-eyed children stared at them from doorways and alleys, their pale faces smeared with dirt. Addy's clean clothing and neat bonnet stood out amongst their ragged garments.

Everton was a district of endless uphill streets, steep lanes, and cramped courtyards where the houses were packed in as tightly as possible to make room for the growing city. There was no regard for comfort or space for the people who sought shelter in them. There were no gas lamps or running water here, only public fountains on the street corners. Women waddled along the road, each carrying a bucket. They formed a scruffy queue. One by one, with a careless motion, they tossed the filthy wastewater into the grid on the street. Addy drew alongside the last woman and jumped back just in time as the stinky liquid splashed across the cobbles towards her.

Every turn into a new street revealed another grim sight: men with sunken faces carrying sacks on their shoulders, their oilskins reeking of fish as they passed. Their insidious eyes keenly watched Henrietta and Addy as they moved by.

They turned into Cavendish Row.

The street was lined with tall buildings that loomed

three or four stories high; the bricks darkened with soot. Damp and rot permeated the air here. Folks lingered in doorways, in corners, on steps, watching them. Their faces were despondent, eyes sharp and knowing.

One man stood out. Balding with lank and greasy hair that touched his shoulders, his pale, unblinking eyes were locked onto them with an unnerving intensity that sent a shiver down Addy's spine. He watched their progress up the street, elbowing off the wall as they neared him.

"Mrs Hill?" His broad Liverpudlian accent thickened his voice. "I'm Jed Buswell."

Their new landlord. Addy's heart sank. Instinctively, she moved closer to Henrietta, seeking to anchor herself to something reassuring under his assessing stare.

Henrietta came to a halt a few feet away from him. The landlord's head tilted as he waited for her reply.

"Are you Henrietta Hill?"

Addy looked expectantly at her mother, though she remained mute.

"I am Adelaide Hill," Addy injected as much confidence as she could muster under the greedy, calculating look that lingered on her mother just a moment too long. "This is my mother, Henrietta Hill."

Jed Buswell spared Addy a mere glance before he grunted, "You're late."

Henrietta seemed to shrink under his glare. "It's – it's a long walk from Fletcher Street, sir."

His mouth twisted cruelly. "Then you should walk faster, Mrs Hill. I'm a busy man and can't abide tardiness. The rent is three shillings a week and due upfront, a week in advance."

"Of course," her mother's hands trembled as she shook out the coins from the leather pouch.

He grasped the money and then held a huge iron key towards her. "Up the stairs to the top floor. Your room is the last door on the left," he muttered gruffly. Henrietta held out her hand for the key, but Jed Buswell didn't hand it over right away. Instead, his eyes meandered over Henrietta one last time.

Finally, he relinquished the key. "Your rent is always due on a Monday," his smile was more of a sneer. "I look forward to seeing more of you, Henrietta."

Henrietta didn't say a word. Addy watched as the landlord strolled through the courtyard. The remaining occupants visibly retreated as he walked past them.

"Come, Addy."

Addy turned back to find her mother reaching for her. She didn't miss the way her fingers shook as she grasped the edge of Addy's coat and pulled her inside, shutting the door behind them with a sharp click.

In the ensuing gloom, Addy had to wait a moment for her eyes to adjust. The sounds of life pressed around her as the smell of dank decay stung her nostrils. Her mother was already halfway up the stairs before Addy had truly registered the sounds of crying babies, raised voices, and the din of life in general.

"Adelaide!" Henrietta called sharply. "Now, please!"

She flew up the stairs, the wooden treads dipping deeply under her feet, as if they would give way at any moment.

As she reached the landing of the first floor, Addy swallowed a scream when a rat popped out of a jagged hole in the skirting, its fat, wiry tail whipping behind it. It scurried along the floor before vanishing into another gap further down the corridor. Heart pounding, Addy gave the hole a wide berth, eyeing the dark opening as she rushed to keep up with her mother.

"Mama, wait for me!" she called out as her mother disappeared up the stairs to the top floor. The stairs dipped and creaked again. Addy pressed a steadying hand to the wall only to snatch it back. Her hand came away wet. The shrill wail of a baby drifted through one of the closed doors, followed by angry shouts as Addy rushed down the gloomy passageway.

Her mother reached the door that was furthest along the top corridor. Her hand shook greatly, and it took several attempts to unlock the door. Eventually, the door to their new home scraped open, revealing a single, small room. The window was so coated in grime that it barely let any light through, and the room was filled with a strange pale glow. Through the gloom, she spied bare floorboards that had splintered in places. Up here, the air was chilly and musty. It was empty save for a rickety wooden table, a grubby armchair and a single mismatched chair that wobbled precariously on uneven legs as her mother set her bags down on it. In the far corner, a rusty potbelly stove was caked in a heavy layer of dust.

Addy made a slow inspection of the room. No hearth, nothing that resembled any of the comforts they once knew.

"Mama," Addy whispered, "we can't live here."

Her mother turned to her with weary eyes. There was no bluster, no trace of the woman who had demanded the highest of standards from her daughter and who once mingled with society's elite. "We have no choice, Addy," she replied dully.

Addy glanced around. "But where do we sleep?"

Henrietta didn't answer. Instead, she shoved the bag off the chair. It clattered to the floor as her mother sank onto the wobbly chair. With her back hunched and her thin hands covering her face, her mother began to sob.

CHAPTER 11

Life in Cavendish Row was unlike anything Addy had ever known.

Their building was cramped and chaotic, teeming with the incessant pandemonium of people living in close proximity. Each house on the street was crammed full of people until the buildings were bursting at the seams. Families lived on top of one another, forced into quarters that were far too small.

The Everton area had swelled with an influx of people lured by the promise of work in the factories and at the docks, which employed thousands.

Each morning, much as she had at Lowther House, Addy was woken by the rhythmic thudding of dockers' footsteps as they flowed from the building, heading to work before dawn. It was a dull vibration that resonated through the walls.

Addy had managed to source a straw mattress that she shared with her mother in the corner of their room. Each night, they gathered around the small stove, burning coal piece by piece to ensure it lasted throughout the week. Food was scarce and Addy would often go hungry.

She knew not to complain about the gnawing pangs.

Cavendish Row itself formed a courtyard. Rows of houses backed up to the next row so that every square inch of space was occupied. Despite the tight space, there was always someone willing to pay for it. Addy learned that the renters would often charge eightpence a week for floor space alone – anything that would alleviate the steep room rent.

Henrietta refused to consider that as an option.

The yards behind the houses were shared, small patches of dirt that served as a playground for the children who lived in the tenement buildings. People strung their laundry between the narrow alleyways. The courtyard itself was always littered with the detritus of life. The rows of houses formed a self-contained community, though Addy quickly learned it was one where trust was in short supply.

The downside to living with thin walls was that she heard much and saw plenty. She quickly understood that people would do anything to make their rent payments, even harming others if it meant keeping a roof over their heads or making the rent.

In Cavendish Row, it was every man for themselves.

Addy had also learned to dread Mondays. Every Monday, Jed Buswell would make his rounds.

On those days, his presence brought about more tension as he made his way along the street.

The rent collector liked to linger against the doorframe with an air of arrogance, his insidious gaze sliding over her mother's slight form. Addy learned to always be at home on Mondays.

"How are you settling in?" he would ask them each week. Over time, the tone changed when he said, "A woman of your quality could do a lot better for yourself in Cavendish Row. I would treat you very nicely, Henrietta." His oily tone was full of indecorous suggestion that made her skin crawl.

Her mother, with her polite upbringing and sense of propriety, was too well-mannered to simply slam the door in his face. Instead, she would smile tightly and offer out the small pile of coins to cover their rent payment. Her hand was quickly snatched back so as not to touch the rent collector's.

His words always carried an unspoken insinuation that there were other ways to pay the rent. Addy's stare turned baleful more than once as the rent collector lingered in the doorway. He had to know how her mother was struggling and that she was vulnerable, and he seemed to use that knowledge to twist the knife.

The situation fuelled Addy's desire to protect her mother at all costs. She had to find work to ensure that they could pay their rent and keep Jed Buswell on the other side of the door.

But finding work was more difficult than she could have imagined. Often, she thought about Mary and how the young girl had worked diligently to maintain her job. And Addy finally understood where that determination and grit to keep going no matter the cost came from.

Day after day, Addy trudged through the snowy

streets. She ignored the hunger and the drizzle that seeped through her clothing. She traipsed around many shops, each doorbell ringing with hope that this time, something would be different.

But every day was the same. Shopkeepers barely spared her a glance. Market stallholders would swat her away as if she were a fly.

"Get gone, girl!"

Each night, she would make her way back to Cavendish Row. She became adept at blending into the streets as much as she could. When she did so, it meant that she could pinch scraps of food and rotting fruit that the market stallholders had set at the back of their stalls.

Each night, she returned home, her soaked clothes clinging to her body.

Each night, Addy found her mother sitting in the same place, staring vacantly at the grimy window. She tried coaxing her mother into finding work, but Henrietta merely shook her head. Once fierce, her spirit had evaporated, and her mother was filled with despair. Gentle urging fell on deaf ears.

Even when Addy persisted, Henrietta no longer scolded Addy. She had become a shell, passive as the sun rose and set.

Addy had traded almost everything they had brought from Fletcher Street. The last few pieces of jewellery that her mother had desperately clung to, the extra coats, and the silver brush that had been a gift from her grandmother.

No matter what she sold, it was never enough. Finally, the day arrived when there was nothing left.

Jed Buswell had bellowed threats through the

locked door. When his footsteps finally receded down the stairs, Addy turned to look at her mother. Henrietta sat listlessly in the armchair, her eyes glazed, her hands limp in her lap.

Addy knelt before her mother. "Mama," she whispered into the thick silence. "You heard what Mr Buswell said. We need to leave. We can't stay here any longer."

His threats of faceless men who would come and drag them out filled her with terror.

Henrietta remained expressionless. "Let them come. What else can they take? There's nothing left."

Addy bit back a sigh. There was still something left for them to take. In the courtyard below, Addy had seen the women who traded their bodies in exchange for rent. She couldn't let that happen. She quickly gathered up the remainder of their items, which now all fit into a single leather satchel.

"Stand up, Mama. Here. Put your coat on. It's cold out."

Henrietta stood docilely. "Where are we going?"

"You'll see," Addy said, fastening the toggles. She opened the door and checked it was empty. Hurriedly, she led her mother down the spongy steps and out into the courtyard.

Clutching the small leather satchel, Addy pulled her mother along the streets of Liverpool. Snow crunched underfoot, and she felt the sharp sting of it on her cheeks, freezing her toes. Both were silent. Folks hurried by them, ducking against the biting winds that slapped at the snowflakes. Addy could barely feel the tip of her nose as she finally turned onto Mount Pleasant.

The workhouse on Brownlow Hill loomed ahead of them.

The imposing building seemed vast, long and stark. A mansard roof with an onion dome in the middle. High black walls separated the undesirable people from the rest of the world, with small, narrow windows covered with heavy iron bars. The spike of a church tower on the end of the building closest to them.

Faint plumes of smoke curled from a couple of the chimney pots, the only evidence of life within the structure. The entrance appeared paradoxically grand as that in any palace, with a stone archway and huge doors – open maws that consumed the destitute.

She'd heard the other children at school speak about almshouses. 'Workhouse' was a dirty word when in company.

Henrietta ground to a halt. It seemed as if her mother had aged years in their short walk from Cavendish Row. A chill, not from the cold wind but from fear, trickled down her spine as she looked up at the daunting facade.

Henrietta glanced back as if seeking an escape. People shuffled past them, life eddying around them both as their world fell apart.

"Mama, what's the matter?"

"I can't do it, Addy." Misery threaded through her voice. "I can't... I've been a fool. A terrible fool. This is all my fault."

She looked down at her daughter, shoulders sagging. "I let things go too far. I thought I could make it right, but..." she shook her head, struggling to find the words past the tears that filled her eyes. "And now, you'll never have the life I wanted for you."

Addy lifted her mother's gloved hand to her cheek. "We still have each other, Mama. We'll be fine."

Henrietta pressed her lips together, tears steadily tracking down her face. Together, hand in hand, they approached the imposing gates of the Liverpool Parish Workhouse.

CHAPTER 12

"You can't just turn up here and ask for a bed for the night," the receiving officer at the workhouse groused at Henrietta. "It's not that simple. There's a process you have to go through. You must apply for relief, fill in the paperwork, and your application must be approved by our Board of Guardians. They don't meet again until next Wednesday."

The grumpy man seemed put out by their arrival, his face contorting into a look of distaste as he inspected the two sodden forms standing in the open doorway. Henrietta's face crumpled into tears again, and she began to weep openly. After a brief hesitation and a noticeable scowl, he reluctantly pushed open the door to admit them into the room behind him.

They stepped into the meagre warmth—the first threshold in the bureaucracy of the workhouse. "Where are you from?" he demanded.

"We live in Cavendish Row, sir," Henrietta replied, her teeth chattering.

"Sit over there and wait," he barked, then scowled at the puddles of melted snow forming around their feet. "And try not to make too much of a mess on my clean floor."

He was tall and spindly, his head hunched into his shoulders as if trying to make himself shorter. Henrietta collapsed onto the bench along the far wall. Addy looked longingly at the roaring fire that filled the hearth, too frightened to move closer to its warmth.

Soon enough, the gangly man returned, followed by another man whose demeanour was far less imposing. The new man was heavyset, dressed in a natty suit. His thick brown hair brushed against the starched collar of his white shirt. His steady, assessing gaze swept over the two shivering forms.

"Who do we have here then?" His voice was smooth and unexpectedly gentle.

"Henrietta Hill," the relieving officer pointed towards her mother with an extended bony finger, "and her daughter, Adrianne."

"Adelaide," Addy corrected politely, straightening under their watchful gazes.

The heavy-set man nodded once, his concerned gaze settling on Henrietta. "What are the circumstances that have befallen you both to bring you to the doors of my establishment?" he asked kindly.

A fresh wave of tears swept over her mother.

"My papa died," Addy murmured, her gaze on the growing puddle at her feet. She had to swallow several times to try and loosen the knot of emotion in her throat.

"I see," the man murmured solemnly. He studied them both a moment longer before crossing to the wide, dark wooden desk in the corner. "My name is

Mr Gordon Fishman," the chair creaked as he sat down. He pulled a ledger towards him. "This is Mr Scott, the receiving officer. As I'm sure he has explained, the normal way of admission is presenting your case to our board, but occasionally, I can offer temporary relief until the board meets."

The receiving officer clicked his tongue in disapproval, and the warden, without looking up, said, "Would you have me put a lone woman and her child out on the street in this dreadful weather, Mr Scott?"

"It's not the done way, is all," Mr Scott muttered.

Mr Fishman selected a pen and drew an ink pot closer to him. His gaze settled directly on Henrietta. "I will admit you, but your position won't be confirmed until this coming Wednesday," he stated. "Your name is Henrietta Hill?"

Henrietta nodded.

He scratched into the ledger, and then he turned to Addy. "And you, young lady, your name is Adelaide?"

"Yes, sir, Adelaide Hill," she spelt out her first name and a curious glance crossed his face.

He set his pen down and linked his fingers. "You can spell?"

Addy nodded. "My Papa always said it was important. He told stories of how being able to read and write had changed his life."

A hint of a smile flickered around Mr Fishman's mouth. "You read, too?"

"Just the classics," she replied nervously, worried she had said the wrong thing.

His smile widened. "It warms my heart to see a young person educated. A girl no less."

"Yes, sir," Addy said politely. "Thank you, sir." She hesitated, glancing nervously over her shoulder at her mother. Henrietta wasn't paying attention to her. She was staring into the fire. "Perhaps..."

Mr Fishman nodded encouragingly.

"Perhaps we might get some soup? My mother... We've not eaten a morsel in days."

Mr Scott scoffed, earning himself a stern look from the warden. The smile he gave Addy held none of the receiving officer's cynicism. "We have some paperwork to complete, Adelaide, but I shall see to it that you get a meal. Tell me, where were you living?"

"Cavendish Row," Addy explained. "Before that, Fletcher Street, and before that, Whitehurst," she watched him scribble the information into the ledger.

"And now," looking up, "this question can trip up some people so I might ask your mother. When is your date of birth? I need the information to confirm your identity."

"The twenty-fifth of February," Addy replied quickly.

He set his pen down once again, a shadow moving over his face. "Happy birthday, Miss Hill."

CHAPTER 13

As promised, they'd been provided a meal. They ate it in what was called the receiving ward, a place where admissions could occur in relative privacy. The thin broth and dry bread might have been plain, but to Addy, it was the most delicious meal she had ever eaten. However, Henrietta barely touched hers. Despite Addy's attempts to comfort her, her mother hadn't stopped crying since they arrived.

The matron in charge of their induction, Mrs Fishman, carried herself with the same kindness and compassion as her husband, speaking to them firmly yet with much patience. The admission process took much longer than Addy had expected. Both she and her mother were required to bathe, though the matron allowed them the dignity of privacy, which Addy was grateful for.

As they dried off with rough, coarse towels, a young girl entered the ward. She wore a stiff, plain brown uniform, and her long dark hair was plaited down her back. She offered up two string-tied bundles that were the same colour as her uniform.

"Thank you, Sally," Mrs Fishman instructed. Their own clothes were taken away for cleaning and storage, a standard practice as everyone who sought relief from the workhouse had to relinquish their possessions. They were now like everyone else under the roof, wearing the same uniform and expected to pay for their upkeep through hard labour. Perhaps the most distressing moment for Addy was having her long auburn curls chopped off. She peered at her reflection in the cloudy-looking glass, touching the ends of her short, choppy hair sadly. Her mother, drained by the whole ordeal, didn't even protest.

As evening approached and the lights outside faded, gas lamps were lit around the room. Sally was summoned by the matron once again, and the reality of their new life settled heavily on Addy as she realised that she was to be separated from her mother. Henrietta was to go to the women's ward, and Addy, because she was under the age of fourteen, was to be taken to the children's ward.

Addy held onto her mother tightly, her eyes shut tight as she vowed to herself that she would not cry. Her mother patted her back absently, and Addy got one last glimpse of her mother before the door to the receiving ward closed.

"She'll be okay," Sally tried to reassure her. "Mrs Fishman will see to her. She's a kind enough woman. It takes people a little while to get over the shock of being here. I see it all the time."

Addy wasn't so sure, but she followed Sally, nonetheless.

Sally held the oil lamp aloft as they made their way

along a stone corridor. The stark, bare walls lent themselves to a cold and austere existence within the workhouse. It was vastly different from anything Addy had experienced and a world away from the luxury of Lowther House. Sally led her down a maze of corridors through a series of buildings and up narrow staircases, pausing at one of the barred windows to point out the yard below. Surrounded by a high brick wall, water collected in the corners and divots within the yard.

"There's the infirmary and the refractory. The church and the dining hall," Sally explained as she pointed to the buildings that abutted the perimeter walls. She also indicated various doors that led to the washhouse, slaughterhouse, piggery, bakehouse, and laundry room, still active even at this late hour. Drying stores, stables, a garden and a fire engine house. Addy marvelled at the town within a city.

"Everything produced here is used to feed us, or the governor, Mr Fishman, sells it to make money for the upkeep of the building and the inmates," Sally said.

Addy tried not to stare at the inmates wandering around in the yard below her, each one dressed in the same coarse brown cloth that marked them as workhouse inmates.

Sally continued along the corridor. "Be sure to hand in your uniform before you leave," she warned, "else you'll be done for theft and off to see the local bobby before you can say Jack Robinson."

Sally paused at a door, her playful glint in her eyes contrasting with the sombre setting. "Are you ready?"

Addy inhaled sharply and gave a brisk nod.

Sally pushed the door open, revealing a long room with high ceilings and more barred windows. The girl's dormitory. A sea of pale faces turned to watch them as they entered, silently observing as she walked past the rows of iron bed frames packed closely together. Each bed had a thin mattress and a threadbare woollen blanket.

Sally stopped at one of the beds. "Put your shoes in the box under here," she instructed, indicating the small wooden crate with the toe of her shoe. "Keep it tucked out the way, or Matron will have your guts for garters."

With that, Sally moved on to one of the empty beds further down the room. Feeling adrift, Addy avoided the weight of the stares that came from all directions. Instead, she dropped her boots into the box and pushed it back under the bed. Slowly, she sat down on the mattress and pulled the threadbare blanket up over her head.

In the small cocoon she made for herself, away from the stares, she allowed her tears to come. She might be surrounded by strangers, yet she had never felt so utterly alone.

She wished she could be with her mother.

She wished Fred Latchford hadn't taken her father's money and left them to this fate.

But most of all, she wished with all her heart that she could be anywhere else but here.

CHAPTER 14

It was the sound of crying that drew Addy from her restless sleep. Almost as if the sobs had come from within herself, she woke, listening to the heartbroken sounds. She sat bolt upright, dragged into consciousness. Blinking into the darkness, she felt disoriented as she looked around the unfamiliar dormitory. The room was bitterly cold, the small stove having gone out hours before.

Her eyes adjusted to the gloom, and she began to make out the shadows and shapes of the room. Most of the beds were still occupied by sleeping girls. She squinted in the direction of the crying, and her heart pulled with sympathy. Whoever was crying was trying to smother the sobs, and Addy felt a kinship with that emotion, having cried herself to sleep only hours before.

"Be quiet!" came a sharp hiss from across the room.

"Do you want matron to hear you? Shut up, before I come over there and shut you up!" Another voice, louder and more threatening, followed.

The crying didn't stop, though it was muffled now as if a hand or fabric had been pressed over a face to quiet the sound. Addy pushed back the thin blanket, gooseflesh rising on her bare arms as her feet touched the cold stone floor.

"You! Get back in bed!" The deeper voice warned again. "You'll get into trouble if you're caught out of bed!"

She ignored the warning, knowing she couldn't leave the poor girl alone. Tiptoeing across the floor, she moved along the narrow rows of beds until she found the source of the sobs. The young girl was sitting up, her face buried into her knees, which were pulled tightly against her chest.

Addy reached out a hand in comfort. "Hush," she whispered softly.

The girl jolted, and Addy could just about make out her tear-filled eyes looking up. "What's wrong?" she asked gently.

The girl tried to stifle her sniffles, her small frail body shaking. "I had a bad dream," she hiccupped as she wiped her nose with the back of her hand.

Addy sat on the bed beside her. "You're okay," she murmured soothingly, placing an arm around the girl's shoulders. "You know, I used to have bad dreams too, but my dear papa told me a story that helped me. Do you like stories?"

Addy could feel the girl staring up at her and saw a slight nod in response.

More of the girls around them began to stir, sitting up silently.

"Bad dreams come from the land of Morpheus. Have you heard of him?" Addy asked.

The young girl shook her head.

"Morpheus is the god of sleep," Addy explained. "He leads the Oneiroi, and he sends us dreams – sometimes beautiful ones. But occasionally, he lets his brothers, Phobetor and Phantasos, take over.

"Phobetor is the mischievous one who brings nightmares, the kind of dreams that make our hearts race and fill us with fear. But dreams, even the bad ones, are just shadows. They cannot hurt us. They're like the stories we read, and just like stories, they pass. Even the darkest night will always give way to the dawn. And dawn brings with it a new day, a fresh chance for us to live."

The young girl sniffled but allowed Addy to ease her back into bed. Her voice was gentle as she tucked the blanket around the trembling child. "Do you feel better now?"

"Yes," the young girl murmured into the darkness.

"The posh girl thinks she's better than us paupers," someone muttered, the words dripping with disdain. "All this talk about gods."

The murmur of whispers spread through the room, little pockets of resentment sparking.

"I'm not better than any of you," Addy said into the darkness, addressing the room at large. "I'm the same as all of you."

The murmurs grew louder.

"Wait till matron hears about her being out of bed," one voice sneered. "She'll be for it when I tell her she's spreading witchcraft in the room."

Addy frowned into the darkness. "I'm doing no such thing."

"Shut up, all of you!" a louder, sharper voice cut through the noise. "I'm trying to sleep."

Addy recognised Sally's voice immediately.

"Tell her, Sally," another said. "She's out of bed and you know that's against the rules. The new girl's breaking the rules!"

In the faint light, Addy could just make out Sally sitting up in bed. "Addy," her voice carried easily through the darkness. "What are you doing?"

"This little girl is upset," Addy swallowed hard, her voice soft.

"So?" came Sally's blunt reply. "Get back in your own bed, right now."

Addy glanced down at the small form of the girl, whose wide, frightened eyes were staring up at her. Addy's stomach knotted nervously.

"Are you alright now?" she whispered.

The girl nodded, though her eyes remained wide and scared.

As Addy padded back past the rows of iron beds, she could hear the whispered insults following her in the dark.

"Sleep!" Sally barked. "All of you. This instant!"

The room fell silent. The iron bed squeaked noisily as Addy climbed back in, all traces of warmth having leached from it. She pulled the blanket up to her chin and lay in the darkness. It was her first night, and she'd already broken one of the rules. The thought of being punished by the matron made her stomach twist with dread. She squeezed her eyes shut, waiting for the first rays of dawn to chase away the shadows.

~

THE NEXT MORNING, Addy followed the crowd, lingering at the back of the group, unsure of the routine. They washed in bowls of ice-cold water, filed out of the dormitory along the corridor, past the milk store, and into the dining hall. After saying a prayer as a congregation, they queued up to collect their meal. A dollop of oatmeal was plopped into her bowl, and she followed the line to the benches. Her mouth watered as the steam rose from the sweet, milky pudding, although her stomach churned as she overheard the other girls whispering tales to the matron.

Mrs Fishman's eyes found Addy, and she felt shame crawl over her cheeks.

Mrs Fishman broke away from the three girls and made her way towards Addy, though her progress was interrupted as another child stepped in front of the matron.

"It wasn't the new girl's fault," the young girl announced loudly enough for everyone to hear, drawing attention. "Lucy was crying and keeping us all awake. She was the only one brave enough to comfort her, Mrs Fishman."

"I see," Mrs Fishman said, taking in the information. She turned to Addy. "The rules are there to ensure you don't hurt yourself by moving around the dormitory at night. There isn't much light, and you could easily stub your toe or trip over something."

Addy looked down at her boots, mumbling, "Yes, miss."

"Well, now you know for next time," Mrs Fishman reasoned. "Alright, children. The day is getting on, and we all have jobs we must do. What does many hands make?"

"Light work," came the chorused reply.

"That's right, so let's get some jobs assigned for the day. Janey, perhaps you could show Adelaide where the kitchen is. You'll both be working there today."

Mrs Fishman spoke to the young girl who'd spoken up.

"Come along, then," Janey called, her voice firm as she gestured for Addy to follow. Addy felt the scornful looks of the other children as she hurried past them.

Janey held the door, her brown eyes staring at the long line of girls glaring at Addy. Her stance was bold, almost defiant, as she gestured at them. "Get to it, then!"

The door swung closed behind them.

"Thank you for sticking up for me," Addy offered Janey a smile.

The young girl shrugged and then struck out along the long stone corridor. "Some of those girls think they need to be toady, but the Matron here doesn't work like that. She's a fair woman when you work hard," her nose wrinkled at Addy. "At the last workhouse I was at, the Matron was a witch. She'd swipe at you as soon as look at you."

Addy had to trot to keep up with Janey's long strides. "You've been to another workhouse?"

"Yes," she shrugged, "though I've been here for a few years now. My Da died."

"My Papa died, too," Addy panted.

Janey spared her a sad look. Her brown hair was cropped short, sticking out from her head in wild curls. She couldn't be much older than Addy, yet she walked with the confidence and purpose of someone who knew their place and was comfortable with it.

"The kitchen's this way," Janey pointed. "Cook's got a temper on her. Mind your p's and q's around her—don't ever answer back and try not to get in the way."

Addy nodded as Janey barked the instructions over her shoulder, drawing up short when Janey held the door open to admit her. The kitchen beyond the open doorway was vast, her mouth popping open as she stared about her. There wasn't much time to take it all in as a hand on her back urged her through the doors,

The room was bustling with activity. Copper vats and pans bubbled away on several long ranges, steam filling the space, obscuring the gleaming pots and utensils hanging from the ceiling. Row upon row of shelving was filled with more utensils – jugs, plates, menacing-looking equipment.

Long lines of women stood as they peeled vegetables into buckets at their feet. The space was crammed with inmates working hard, a choreographed dance overseen by a minute woman with a sharp tongue.

Remembering Janey's advice, she listened carefully, copying the actions of the older girl. Even though it all seemed so confusing, Cook kept a careful eye on the mutton stew and apple tarts, knowing exactly where each stage of the process was.

The morning passed by quickly and without an event, yet Addy still breathed a sigh of relief when she stepped out of the workhouse building and into the frozen yard. The air was filled with joyful shouts and laughter.

Addy paused to look about her.

Mothers and children hugging close, a moment in time when the harsh rules of the workhouse seemed forgotten. Her eyes tracked the brown uniforms until her gaze settled upon the slight form of her mother.

Overcome, Addy forgot decorum and raced over the packed snow.

"Mama!" Without waiting for permission, overcome with relief, Addy wrapped her arms around her mother and began to sob.

CHAPTER 15

Henrietta's once comforting smile did little to soothe Addy's discomfort as she joined the rest of the children streaming into the dark, low-ceilinged building beneath the church. The makeshift classroom was dimly lit, its walls roughly hewn from stone and crudely whitewashed. Rows of desks filled the space, and at the front, a large blackboard was being written on by a stern-looking man.

He eyed the children as they filed into the room, his dark eyes sweeping over the ragtag group.

"Inside," he commanded, "and do it in silence!"

The children settled quickly, heads down as he peered over the top of his wire-rimmed glasses that perched precariously on the end of his nose.

Addy hesitated at the back of the room, desperately trying to remain inconspicuous as the hawklike gaze settled upon her.

His dark eyes narrowed as he studied her unfamiliar face. "What is it, girl?"

Addy's heart leapt into her throat as all eyes turned

to her. "I– I'm sorry, sir," she stammered quietly. "I'm new. I don't know where to sit."

"Sit there," he pointed to an empty desk towards the back of the room, "and be quick about it."

Addy quickly obeyed, slipping into the seat as quietly as she could.

"Name?"

"Adelaide Hill," she replied.

"Speak up, girl!" His bark made her jolt.

She repeated her name louder, her face flushing with embarrassment.

He watched her for a moment, his gimlet gaze unchanging. "The school rules are on the wall behind me. I want you to read them out loud and make sure I can hear you!"

Her heart pounded as she looked past him to the neatly written words on the sign to his left. She took a deep breath and began to read.

"Number one, silence at all times during lessons. Number two, punctuality is expected, and tardiness will not be tolerated." She swallowed over the strange wording. "Number three, raise your hand to speak and only speak when spoken to. Number four, the three R's are a child's path out of the workhouse. Number five, cleanliness is next to godliness. Number six, desks, writing slates, and books are the property of the workhouse master. Any damage will be paid for through hard labour and fines."

Her voice steadied as she read each rule, her confidence building with each word. She glanced at the schoolmaster as she finished, relieved to see a faint glimmer of approval in his eyes.

He seemed satisfied with her response. "My name is Mr Nelson," he declared. "I am your schoolmaster.

For three hours a day, you will read and write. You've already shown me that you can read. Let's see how your writing skills are. Children, please take out your writing slates."

With that, he turned, and the lesson began.

Addy watched as the other children lifted the lids on their desks and pulled out small slate boards. She copied their movements, fumbling slightly as she pulled out her own slate and set it on top of her desk.

Mr Nelson began to write a sentence on the board.

"Neatness and precision will be rewarded. I want to see this sentence written exactly as I have," Mr Nelson announced.

Addy's hand trembled slightly as she picked up the slate pencil and pressed it carefully into the dark, grained surface. She loved learning and quickly settled into the lesson.

Mr Nelson's footsteps clicked against the cold stone floor as he moved along each row of desks. Addy held her breath as he leaned over her shoulder to inspect her slate. She had taken extra care with her letters, trying to form each one as neatly as she could, but his face was unreadable as he studied her careful loops and lines.

He made a noncommittal grunt and moved on. Addy exhaled in relief and returned her concentration to her slate. The classroom was silent, save for the occasional cough or deep sigh, until Mr Nelson's voice cut sharply through the air.

"This," he sneered, holding up a slate for the entire class to see, "is what happens when a person lacks discipline." He thrust the slate under the nose of a child and barked, "This is a disgrace! You haven't even tried."

Addy worried her lip as she stole a glance and felt a

pang of dread when she recognised Janey's profile. From this angle, she could see the crooked, smudged letters—the hurried marks of someone who hadn't quite mastered the art of writing. Janey's face was a furious shade of red, her head bowed into her shoulders as Mr Nelson heaped disdain upon her.

"Pathetic," Mr Nelson continued. "You are only fit to scrub floors with writing like this. You'll stay behind after class, and you'll rewrite this until it's passable. Perhaps that will teach you the value of making a proper effort."

Addy jolted as Mr Nelson dropped Janey's slate back onto her desk with a clatter. Janey's chin trembled as she fought back tears, and the room was once again filled only with the scratching of pencils against slates. Each child silently thanked their luck that they'd escaped the schoolmaster's wrath.

When Mr Nelson finally rang the bell to mark the end of the lesson, Addy set down her pencil. Three hours of constant studying had made her hand ache. The children obediently formed a single line and filed out of the room, their footsteps echoing against the floor in a steady rhythm. As she was at the back of the line, she was the last to leave.

She lingered, wanting to wait for Janey but remembering her friend had to stay late for punishment. She hesitated by the door, but Janey was hunched over her desk, head down.

She wanted to stay, but Matron's sharp reprimand changed her mind.

"Adelaide! Off to the kitchen with you, right this minute," she ordered, waving Addy along.

Addy returned to the kitchen and resumed her tasks. The rest of the day dragged by in a blur of scoldings and chores. When Janey didn't appear at suppertime, Addy began to worry. She didn't see her friend again until all the children were back in the dormitory.

The other children were chatting in clusters, but Janey sat away from them all, alone on her bed, shoulders hunched as if she were trying to disappear.

Tentatively, Addy made her way over to Janey's bed. "Janey?"

When Janey didn't move, Addy reached out and gently touched her friend's shoulder.

"Go away," Janey muttered.

Addy hesitated. "Please, Janey. I just wanted to check if you're alright. You've been so kind to me here... I just wanted to make sure you were okay."

Janey shrugged suddenly. "Do as you like."

"May I sit down?"

Janey sighed heavily, her gaze resolutely fixed on her feet. "Free country, isn't it?"

Ignoring the curious glances from the other girls, Addy carefully sat down beside Janey.

Addy dipped her head lower so that her face would appear in Janey's line of sight. "I didn't care for what Mr Nelson said to you," she said gently.

Janey's eyes flicked up, and Addy could see the redness around them, signs of the tears she'd tried so hard to hide. She met Addy's gaze for a moment before dropping her eyes back to her hands. "It's true though, isn't it? It's alright for the likes of you. I'm only fit for the workhouse."

Addy shook her head. "That's not true. You're bright and quick."

Janey rolled her eyes. "I'm thick as a log. Can't even read as well as you, nor write my own name."

"I could teach you," Addy offered quickly, "if you'd like me to."

Janey stared at her for a moment, her expression guarded, before her gaze dropped back to her hands, where she was picking at the cuticles around her thumbs. "No point, is there?"

"There is," Addy insisted. "You might start scrubbing floors, but the housekeeper in our home started out her working life as a scullery maid. She became the housekeeper because she could read and write. There's nothing wrong with scrubbing floors if that's what you want to do, but reading and writing can help you get better jobs if you want them."

Janey plucked at her skin until Addy laid a gentle hand over hers to still the movement.

"Please, Janey. I think with just a few lessons, we'll get you there."

Janey didn't move, but Addy sensed she had her attention.

Addy leaned in close, so only Janey could hear. "Wouldn't you like to prove Mr Nelson wrong?"

Janey's lips twitched. Her eyes lifted to meet Addy's, and Addy saw a glimmer of defiance in them.

"Alright," Janey whispered, her voice low. "How would we do it?"

CHAPTER 16

The bell tolled every morning at precisely five o'clock, its harsh clang wrenching Addy from her narrow bed. Her body, still aching from the previous day's work, protested as she rolled out. But she knew better than to linger; any delay would be met with a sharp reprimand from Matron Fishman.

Life in the workhouse followed the same regimented routine every day. Every hour was accounted for—work, meals, lessons—all slotted into a schedule as rigid as the walls that surrounded them.

After the bell sounded, the children were to wash and then line up, groggy and yawning, to receive their meagre breakfast. Lessons were the only part of her day that Addy truly looked forward to.

Mr Nelson, though strict and quick to wield the birch branch when his patience wore thin, introduced her to books and stories she had never heard of before. Much like the time she'd spent with her father, tales of far-off places and thrilling adventures captured Addy's imagination. But she was careful to keep her enthusiasm subdued, for Mr Nelson had a quick temper, and the birch branch was never far from his reach, ready to strike any child who dared to speak out of turn or failed to meet his exacting standards.

Even free time was scheduled. Three times a day, they were allowed outside, and whenever they were granted time in the yard, Addy would pull Janey aside to teach her to write. They would find a quiet corner where silt had collected and crouch down, painstakingly tracing letters in the mud with sticks. Slowly but surely, Janey's letters grew steadier, and Addy was certain she would never forget the proud grin on Janey's face when she managed to write her own name without any help.

The two girls had become inseparable, a quiet alliance in a place that was bleak and unfeeling. Janey became Addy's protector; whenever someone taunted Addy for her polite elocution or ability to read, Janey would appear, shoulders squared and fists bunched, ready to defend her friend. In turn, Addy helped Janey in every way she could and clung to their friendship like a lifeline.

Alongside the other girls, Addy was taught needlework, mending garments and sewing in straight lines with tiny, precise stitches. Any and all skills that would both make the workhouse money and prepare her for a life in service. They scrubbed in the kitchens and toiled in the laundry rooms, working until their hands were red and raw, and their arms ached. Addy kept her head down, completing each task to the best of her ability, knowing that these skills might one day offer her a way out of this place.

Days were long and monotonous, each one blending into the next as winter gradually faded, though the arrival of spring brought little change to the cold granite walls that enclosed them.

Other than her time with Janey, the only other part of Addy's weekly routine she looked forward to was seeing her mother in the yard. Around them, families congregated, filling the air with laughter and squeals of joy. Yet Addy often found herself sitting beside a subdued Henrietta. More often than not, Henrietta would stand in the corner of the yard, sitting on an upturned bucket or keeping to herself, away from the joyous reunions. Her fingers were stained from the oakum work that the women were required to do—picking apart tarred rope fibres. A tedious, endless task, with the end product sold back to the dockyards for use in caulking ships.

One day, hoping to cheer her mother up, Addy brought Janey over to meet her.

"This is Janey, Mama," Addy nudged her friend forward. "She's a very good friend of mine and has been looking out for me here."

Henrietta's gaze drifted over Janey, her smile faint. "Hello."

"I'm helping her with her writing, Mama, so that one day she can leave here too. Because we won't be here forever, will we?"

Henrietta turned to her daughter, absently brushing a hand over her shorn head. "Why did you cut your hair?"

Addy blinked, fighting the sudden sting of tears. It had been cut almost two months ago. "One of the girls had lice," she lied, glancing helplessly at Janey.

"That's nice," Henrietta murmured distantly.

Addy tried her best to lift her mother's spirits, sharing stories about her day and the things she'd learned, but nothing seemed to break through Henrietta's shroud of melancholy.

"I'm scared, Janey," she admitted as they headed back to the laundry room. "It's like she's... fading away."

"It happens to some," Janey replied. "This place can break people's spirits."

Addy didn't like the sound of that. "What else can I say to her?" She glanced back at her mother, who was staring vacantly into the distance.

Janey shrugged. "The workhouse crushes some, not others. Some stay their whole lives, others leave after a short stint. They come and they go, sometimes on the same day, returning at night when their fortunes fail."

Addy stared at her friend.

Janey smiled knowingly. "They stumble back, smelling of ale from a day spent at the inn. But those people get a glimpse of life outside, and that keeps them going."

Addy frowned, wondering if a break from the workhouse might help her mother, though she couldn't imagine Henrietta spending the day in a public house. She wished she could do something—*anything*—to ease her mother's pain.

Janey slung an arm over her shoulders, giving her a reassuring squeeze as they waited for the other women to enter the laundry. "Don't worry too much. She's your mama. You're tough, so I'm sure she'll be fine."

Meals were eaten in silence after prayers. The food was measly, barely enough to satisfy her hunger—watery gruel, watery broth.

Addy would fall asleep dreaming of the feasts they

used to have at Lowther House, knowing that such thoughts only made her growling stomach worse, yet she couldn't help herself. Even on the rare days when they were given meat and cheese, the hunger never quite disappeared.

As spring gave way to summer, the longer daylight hours brought an extra hour of work each day. Janey and Addy crouched in the yard corner; Janey's attention focused on the letters she painstakingly scratched into the thick mud. A shadow suddenly fell over them, and Addy looked up, dread zipping through her. But rather than the scolding she expected from Mrs Fishman, the matron's grave expression filled her with a different kind of fear.

"Addy, you must come with me."

Addy exchanged a puzzled look with Janey, then obediently followed the matron. She was led through the dingy hallway, but instead of being taken to Mr Nelson and his waiting birch branch, the matron directed her toward the master's office.

The matron knocked, a quick tap-tap, and waited for her husband's muffled response before opening the door.

"Adelaide Hill, Gordon."

The workhouse master let out a sigh that sounded more like resignation, doing nothing to ease the trepidation pooling in Addy's stomach.

Mr Fishman leaned back in his seat, his fingertips tapping a quick rhythm on the mahogany desktop. "I shan't take much of your time, Adelaide. I'm afraid I have some sad news."

It was the hesitation that undid Addy. Her gaze darted between the two adults, and she knew, even before he spoke, what he was going to say.

The world tilted beneath her feet, her pulse pounding in her ears so that she barely heard his words.

"Your mother was found dead in her bed this morning."

CHAPTER 17

Life for Addy had irrevocably changed, and yet she didn't have much time to dwell on it.

The workhouse routine dragged on relentlessly, an endless daily loop of chores, lessons, and paltry meals.

There was little time for something as significant as grief.

Addy drifted through each day as though watching everything from behind a veil, seeing it all with a dull detachment. She longed to be left alone to mourn her mother properly, but there was no time for such luxury, certainly no space for solitude within the rigid schedule.

Dragged along by the regime, the days blurred as the seasons shifted outside the stark stone walls. Arguments between the children over trivial matters, disputes in the dormitory over who was right or wrong—all these squabbles seemed hollow and unimportant to Addy now.

She was an orphan, like so many of the children she shared the dormitory with.

Perhaps that was why most of the bullies now left her alone, though she suspected it had more to do with Janey's fierce protection.

Addy felt the loss of her mother most keenly on days when the children shared the outside yard with their mothers. She would watch the warm embraces between mother and daughter, and her chest would ache. But Janey was always there, gently tugging her away to their quiet corner so that she could practice writing in the dirt with the stubby stick they tucked into the wall's crevices for safekeeping. The snow came and melted. Spring warmed the air. It thickened with stifling summer fogs, then turned crisp again as autumn crept back in.

The same routine, day in and day out, that you could set a watch by. In some strange way, it was almost a comfort.

It wasn't until the yard was blanketed in white snow that something finally broke through Addy's indifference. It happened during one of Mr Nelson's lessons.

He held up a slate for the class to see and declared in his booming voice, "Hard work and dedication pay off! Look at this. Why can't the rest of you write this well? Are you even trying?"

Blinking to clear the melancholy, Addy saw Janey's triumphant grin as she looked over at her. Addy's heart skipped a beat when she saw Janey's name neatly scrawled across the top of the slate, her letters steady and clear against the black surface.

That evening, the dormitory buzzed with excitement over Janey's success. Animated chatter, whispers, and giggles filled the air as the other girls admired all the hours of secret lessons that had paid off. Janey tried to shrug off the attention, but Addy encouraged her to take pride in her efforts.

"But you helped," Janey pointed out, and Addy felt a quiet warmth spread through her chest that she hadn't felt in a long time. She felt a small hand on her shoulder and turned to find Rose, a slight girl with mousy brown hair and a dusting of freckles, beaming up at her with a crooked smile.

"Will you teach me?" Rose asked.

And so it began.

Each day, during their brief and precious moments of freedom in the yard, Addy found herself in one corner or another, surrounded by a small cluster of girls scratching letters into the dirt with sticks. Soon, all four corners of the yard were occupied by little hubs of activity. Addy moved from one group to the next, offering gentle corrections and encouragement. For Addy, it filled her with something that felt close to hope.

The workhouse, for all its cruelty, couldn't crush their desire for something better.

"Addy, tell us a story," one of the girls would often plead as night settled over the workhouse.

And so, night after night, long after Mrs Fishman had extinguished the candles, Addy's soft voice would fill the room. She wove tales of strange creatures and powerful gods who argued over the fates of mortals, stories from her imagination mingled with those her father had once told her. Tales of resilience, grief, and love, to ward off bad dreams and soften the harsh reality of their lives.

"In the beginning," she would always start, closing

her eyes as images unfurled behind her lids, "there was a girl who fell in love with a mortal. But the other gods were jealous of their love. They saw it as a betrayal…"

For a short while, her stories transformed the dormitory, filling it with whispers and gasps, as the girls listened to tales of daring deeds, unimaginable odds, and love that endured through grief and struggle. These stories made them feel a little less small, a little less forgotten. They became the adventurers, the voyagers in a world that stretched far beyond the high grey walls enclosing them.

It was a balm for Addy, too—a way to weave her grief and loss into tales. She felt a flicker of her old self returning when she found solace in helping and storytelling.

Addy's stories gave them the courage to hope that perhaps one day, they would all find a way out of the workhouse.

Until the day came when Addy was summoned to the workhouse master's office.

CHAPTER 18

Addy trotted alongside the matron as the older woman strode briskly through the maze of stone corridors. She tried repeatedly to steal glances at the matron's face, hoping to catch a hint of what was to come, to gauge just how much trouble she might be in—though she wasn't sure why. Speaking to the workhouse master was never a good sign, and her mind was restless, flitting back to the lessons in the dirt, the whispered stories at night.

Her stomach twisted.

The workhouse master's office lay at the end of the hall, past the male and female waiting rooms. Its door was polished dark wood, distinct from the whitewashed, worn doors of the other rooms. Matron knocked three times and waited until granted access.

The office was panelled with dark wood, like the door. The wooden floor was clean but scuffed, bearing the marks of many who had come seeking help from the man behind the desk. Behind him, shelves were packed with ledgers and various leather-bound tomes.

The air felt stale, tinged with dust and a faint bite of lamp oil.

"You wanted to see Adelaide Hill," Mrs Fishman announced.

"Come in, come in, Adelaide," the workhouse master said briskly. Addy stepped further into the room, only to notice there were others present. Alongside Mr Fishman stood Mr Nelson, his usual scowl replaced with a somewhat satisfied expression. Beside him was an elegant woman Addy had never seen before. Dressed in deep violet satin, she radiated a composed aura that seemed out of place in the austere surroundings. The door clicked shut, and Addy realised Mrs Fishman was staying in the room with her.

Her thoughts scrambled, trying to come up with something to say to explain the yard writing or storytelling, but Mr Fishman was already speaking, his tone overly hearty.

It took a moment for Addy to catch up.

"This is Mrs Margaret Scorby," Mr Fishman was saying, gesturing towards the woman. "She and her husband are longstanding members of our board of guardians."

Addy's eyes took in Mrs Scorby's attire—the violet gown and matching hat, with fat, yellow gems sparkling at her throat, as well as a brooch pinned just below her shoulder. Raven-black hair framed her face, and her sharp blue eyes, bordered by dark lashes, seemed both welcoming and formidable.

A nudge from Mrs Fishman reminded Addy of her manners.

"Good morning, Mrs Scorby," she said politely.

"Hello, Adelaide," Mrs Scorby replied, her gaze

assessing as it swept over Addy's drab uniform. Addy had the distinct feeling she was being sized up. "Mr Nelson was just telling me about your attitude in the classroom. Do you enjoy learning?"

"I do, Mrs Scorby," Addy replied, glancing quickly at Mr Nelson, who gave her a strange smile.

"She's one of our brightest students," Mr Fishman added with an approving nod. "In fact, my wife tells me she's been helping the other students in her spare time."

Addy's heart pounded. *Mrs Fishman knew about her secret lessons—and had said nothing?*

"She's helped several of our girls improve their writing," Mr Nelson confirmed.

Mrs Scorby raised an eyebrow, looking impressed. "Is that so?"

"Yes," Addy replied, her voice soft but steady.

"And why do you do such a generous thing?"

Addy hesitated. "I believe... if we could all help each other just a little, the world would be a much better place."

Mrs Scorby's expression warmed. "A lovely sentiment for someone so young."

"She's bright," Mr Fishman remarked approvingly. "And she's a quick study. I doubt she'll give you any trouble."

"Well, Mr Fishman, you've yet to steer me wrong," Mrs Scorby said as she stood up. "I shall make the donation for her indenture today, and then we'll be on our way."

"You're taking the girl now?" Mr Nelson interjected, surprise crossing his face.

"I don't see the point in delay, do you?" Mrs Scorby

replied smoothly. "The early bird catches the worm, after all."

The adults moved around her with practised ease, leaving Addy glancing between them all, still bewildered. Before she could fully grasp what was happening, Mrs Fishman was guiding her from the room.

Instead of heading back to the familiar hallway towards the laundry room, Matron steered her towards the waiting room.

"Where... where am I going?" Addy asked, voice shaking slightly.

"Come along," the matron replied curtly. Addy's mind scrambled, her steps faltering as they passed the vestry clerk's office and the porter's residence. Her anxiety grew with each step.

"Matron," Addy said with a tremor, "I... I must get back to work."

The matron gave her an exasperated look, somewhere between amusement and irritation. "Don't you get it, girl? Your services are needed elsewhere."

Another door opened, and Addy was propelled inside. She found herself in the same room where she and her mother had first waited. Her mouth went dry as her eyes landed on a small pile of clothes laid out on the bench against the wall: a blue dress, stockings, shoes, and a grey woollen shawl.

Her own clothes—the ones she hadn't seen since the day they'd arrived.

"Matron, what's happening?" Addy whispered, her voice barely audible.

Mrs Fishman sighed, placing her hands on her hips with a look of diminishing patience. "You're leaving here, Addy. You're starting a new job in service for Mrs Reginald Scorby."

CHAPTER 19

Sitting in a carriage once more felt strange and unfamiliar.

The scenery passed by in a blur that Addy barely registered. All she could think about was the friends she'd left behind. She hadn't been given a chance to say goodbye to any of them, and when she protested, Matron had grown cross with her.

Most of all, she was upset that she hadn't been allowed to tell Janey that leaving hadn't been her choice and that she hadn't wanted to abandon her. Matron had insisted it wasn't a matter of choice and that she should be grateful Mrs Scorby was giving her a chance.

Mrs Scorby travelled with a lady's maid, a woman with a perpetual frown that gave her a look of distaste whenever Addy met her gaze. Mrs Scorby had introduced her as Hopkins. Each time Addy caught her eye, Hopkins gave her a frosty stare that seemed to measure and judge her.

"I dare say you'll find it a bit different now, given

what you're used to," Hopkins sneered as the carriage trundled along the road.

Addy turned her gaze to the carriage interior. "Yes, miss."

"Actually, Hopkins," Mrs Scorby interjected, "Adelaide grew up in a big house near Manchester."

"Not as grand as Longhaven, though, Mrs Scorby," sniffed Hopkins, clearly unimpressed.

Mrs Scorby and Addy exchanged a smile. "You'll have to forgive Hopkins," Mrs Scorby said. "She's very loyal to the family."

"With good reason," Hopkins added primly. "The family are very good employers."

Mrs Scorby's eyes sparkled at the praise. "Yes, well, we do try." Her gaze settled on Addy. "You'll settle soon enough, I'm sure."

"Yes, miss," murmured Addy, though her stomach twisted with uncertainty.

The countryside beyond the window was achingly familiar, yet entirely new. Gone were the city haze and pungent smells, replaced by rolling hills, lush and vibrant with spring growth, and fields bathed in sunlight. Stone cottages and small farmsteads dotted the landscape, and as they passed, Addy's chest ached for all that had once been.

Villages and hamlets slipped past until the carriage slowed, turning into a wide, sweeping drive lined with ancient oak trees. Ahead, a grand manor house came into view, its grey stone walls gleaming in the afternoon sun. It was breathtaking—a vast Italianate-style edifice, and was much larger than any house she'd known, with rows of sparkling windows catching the light.

Addy couldn't help but stare at its grandeur, the

symmetrical lines, and the imposing columns. The carriage pulled up alongside the front steps, and two footmen appeared at the double doors, dressed impeccably in livery with double-breasted coats, waistcoats, trousers, and small black ties knotted at their throats. They moved with practised grace, one—an older man—opening the door while the younger one stood at attention.

"Afternoon, Mrs Scorby," the older footman greeted her with a slight bow.

"Hello, Charlie."

A distinguished-looking man with neatly combed silver hair appeared in the doorway and descended the curved stone steps. "Good afternoon, Mrs Scorby. I trust you had a successful trip?"

The older footman extended a hand to help her down.

"Yes, I'm certain Mrs Burgess will be pleased," Mrs Scorby replied. She paused to pluck off her gloves and hand them to the footman. She chatted to the butler, their voices fading as they disappeared through the front doorway.

Now that Mrs Scorby had gone inside, both footmen seemed to lose their solemnity. They shared a quick look and then turned to stare openly at Addy.

The younger one's gaze was filled with curiosity. "And who do we have here, then?"

Hopkins rolled her eyes disdainfully. "Another street rat from the workhouse," she muttered scornfully. "Why she can't hire a proper maid, I'll never understand."

"Now, now," the older footman replied, undeterred. "You never know. This one might be different from the others."

Hopkins scoffed. "I'll be a monkey's uncle if that's true."

The driver, unimpressed, cut in. "Haven't you all got better things to do than gossip like fishwives?" He jerked his head towards the bags. "Get on with it. I've got to groom, feed, and stable these horses for the night before I lose the light, so quick as you like."

Suitably chastised, the two footmen grabbed up the several bags and carried them inside. Hopkins collected another and began walking around the side of the house. Under an ivy-covered stone archway, she paused and looked back at where Addy stood, clutching her leather satchel.

"Hurry up, then. You can't clean fireplaces from there, and if you stand in one spot for much longer, you'll grow roots," Hopkins barked before marching around the corner and disappearing.

Addy glanced at the driver, who offered her a small, sympathetic smile. "Typical lady's maid," he muttered. "Far too above her station, that one. My name is Griff."

"Addy," she whispered, a reluctant smile tugging at the edges of her mouth.

Griff climbed up into the driver's spot and gathered the reins. "Best go on and get yourself inside. Keep your head down and your nose clean, and you'll do all right."

CHAPTER 20

Addy stood wide-eyed in the cavernous kitchen of Longhaven. Though it was much smaller than the workhouse kitchen, it was run with the same clockwork efficiency. She reminded herself that the purpose of this kitchen was not to feed hundreds but to create gourmet meals for a single family.

The cook, a broad woman in a light blue uniform and white apron, scrutinised her closely. A halo of frizzy brown hair topped with a mob cap framed her face.

The housekeeper, a neat and slender woman named Mrs Burgess, breezed into the kitchen. "I see you've met your new scullery maid, Mrs Porter," she announced, glancing at Addy.

"She's not much to look at, is she?" The cook's scepticism was evident. "Barely looks strong enough to hold her own weight, let alone carry a bucket of ashes up and down the stairs."

Addy kept her head down, clutching her satchel a

little tighter to her chest. She was used to being spoken about as if she wasn't there, but she didn't like it. However, she kept her mouth shut, especially now that she no longer had Janey to protect her.

Mrs Burgess looked at Addy as if seeing her for the first time, though Hopkins had marched her past the housekeeper's sitting room not five minutes earlier. "She comes highly recommended by the workhouse governor."

Mrs Porter didn't look impressed. "Time will tell, won't it?"

Mrs Burgess agreed and turned to Addy. "We don't have all day."

Addy followed, hefting her satchel up higher. The housekeeper led her down a narrow corridor lined with doors and openings leading to various rooms: a larder with stacked shelves, a spacious storeroom, and the butler's sitting room. She caught a brief glimpse of the service hall, a low-ceilinged room with a long table where the staff gathered for meals. Each doorway offered her a peek into this new world, one that was both strange and yet somehow familiar.

She understood the routines of service, but this would be her life now.

They paused at a doorway leading to a smaller room filled with the smell of soap and stone.

"This is the scullery," Mrs Burgess announced. Addy peered inside. Shelves lined the walls, holding an assortment of pots, brushes, and other tools. Two deep stone sinks sat beneath a small foggy window, and a narrow, sturdy wooden table held dirty pots and pans, set apart from the pristine main kitchen. "This is where you'll be doing most of your work. I expect it to be kept spic and span. The scullery maid might have a lonely position, but the work is essential to helping the house run smoothly. Do you understand?"

"Yes, ma'am," Addy replied quickly, remembering Mary's words.

"Come along then," the housekeeper said, leading her further along the hallway to another door. Here, a constricted winding staircase spiralled upwards, the stone steps worn from years of use. "You will only use these stairs," she said over her shoulder. Her footsteps echoed as she climbed. "These are for the servants. Family and guests use the main staircase." She paused on a landing to look back at Addy. "That's one rule I don't like to see broken."

They continued up, the stairwell narrowing as they reached the attic floor. A long, plain hallway stretched out before them, lined with doors on each side, ending in a heavy locked door in the middle. Through the glass, Addy could see that the hallway continued on with matching doors on the other side.

"This side is for the girls," Mrs Burgess told her. "The men are on the other side, and you are never to go across there. Only I am permitted to open that door." She paused, looking pointedly at Addy. "Do you understand?"

Addy nodded quickly.

Mrs Burgess carried on. She opened a door at the far end of the hallway and led her inside. The room was small and sparsely furnished, with two beds covered in dark blue blankets. A single wardrobe stood against one wall, and under the lone window was a small washstand with a jug and a bowl for washing. Two candleholders sat atop a narrow set of drawers.

"The water closet is down the hall," Mrs Burgess said, casting a critical eye over the room. She pointed to a red-and-white striped dress laid neatly across one bed. "That's your bed and your uniform." There was a starched white apron and a cap folded beside it. "I expect you to maintain that dress. Any holes you make, you repair. And you are to remove any stains. It may be a bit big for you, but you'll grow into it soon enough." She paused, raising an eyebrow as she inspected Addy. "You have the day to settle in. You'll get half a day off on Sundays. Your wages are paid quarterly. Our supper is before the family eats, always at six o'clock sharp in the service hall. If you're late, you don't eat."

Addy swallowed. "T-thank you, Mrs Burgess," she managed, though nerves fluttered inside her.

With a final appraising glance, Mrs Burgess left. The door clicked shut behind her, leaving Addy alone in the room.

Slowly, she lowered herself onto her mattress and set her satchel down by her feet. Her gaze lingered on the unfamiliar room. This place was her new world. A pang of guilt hit her as she thought of Janey and the other children she'd left behind. Who would tell them the stories now? She wondered, as she contemplated her new surroundings, what would become of her life here?

CHAPTER 21

At first, life at Longhaven felt overwhelming. The Lowther family had seemed wealthy to her, but Longhaven was three times the size and required a team of staff that dwarfed those at Lowther Manor. Addy knew wealth but never on the scale of the Scorby family's fortune.

Below stairs was like a never-ending carousel of staff, with footmen, maids, stable hands, hall boys, and delivery boys rolling through the lower half of the house in a constant ebb and flow. The butler, Mr Smale, oversaw the male staff, while the housekeeper managed the female staff.

There was a hierarchy to the servants. The scullery maid was on the bottom rung. However, most of the staff were kind and supportive of Addy. Working in service was considered a respectable career choice, often pursued for a lifetime. There was a collective sense of pride among the staff, as serving a wealthy and prominent family also elevated their own status within society. The only exception was Hopkins. As the lady's maid, she held a higher position in the household and did not hide her disdain for the other maids. She was all too eager to remind them of her elevated position, though never within earshot of Mrs Burgess.

The servants' hall was always bustling, full of constant chatter and whispered tales that painted a social tapestry of the family estate.

Reginald Scorby owned extensive properties and held stakes in various businesses, from shipping to farming. He was often away on business, and when he was home, the family entertained frequently. Guests ranged from landed gentry to the occasional duke, and the staff worked tirelessly to prepare lavish meals and maintain the spotless rooms.

Platters flowed constantly up and down the staircase, with the footmen donning white gloves to serve each course.

Addy kept out of the way, tucked away in the scullery. Though she did listen eagerly to the gossip as the footmen relayed snatches of conversation from the family's table.

Life below stairs was different, yet familiar, and just like at Lowther House, she found herself more comfortable down there than in the grand rooms above.

Addy wasn't afraid of the hard work. She'd learned long ago that if she did her tasks to the best of her ability, those in charge were pleased — and the same held true with the senior staff at Longhaven.

Mrs Porter kept a sharp eye on everything, and it didn't take long for her to notice that Addy had a knack for getting things done before she even had to be asked.

Unlike the others, Addy didn't once complain. No one understood the importance of having a job better than she did.

For the first time in her life, she was earning money that was her own.

Her working day began early, and she was often the first one up. Mrs Porter had high standards, and while the woman was quick with a scolding, she never lashed out physically.

Addy shared a room with another maid named Lucy. Older than Addy, she was proficient in her duties. A local girl, Lucy was shy and had a gentle way about her. She was the youngest of eleven children. Her parents, not needing another mouth to feed, seemed happy to send her into service. Living with Lucy was easy; she kept her side of the room tidy, was quiet as a church mouse, and focused on her work.

Lucy had shown her the ropes, helping her quickly get up to speed with her duties.

"Never fill your bucket more than halfway," Lucy said as they quietly made their way along the hallway. "Filling it up too much makes it too heavy—and you don't want to be like Maude, do you?"

Addy frowned at her new roommate. "Who's Maude?"

Lucy paused in front of a closed doorway, lowering her voice to a whisper. "Overfilled her bucket once and ended up dropping it down the back stairs," her dark eyes sparkled with mirth. "Mr Smale almost bust a gut over the mess, and she was dismissed instantly."

Addy certainly didn't want to end up like Maude. Mr Smale was a formidable presence in the servants' hall, and she wanted to do her best to stay on his good side.

Lucy knocked twice on the door, waited a moment, then opened it a crack and peered inside. She pressed the door all the way open and gestured for Addy to enter. The tin bucket clanged as Addy stepped into the room, and Lucy held a finger to her lips. "We must be quiet at all times. We don't want to disturb the master or the mistress, now, do we?

"Always knock on the door to check. Most of the time, these rooms are empty, but Mrs Burgess will be up later to check that you've done your job properly. The master's bedroom is at the other end of the corridor, with the mistress's room next to it. Young Master Henry's room is a little further along, and those are the rooms that are occupied each night. Then there's the tutor's room, but we always leave those until last."

Learning that there was a tutor in the house filled Addy with dreaded memories of Miss Fisher, Marjorie's cantankerous governess, but this tutor seemed far less intrusive. He schooled young Henry Scorby in the three R's, as well as history, Greek and Religion, all fine subjects for a young man of such an upstanding family before he went off to public school.

She quickly set to work emptying the ashes. Remembering Mrs Burgess's words, she kept close to the edge of the corridor as she carried her tin bucket up and down the narrow, twisting servant's staircase. She left the ashes in the pit next to the outside water closet before climbing back up to the first floor.

Lucy worked swiftly through her tasks, changing the beds and making them neat. She also tidied the rooms and tied back the heavy curtains. It was Addy's job to clean out and lay fresh kindling in the fireplaces in each room, plus keep them stoked throughout the day. Quite often, Lucy finished on a floor and moved on, leaving Addy alone to complete her work.

The last room on the first floor was young Master Henry's.

As instructed, Addy knocked and waited; as expected, the room was empty. In contrast to the grand opulence of the master's and mistress's rooms, this room, while nicely furnished, had the unmistakable appearance of a child's space. The wall colours were muted. Lucy had already tidied the clothes away, hanging them neatly in the cherrywood wardrobe.

Just as Lucy had warned, Mrs Burgess came upstairs to check on her as she was finishing up young Master Henry's fireplace. Addy didn't have time to worry about whether she'd met the housekeeper's exact standards before she was hurried down the back stairs to the scullery. The small table, cleared of everything before she'd started on the fireplaces, was once again covered in dirty pots and pans. A bucket of vegetables waited to be peeled on the floor by one of the sinks

And so, it went on. Unlike the workhouse, where tasks had been spread among many children, the work here seemed endless. Just like in the workhouse, she rose at first light, her body still aching from the previous day. Though Longhaven's kitchen was smaller and catered only to the family and guests, it still ran with the precision of a well-oiled machine.

By the time she climbed into bed each night, she was exhausted.

Before she slept, she would say a prayer for Janey and Rose, and bless her parents. For she missed them all very much.

CHAPTER 22

Sundays became Addy's favourite day of the week.

After the morning church service, she was granted a few hours of free time, which she used to wander the fields and explore the woods surrounding Longhaven.

She climbed stiles and fences with abandon, delighting in the natural ponds and the rabbit warren of lanes connecting the local area. The estate grounds sprawled with red-brick barns and large stables holding a team of horses owned by the household. Griff, the groom she'd met on her first day, would indulge her, letting her feed the horses an apple she'd scavenged from the stores. He didn't laugh at her if he overheard her chatting to the chickens and pigs as she fed them scraps during the week.

One of her favourite spots was the dovecote, a round stone structure on the edge of the estate. It had small openings high up where doves and pigeons perched. Inside, rows of nesting boxes lined the walls, and the gentle cooing of the birds filled the air as they watched her from above.

Spring passed quickly, and Addy revelled in the warmth of summer. Meadows filled with wildflowers became her sanctuary, where she would lie in the grass, watching clouds drift by on lazy Sunday afternoons. She saved every penny she earned, delighting in watching the coins pile up as the chill of autumn crept in. Finally, after setting aside all she could, she indulged in a small present for herself. It felt strange to make such a luxury purchase after years of scraping by, but when she went to the servants' hall to pick up her lunch, she was thrilled to see her parcel had arrived. She set it down and eagerly tugged at the string, excitement bubbling up inside her.

Before she could open it, though, Charlie, one of the footmen, snatched the parcel from her hands with a mischievous grin. "What do you have there, Addy?"

"Please," she stretched for it, "give it back."

Charlie held the book aloft, dangling it just out of her reach, and then tossed it to Samuel, another footman, when he strolled into the servants' hall.

The older lad took in the scene and quickly joined in the teasing. *"The Pilgrim's Progress?"* Samuel mocked as he read the title, "Well, how do you like that for a scullery maid?"

Addy reached again, but Samuel tossed the book to Bertie, the hall boy.

"You're going to rip it!" Addy said desperately. "That cost me three months' wages!"

The other servants were laughing, drowning out her pleas, but the laughter died as a sharp, authoritative voice sliced through the room. *"What* is going on here?"

Everyone's eyes widened as Mr Smale's severe expression swept across the room.

Red-faced, Bertie quickly set the book down on the table, his gaze fixed on his feet.

Mr Smale picked up the book and glanced at its spine. "What is this, Albert?"

"The boys were teasing Addy," Lucy piped up, "because she used her wages to buy herself a book."

Mr Smale's bushy black eyebrow arched as he gave each of the three young men a stern look. "And why were you teasing her, Albert?"

"Samuel started it," Bertie mumbled into his chest.

"Charlie gave it to me," Samuel added quickly.

"Don't you three have better things to do? Or would you rather find employment elsewhere?"

"No, Mr Smale!" They chorused.

The butler continued, "Perhaps you should take a leaf out of Adelaide's book and better yourselves by expanding your horizons. Unless you want to stay a hall boy or a footman for the rest of your lives."

He held out the book, and Addy took it, relief washing over her. "There are books in my sitting room, Adelaide," he said, giving her an approving nod. "You're welcome to borrow one and save your money if you like. I do expect them to be returned in the same condition as you take them."

"Thank you, Mr Smale," she replied, clutching the book to her chest.

Mr Smale swept his gaze across the room once more. "Back to work, all of you."

He stalked out of the servants' hall, and murmurs of discontent rippled among the other servants, irritated at being reprimanded because of Addy.

But she didn't care. She'd heard much worse in the

past and their words rolled off her like water off a duck's back.

~

THOUGH ADDY HAD HEARD all about young Henry Scorby and the lofty path he was already set upon, she had yet to meet him.

By the time she reached his room to tend to the fireplace each morning, the young master was already deep in study elsewhere within the grand house. She'd listened to the servants' chatter and gathered that next summer, young Henry would turn thirteen, meaning he'd be off to boarding school—likely Eton or Harrow—to study languages, law, and more. They speculated if he would go on to university, too.

She found herself wondering what cities like London and Edinburgh looked like. What it would be like to experience learning in such places. She thought of her father, who had cherished education as a path to opportunity. He'd used his education to raise his social status from the miner his father had been.

What choices would the young master make when he already had the world at his feet?

One morning, as Addy was finishing her tasks, she picked up her tin bucket and turned, scanning the room out of habit. Her gaze drifted over the desk, falling upon two neat stacks of books. She couldn't help herself and set the bucket down, crossing the room to inspect the titles.

A small smile tugged at her lips as she recognised several. One pile contained texts on history and literature: *Principles of Political Economy*, *The Life and Letters of Lord Macaulay*. The second stack held more indulgent selections: *A Tale of Two Cities* by Charles Dickens and *The Iliad* by Homer. She plucked *The Iliad* from the middle of the pile, flicking open the cover. As her eyes scanned the opening lines, the walls of Henry's room faded, and she was back at Lowther House, curled up in her bed, hearing the words in her father's voice. The memory brought a sharp pang of sorrow as the familiar words swam before her.

"What are you doing?"

Addy jolted violently, nearly dropping the book as she spun towards the voice. Expecting Mr Smale's stern gaze, she instead found herself staring into the bluest eyes she had ever seen, framed by long, dark lashes that made them even more striking. The young master was watching her, studying her with equal intensity.

"I… I'm sorry, sir," Addy stammered, hurriedly setting the book back in place and aligning its edges with the others. "I was just…"

"Reading?" Henry took a step further into the room, a hint of incredulity in his voice that made her bristle slightly.

She quickly knuckled away the moisture around her eyes. "Actually, yes."

The young master closed the door, resting his hand on the handle as he looked at her in surprise. His resemblance to Mrs Scorby was evident: the same raven hair and finely shaped face, though his still retained the softness of youth.

Tilting his head, he checked the title of the book on top of the pile as he walked towards her. "You read *The Iliad*?"

"I haven't, not in a long time," she admitted, glancing down at the familiar cover. "My father read it to me when I was young. It was..." Her voice grew husky, trailing off as she struggled to keep her emotions at bay. She cleared her throat, trying to explain. "I meant no harm, sir."

Amusement flickered in the blue of his eyes. "I don't care much for Homer myself. His story has too many heroes with fragile egos fighting over stolen women and glory. I don't find it very realistic."

As he scanned the book titles, his fingers brushed over the leather covers. He was taller than she was, his wild, jet-black curls tumbling over his brow in careless disarray, giving him a slightly rebellious look. His lips quirked in a crooked smile when he caught her looking at him again. "What did your father do for work, if he read to you?"

"He was a land agent," she replied quietly, "for a man named Mr Chester Lowther."

"Lowther," Henry murmured thoughtfully. "I've heard of that name. Isn't he in textiles?"

"That's right, sir," Addy said. "He owns cotton mills in a village called Whitehurst, just south of Manchester."

Henry's lopsided smile reappeared. "Seems strange to be called 'sir' when I'm hardly older than you."

"Mrs Burgess would expect it... sir," she replied timidly.

He let out a soft sigh, shaking his head. "Well, we wouldn't want to upset Mrs Burgess now, would we?" His warm chuckle drew a smile from her. Curiosity burned in his eyes as he studied her anew. "What's your name?"

"Adelaide," she said, glancing up at him through her lashes. "But most people call me Addy. I'm the new scullery maid."

"I'm Henry," he replied. His gaze flicked briefly to the pile of books before looking at her again. "Do you like to read?"

"When I can," she said. "But I don't have much time for it, being as busy as I am, sir."

He continued to study her as though she were an unfamiliar creature he'd just encountered. She remembered that she still had one more hearth to clean out as well as a bucket full of vegetables to peel. Feeling self-conscious, she ducked her head and grabbed her bucket from the floor. "If you'll excuse me, sir, I'd best be getting on. Otherwise, Cook will be sending out a search party for me." She made it to the doorway and paused, turning back to meet his avid gaze. She hesitated, then said, "Begging your pardon, *The Iliad* isn't just about heroes fighting for honour. It's a story of resilience and grief... and the cost of war. It shows the strength of people, not just their weaknesses."

She slipped through the door, but not before she caught the surprised smile that spread across young Master Scorby's face.

CHAPTER 23

As the months rolled by, Addy fell into the rhythm of working within such a large team. The work was backbreaking, and as winter set in, her hands grew red and raw, covered in chilblains from being in and out of cold water.

She didn't moan. Despite the gruelling work, life in the servants' hall felt like being part of a family once again.

There was a clock in Addy's room, though she never had cause to use it. Her two years in the workhouse, waking to the bell at five o'clock had conditioned her body to rise without needing to be prompted. And it was just as well, as Addy had always been given the earliest jobs, meaning she needed to be the first out of bed.

She stood out among the staff in her red-and-white striped uniform; the other maids wore crisp black dresses with starched white aprons and caps.

In the depths of winter, Addy's tasks expanded to include keeping on top of the endless laundry, scrubbing the clothes clean of soot and mud splatter. The long days of washing, peeling until her hands were sore, and hefting her tin bucket up and down the servants' stairs had toughened her body.

Before their encounter, she had never seen Henry Scorby, but now he was often in his room whenever she came to clean his fireplace. He was usually sitting at his desk. When she walked in, he'd offer her a brief smile before returning to his studies, and she'd quietly tend to the hearth.

Until the day she found him with his books spread all out across the carpet. Some were even upended. If she didn't know better, she would guess that they'd been thrown and left wherever they landed.

Rather than his pleasant smile, he scowled at her as she walked in. "You're late."

She flinched at his brisk tone, her timid reply automatic, "Yes, sir."

He was silhouetted at the window, the wintry lands behind him were a whiteout from the snow. "Hurry up; it's freezing, and I've got exams to revise for."

Addy kept her head down and crossed the floor to kneel by the hearth. "It's snowing outside, so the fires have been burning longer to heat the house," she said quietly.

"I don't need excuses. Just hurry up and leave, will you?"

Trying not to take his sharp words to heart, she set about her work, taking care not to let the brush clang against the tin bucket. She quickly cleared the grate, arranged the kindling, and took the ashes outside to dispose of them. When she returned, Henry was slumped at his cluttered desk, head in hands, his hair dishevelled from running his fingers through it repeatedly.

Addy moved quietly, careful not to disturb him as she lit the fire. When a book suddenly tumbled onto the floor behind her, she jumped.

"I can't do it!" Henry groaned in frustration. He pushed back from his desk and paced across the room, his shoulders tense, fingers tugging at his curls as he stared out of the window.

She watched him, uncertain whether she should say anything. She added more kindling to the fire, thinking about the whispers she'd heard in the servants' hall. A lot was riding on Henry's entrance exams to the prestigious school his father had chosen. She could almost see the weight of those expectations bearing down on him.

"You have it so lucky," he muttered, almost to himself.

Addy tried not to react to the bitterness in his tone. He didn't know her past, her struggles, or what she'd endured.

"You'd probably get top marks with your eyes closed, too. I bet the hall boys would do better than me right now."

"You're talking about the entrance exams, aren't you?" she ventured.

"What do you know of it?" he snapped, turning to face her.

"Servants' talk," she replied with a shrug as she stood up.

"Do they agree with my father? Do they think I'm too stupid to handle it all and that I'll ruin the family's reputation when I fail?"

"No, they don't," she said gently. "They all think

you'll get top marks. I dare say they're envious you have this opportunity to study and learn—something that most of us will never know, especially girls like me."

Henry ran his hands down his face. "How wonderful. Now I'm being made to feel worse by the maid."

"I'm sorry," she offered. "I didn't mean to."

He sighed, his breath fogging the cold glass as he stared outside. "My father never went to Eton. He wanted to, but my grandfather wouldn't allow it."

"Eton isn't the only good school, sir. There's Winchester, Bristol... and of course, Oxford or Cambridge."

Henry rounded on her, blue eyes flashing. "That's all well and good, but when you're too thick for the words to go in, none of it matters. I've been at this for hours, and it just keeps blurring. I'm stupid... not even fit to work down in the mines or at the docks."

"You're not stupid," Addy took a step towards him. "Not by a long shot."

He gave a mirthless laugh. "Tell that to my tutor. Tell it to my father."

Addy looked around the disorder on the floor, noting the daunting stack of books—philosophy, mathematics, history—all advanced and complex subjects. "How long have you been sitting here trying to revise?"

He shrugged. "Hours," his gaze tracked hers around the room. "Since breakfast. Mr Peters, my tutor, is testing me daily now, setting endless tasks for practice. The more I read, the harder it is to take any of it in."

"Well, that's why the words aren't going in." Struck by an idea, she wiped her grubby hands on her apron as she crossed to his desk. "There was a scientist my father once told me about," she shuffled through the papers on his desk. Without waiting for permission, she took a sheet from the pile and began to rip it into a square.

"She hypothesised that taking breaks is just as important for the mind as working hard is," Addy made a fold in the paper. "She discovered that relaxing lets everything sink in properly."

"What are you doing?" Henry asked, curious enough to stand behind her.

Expertly, her nimble fingers folded, tucked, folded again. "Your mind's like a sponge. If you keep pouring water into it, it becomes saturated and can't hold any more. A break lets the sponge dry a bit so that it is then ready to soak up more water."

The paper was covered in black smudges from her sooty hands but as she folded with practised precision, it began to take shape.

Henry leaned in closer.

"This is an ancient art form," she explained as she tucked another corner. "It started in Japan. Soldiers made them to pass the time. Nowadays, they're given as symbols of peace and patience."

By now, Henry was entirely absorbed in what she was doing.

"By giving your mind a break regularly, say if you do something creative or relaxing instead of taxing, it allows your mind to process what you're asking it to do."

With a flourish, she set the delicate paper figure on top of his desk.

"It's a bird," Henry said, his face lighting up with boyish delight.

"A crane," she confirmed with a small smile. "I

haven't made one in years. My papa used to make them when he was puzzling over a problem. He said that by the time he finished, the solution usually came to him because he'd given his mind a chance to rest."

She lifted her green eyes to meet his. "You're not stupid. You just need to take a moment to let the information settle."

Henry picked up the delicate crane, twirling it in the light so that he could study the precise folds with fascination. Addy smiled as he turned it over, trying to work out how she had done it.

Eye shining, he grinned. "Can you show me how to make one?"

CHAPTER 24

The dull December light filled Henry's room as Addy followed Lucy inside, her gaze sweeping over the familiar mess. Henry glanced up from his desk. A small smile tugged at her lips when she noticed several crumpled paper cranes scattered around him.

Wordlessly, the maids got to work. Addy waited until Lucy had finished and moved on to the next bed chamber before she stepped closer to the desk. "How are you getting on with your cranes?" she asked.

Henry looked up mid-fold, a half-formed crane in his hands. "It's helping with my studies, just like you said," he replied with a grin. "Although I'll admit, mine aren't as good as yours."

Addy touched one of the paper birds with the tip of her finger, careful not to scrunch it further. Then, she bent to pick up a few discarded sheets of paper from the floor. "As with everything in life, it takes practice." She carried the discarded paper to the fire and added it to the kindling before beginning to sweep ashes from the hearth.

"Do you mind the work you do?" he asked.

Tipping the ashes into the tin bucket, she replied, "It's hard work, but I don't mind it. It's far easier than where I was before."

"Where did you work before?"

Her movements faltered, and she hesitated. She didn't like talking about the workhouse; it was a word heavy with stigma, especially among the servants. To her, it felt like a shameful mark on her past. Young gentlemen like Henry Scorby did not need to know of such places, nor the hardships the lower classes endured. She thought of Frederick and his betrayal, unwilling to expose that part of her story to the master's son.

Avoiding his curious gaze, she bit her bottom lip, the words lingering unspoken

"Cat got your tongue?" he teased, noticing her hesitation.

"No," she replied, glancing down at the ashes. "It's just... where I was before wasn't my fault. It wasn't anyone's fault, really," she murmured, swallowing down the painful memories of Liverpool.

When her silence dragged on, he said, "I've never known a person like you. You can read. You're bright and clever. You can lay a fire," he laughed. "I dare say you can do so much more than I ever could."

She met his gaze and saw the warmth in his smile. Still, she dithered. She thought of her poor mother, dying alone in her bed, surrounded by strangers and dressed in the itchy brown dress she would have despised so much. Then there was Frederick and his betrayal. Addy was unwilling to expose that part of her story to the master's son.

"You can tell me, Addy," he offered gently. "We're friends, aren't we?"

She decided that she liked Henry best in these quiet moments, when he wasn't burdened by his family's expectations.

"I was in the Liverpool workhouse," she admitted reluctantly, lowering her eyes as she felt the familiar sting of shame wash over her when Henry's blue eyes widened.

"Well, you're not there now," he said after a moment. When she looked up, his expression held no trace of judgment. "That's a good thing. My father always says that hard work and dedication can change a person's life."

Her heart lifted slightly, a faint smile breaking through her guarded expression. "My papa used to say that too."

"I think any man who reads *Homer* to his daughter must be quite remarkable. I dare say your father would have got on well with mine."

Henry was the master's son, and yet, right at that moment, she felt a kinship with him. A warmth that sparked something unfamiliar yet comforting inside. "Thank you for saying that," she murmured. "He was a very remarkable man. I miss him every day."

Gathering up her brush and shovel, she placed them in the bucket, knowing her work for the day wasn't yet done.

As she reached the door, Henry called out, "I'll see you tomorrow, Addy."

Snow fell heavily as midwinter approached. The house was decorated with evergreens, and the pine scent filled the air alongside an excited buzz. The servants worked tirelessly to keep up with the endless flow of dinner parties and distinguished guests for the festive season. Addy's workload grew exponentially as she had to keep up with cleaning the extra grates, as well as peeling more vegetables for Mrs Porter.

On mornings when Henry wasn't in his room, Addy began finding small gifts left for her—carefully tucked into the ashes where only she would notice. A pair of polished buttons, a smooth stone wrapped in paper—small tokens that she kept carefully tucked away in her room. Sometimes, he'd leave a book on the hearth with a paper marker poking out between the pages to mark a passage he wanted to share with her.

Addy would take a moment to read the marked lines, each one carrying a thoughtful message that made her smile, as though he wanted to share a part of his world with her. She would leave the book neatly on his desk, the marker tucked back in the cover, so he'd know she'd read it.

She kept it a secret from Lucy and the others.

She knew it was wrong.

After all, their worlds were aeons apart. Next summer, Henry would embark on a new adventure in boarding school. But for now, she relished those little moments of joy in her day.

Christmas morning dawned clear and cold. Longhaven was draped in festive cheer. Addy found Henry waiting for her in his bedroom. He was smiling, holding a small package wrapped in brown paper and tied with string.

"Merry Christmas, Addy," he said, his eyes bright as he held the parcel out.

She took the package, her hands trembling as she carefully tugged at the string. Inside was a well-worn book bound in dark green cloth with elegant gold lettering: *Jane Eyre*.

"Oh, sir..." she whispered, looking up at him with wide eyes. "This is incredibly generous of you. Thank you." She stroked the cover, holding the book close to her chest. She knew how much a book like this would cost, and the gesture felt overwhelming.

Henry shrugged, a touch of embarrassment colouring his cheeks. "I thought you might like it. It's a story about hardship and overcoming adversity. A story of strength. I thought... I thought you'd understand it better than most."

"It's the first present I've had in... in so long," she said softly, her voice thick with gratitude. "It means more to me than you could ever imagine."

"You've helped me so much with my exams, Addy. It's the least I could do."

That night, as the servants gathered for a lively Christmas celebration in the servants' hall, Addy slipped away to her tiny room in the attic. By the soft glow of candlelight, she opened *Jane Eyre* and lost herself in the world within.

For the first time in years, Christmas truly felt like Christmas.

CHAPTER 25

"You're getting a lot of post these days, Lucy," Mrs Burgess's statement stopped the conversation around the table in the servant's hall. All eyes looked to Lucy.

Addy watched as a deep red coloured the maid's face from her chin to the roots of her hair. Her hands slid under the tabletop, the sinful letter in her hands. "Am I?"

"That's the third letter you've had this week," Charlie chimed in from the other end of the table.

"Is that word from home once again?"

"Yes, Mrs Burgess," Lucy murmured, but she avoided meeting the housekeeper's gaze.

Supper around the table was always a lively affair, with Mrs Porter and Addy among the last to take their seats. As soon as Mr Smale finished his meal and rose from the table, the rest of the staff would stop eating and stand, acknowledging his position with a mark of respect.

Addy waited until later that evening after all her

tasks were finished, and she and Lucy were alone in their bedroom preparing for bed before she brought up the subject of Lucy's frequent letters once again.

"I told you," Lucy said, her tone unusually guarded. "They're from my Ma."

From where she sat on her narrow bed, Addy watched her friend move around the room, clearly uneasy. She folded up a blanket with jerky movements. "No, those aren't the actions of someone just getting a letter from home."

Lucy ignored her.

Addy smirked, sensing the embarrassment that rolled off her friend in waves. "Your brothers are all too busy, and your sisters are too. Come on, what gives?"

The iron bed springs squeaked as Lucy slipped between the sheets, pulling the dark blue woollen blanket up over her. "What's it to you?" she muttered.

Addy couldn't help the grin spreading across her face. "Have you got a fancy man, Lucy Cotton?"

Lucy shot her a glare across the room, though the expression faded as she leaned over and blew out the candle, casting the room into darkness.

"So, what if I have?" she replied softly. "It's not against the law, is it?"

The room was quiet as Lucy settled into bed, the covers rustling as she tugged them around her.

Addy frowned into the darkness. There was no rule against Lucy having a sweetheart writing to her, but she knew that most women left service when they got married. She'd only just gotten used to living with Lucy, and the thought of things changing unsettled her.

"Please don't say anything," Lucy's voice broke the

silence. "If Mrs Burgess says anything to my mum, she'll box my ears. Ma doesn't want me to leave service. It's hard enough to find a good position, let alone in a big household like this."

"I won't say anything," Addy assured her softly.

"He's nice enough," Lucy murmured after a pause. "I just don't know if I like him enough to marry him."

Addy pondered this. Back in the dormitory, the girls would sometimes talk about their fancy for certain boys, but marriage felt foreign to her. She hadn't considered what her own future might hold in that regard.

"You'll see," Lucy added. "One day, there'll be a man who catches your eye, and you won't be able to help yourself."

Addy almost laughed, but in the silence, a pair of striking blue eyes appeared in her mind. She settled into bed, drifting off to sleep, thoughts lingering on that crooked smile.

~

FIRST CAME the carpet of snowdrops, followed by bright bursts of daffodils, their yellow heads bobbing in the light winds as spring crept softly over the land with a quiet promise of warmer days ahead. Leaves unfurled on the trees as life breathed back into the landscape.

Longhaven's routine moved in its usual rhythm. The dinner parties lost the zeal of the Christmas season, yet Mr Scorby still entertained at least twice a week. The biggest change in the household was the preparations for Henry's departure. He had passed his exams, and as the only child, his leaving was a significant event for everyone.

On a rare and cherished Sunday afternoon off, Addy hurried home from church and snatched up the latest book she'd borrowed from Mr Smale. The sun warmed her back as she wandered through the lush grounds of Longhaven.

Birds swooped through the air, their song drifting on the breeze that lifted her skirts. She walked along the small river that wound through the grounds, the water tumbling over moss-covered stones and disappearing into the forest. Deer grazed in the deer park, and a bobbing white tail of a rabbit darted across her path before it disappeared into the long grass that brushed her boots.

She followed the meandering pathway, lost in her own world, when she heard the steady clip-clop of hooves. She spotted Henry guiding the huge bay along the bridleway before he saw her. When he eventually noticed her, a broad smile split his face, and he hailed her.

"What are you doing all the way out here?" he called as he neared her.

"Enjoying my afternoon off," she said with a smile. "It's warm enough, but there's still a nip to the air." She drew her shawl closer around her shoulders to illustrate her point. "The groundsman doesn't mind when I sit in the dovecote and read. It's warm enough in there, and the pigeons don't seem to mind a bit of company either."

Henry reined in his horse, bringing it to a stop where she stood on the path. His eyes flicked to the book in her hand, his head angling to try and read the title. "Another of Mr Smale's collection?"

"He's very kind to let me borrow it."

"Surely there won't be a book left in the house that you've not read soon. Which one do you have? I can't tell from here."

"*The Three Musketeers,*" she replied, holding up the book with a shy smile.

"That's one of my favourites," he grinned.

"It is?"

Henry swung down in one fluid motion, his eyes alight with interest. He looped the reins over the horse's head. "What little boy wouldn't enjoy swashbuckling adventures with his friends?"

As if by tacit invitation, they began walking along the path that curled around the farthest parts of the Longhaven estate. As always, the conversation flowed easily between them.

Henry told her about his trepidation over going to boarding school and leaving all he knew. Addy listened and was able to offer him some sage advice on big changes and how to handle it. After all, she felt she was something of an old hand at such things. He seemed genuinely interested in her answers, and Addy relaxed in his company.

Henry stopped when the dovecote came into view. "I'd forgotten about this place."

"It's probably the quietest part of the estate," Addy struck out across the field towards it. The door was frayed at the edges and required a gentle bump of her shoulder to open.

"Mr Roberts doesn't mind you being in here?" Henry asked uncertainly as he stepped into the warm, dim interior.

Addy nodded. "It was his idea. As groundskeeper, he knows the best places for me to go on damp and cold afternoons. He knows I like to sit and read in my spare time."

Fascinated, Henry studied the rows of nesting boxes tucked under the eaves. Pigeons and doves cooed and flitted overhead, their soft sounds gently comforting. Addy took a seat on an upturned bucket, watching him with curious eyes. "You've never been in here before?"

"I ride past here often. From the outside, it doesn't look particularly hospitable."

Addy smiled. "Sometimes looks can be deceiving, young master Scorby."

Henry gave her a deadpan look. "I suppose you're going to start teasing me again about how sheltered my life is."

Addy's smile was automatic. "Of course."

"Typical. I wouldn't take this kind of abuse of anyone else, mind." Henry picked up a crate and turned it over to fashion himself a seat, too. "I don't suppose you brought any snacks or something to drink?"

Addy drew a small package wrapped in waxed cloth from her pocket. "Mrs Porter made some flapjacks."

"Good, old Mrs Porter," Henry took the package, unwrapped it, and broke the biscuit into two pieces.

"She wouldn't much care for being called old."

Henry held one of the pieces out, his grin incorrigible. "I'll share my biscuit for your silence."

"*My* biscuit," Addy took it. "I suppose you want my book, too."

Henry leaned back and closed his eyes as he chewed. He gestured with what was left of his snack. "No, but you can read it to me."

Addy chuckled. She bit into her flapjack and flipped open the book. She began to read aloud, her melodic voice weaving the story of a young man on the cusp of adulthood, taking up arms for those who could not fight for themselves.

By the time they left the dovecote, the shadows were longer, and the sun had melted into a molten pool of red and gold on the horizon. Henry collected the horse from where he'd tethered it on the edge of the forest, allowing it a long drink.

"We'd better get back," she told him. "Else they'll be sending out a search party for you."

"I often ride out alone on a Sunday. Mother likes to rest, and Father uses the time to catch up on his Sunday reading. Normally, Sunday afternoons are boring, but... I've enjoyed today."

The world around them was painted in hues of blue and gold as they parted ways on the edge of the forest. Addy walked back to her room, trying to remember when she'd last had such a good time.

CHAPTER 26

*D*ays lengthened into summer.

On her Sundays off, Addy made her way to the dovecote. Henry would be waiting; his horse hobbled under the shade of a tree. Addy would make sure to bring enough food for them both. They often sat in the grass, discussing various topics and sharing dreams. They spoke of everything and nothing, hours slipping by in these stolen moments, suspended in time.

He was no longer the master's son; he was simply Henry, her friend.

All too soon, September arrived. The entire manor house buzzed with preparations for Henry's departure. Addy helped Lucy pack the trunks, disquiet settling in her chest as she folded his clothes. The footmen loaded them onto the waiting wagon that would take Henry and his father to the train station.

From an upstairs window, Addy stood in one of the bedrooms, looking down as servants scurried in and out of the house. They lined up to bid farewell to the young master, but as a scullery maid, she wasn't included. Her heart was a mixture of tangled emotions: pride, envy, and something she wasn't quite sure she could name. She was genuinely pleased for him, knowing how hard he'd worked. But she also felt a pang of envy, wishing she could spend her days buried in books, learning and exploring new worlds.

The soft footfall on the carpet behind her jolted her, and she turned to see Lucy joining her at the window.

"Why aren't you down there?" Addy asked.

Lucy stood alongside her. "I dare say the young master won't notice a missing maid, and Mrs Burgess wanted me to crack on with the bedrooms. We're already behind on the summer tasks." Lucy pressed her forehead against the glass to get a better view. "He's really going, then."

"I was just thinking about how different his life will be from now on."

"Not that different," Lucy murmured. "There'll still be people there to fetch and carry for the likes of him."

"I meant that he's leaving the home he's known all his life," Addy replied, ignoring the bitter tone.

"A life meant for his sort, Addy." Lucy turned to her. "We all know you've got a soft spot for the young master, but his life is on a different path to yours."

Addy's cheeks flamed. She opened her mouth to deny it, but Lucy was already turning back into the room. "Come on, there's work to be done."

Addy cast one final glance at the departing carriage. She bid her friend a silence farewell and then she got on with her work.

It seemed to Addy that she was the only one who noticed Henry's absence from the household.

The dinner parties and business soirées carried on as usual. Guests streamed endlessly through the house, and her list of tasks continued without pause. Yet Addy had lost some of the enthusiasm for her work. Without Henry's company, the dovecote and the meadows didn't feel quite the same. For Addy, Longhaven had lost a bit of its sparkle.

Lucy was the only one who noticed the change in her, though whenever she mentioned it, Addy was quick to change the subject. It was easy to do. All she had to do was redirect the conversation to the young gentleman Lucy was still exchanging letters with.

"His family are labourers," Lucy explained one morning when Addy sidestepped the reason she was staring out the window. "The letters are coming more frequently because winter's on its way. He's not as busy as he is in the spring and summer months."

"Is he local?"

Lucy shrugged. "Local enough. The village where his farm is about ten miles away as the crow flies. I met him at a tea dance." Her smile turned wistful.

"What's he like?"

Lucy shrugged again. "He seems kind enough. I mean, he doesn't make much money as a farm labourer, so I won't be moving into a fancy house, but…" Her smile gave away more than she was saying. "He's good enough for me."

"You like him," Addy teased.

Lucy pouted. "He likes me well enough, and that's good enough for me."

"I'm happy for you," Addy replied. "You only need a

kind man to have a good life. That's worth more than all the tea in China."

Lucy laughed, and Addy let the topic go.

∾

Now that Henry had left, Mr and Mrs Scorby travelled to the Scottish Highlands to stay with friends. Reginald took Smale with them.

Most of the staff took the opportunity for some much-needed time off, but as Addy had nowhere else to go, she spent her days working alongside Mrs Burgess, tackling smaller tasks that often went unnoticed in the bustle of daily life.

She sorted linens, polished forgotten corners, washed carpets, and tended to minor repairs. Addy enjoyed the slower pace at Longhaven; the highlight of these quiet days was sharing suppers with Mrs Burgess and Mrs Porter. In the soft glow of candlelight in the servants' hall, she listened as the two women shared stories. Through little snippets—vague references to a husband at sea, mentions of growing up in the East End of London, hints of a romance left behind—their tales were enigmatic. Those evenings reminded her of Whitehurst and made her yearn for her own family.

Shortly after the staff returned from their time off, a travelling fair arrived in the village. Mrs Burgess agreed to let a small group of them go for the afternoon. At first, Addy refused, but Charlie and Lucy encouraged her, insisting she deserved some time off after all her hard work.

Addy found herself swept up in the excitement of the rare treat. The fair was busy, filled with bright colours and cheerful music. Families from nearby flocked to the town. Children darted between stalls, and courting couples strolled arm-in-arm between the brightly painted tents. Jugglers and performers entertained the crowds, and a daring fire eater filled the evening with magic. It was easy to lose herself in the laughter and joy, surrounded by the vibrant energy.

The excitement soured when Charlie, emboldened after a few pints of ale, attempted to steer Addy into one of the quieter corners. At first, Addy was polite, gently extricating herself from his wandering hands.

"Come on," Charlie breathed, his ale-scented breath hot against her face as his hands skimmed up her sides. "A pretty girl like you shouldn't be alone on a night like this."

"Enough, Charlie," she injected a bit more firmness into her tone and pushed him back.

"You're just a scullery maid; you shouldn't be so picky," Charlie sneered, lunging for her again, only to be yanked backwards by Samuel, who stood protectively in front of her.

"Let's head back, Charlie. Mrs Burgess will be wondering where we all are."

Furious, Charlie glared up at Samuel, pulling his jacket back into place. Samuel took a step towards him, and Charlie seemed to change his mind. He scurried off back into the crowd of the fair.

Addy sent Samuel a grateful smile and followed the group at a distance.

"Are you alright?" Lucy murmured later. Addy tried to shove the incident from her mind, telling herself that Charlie had just indulged a bit too much in the celebrations, but the whole thing had left her unsettled.

After the fair, the days grew colder. Mornings filled with mists that lingered over the parklands, and strong winter winds stripped the copper-coloured leaves from the trees until only bare branches remained. Jack Frost crept in, dusting the grounds with ice and weaving delicate patterns on the windowpanes each morning.

Addy made her rounds every morning, thoroughly checking the bedrooms even when they were empty. It was an extra step in her responsibilities but ensured Mrs Burgess remained happy with her diligence. It also gave Addy a sense of pride to know the house she worked in was kept immaculate.

The frost was particularly heavy one morning when she stepped into Henry's room. She swept her gaze over the interior. The bed was neatly made, not a speck of dust remained in the soft winter light.

She noticed an unexpected object in the fireplace. Frowning, she peered through the low light, trying to identify what it was. She stepped closer.

There, nestled among the kindling set ready to light the fire for Henry's return, was a delicate paper lotus, perfectly folded, elegantly crafted. Her heart raced with a flush of pleasure as she reached out to gently touch it, marvelling at the intricacy of the neat folds.

She knew who had left it, even though he wasn't meant to return until the following day. She held it up in the light to study it, recalling the awkward paper cranes Henry had once folded.

Then something caught her eye. Henry was standing in the doorway, a familiar smile warming his face.

"Hello, Addy."

CHAPTER 27

Two Years Later

"Where's the béchamel sauce?" Mrs Porter asked.

"Over there, Mrs Porter," Addy replied briskly, her attention on the three pots simmering on the stove.

As the kitchen maid, she was considered Mrs Porter's right hand. Her quick mind and nimble fingers had made her Mrs Porter's shadow. When Mrs Porter first suggested promoting her to kitchen maid, Addy had her doubts. She could barely boil an egg, let alone whip up the complicated dishes served to landed gentry and nobility. But with Mrs Porter's blend of gentle coaching and scolding, Addy learned quickly.

The new position meant she wasn't above stairs very often, but it was a welcome change from having her hands in cold water peeling vegetables day in, day out. The work was still hard, but she took small satisfaction in knowing she'd moved up in the servant ranks.

Her replacement in the scullery was a young girl named Bess, Mrs Porter's niece from Liverpool. The girl's thick Liverpudlian accent made her the butt of many jokes, though Addy took her under her wing. The accent reminded her of the workhouse and Janey. She wondered what had happened to her old friend and prayed that the lessons she'd given her in the corner of the workhouse yard had helped Janey secure a career in service, too.

Just as she'd done in the workhouse, Addy helped Bess with her reading and writing. Long after the other servants had gone to bed, Addy would sit with Bess in the servants' hall. Rather than using sticks in the mud, Addy guided Bess to write on paper that Mrs Burgess had given them. It was exhausting, but whenever the young girl mastered a new skill, the bleary-eyed mornings were worth it.

"You're wasting your time with that one," Lucy remarked one evening as they got ready for bed. "That girl can't even set a fireplace properly. She won't make much of a life."

But Addy knew the pleasure of being able to read and exchange letters with those she liked. "Everyone deserves the chance, and she's quick to learn. Besides, if I hadn't learned to write, how else would I be able to write to you once you're married?"

Lucy flipped back her bedcovers with a jerky motion, not bothering to hide her glare. "He has to ask first," she grumbled.

"He will," Addy assured her. "When the time is right."

"When I'm on my deathbed, too old to stand, let

alone walk down the aisle," Lucy muttered. "Honestly, he infuriates me. Almost three years and he still hasn't asked me. How much longer do I have to wait?"

Addy hid her smile. "He's busy," she said as she blew out the candle. "It's summertime, and you know how life is for him."

Lucy harrumphed into the darkness. Addy settled into her bed, excited that it was summer—not just for the garden parties and longer days spent outside, but because Henry would soon be home for the long summer break.

She was counting down the days until his return.

Then, finally, he was home. She'd heard all about the homecoming, helped prepare the family feast to welcome him, and tried not to show how eagerly she listened to Smale and the footmen relaying the stories they'd overheard Henry tell in the dining room.

It seemed his life was everything he'd hoped for. He had a flair for law and philosophy, and he enjoyed playing rugby with his school team. At times like this, she wished she could trade places with Bess.

She missed finding the little treasures Henry used to leave in the fireplace.

It was the following Sunday afternoon before she finally saw him. He was standing at the edge of a thicket of trees as she followed her usual path through the estate. Her pulse quickened at the sight of him. He'd changed since she'd last seen him—taller, his boyish frame had filled out, though his gait still held the awkwardness of someone growing into their limbs. He had his father's breadth but his mother's colouring. His piercing blue eyes sparkled as she approached.

"You're late," he called out.

She couldn't keep the smile off her face. "So, you always say."

He laughed and fell into step beside her, towering over her now and adjusting his pace so she wouldn't have to hurry. "How's the new job?"

"It's good," she smiled. "I like to cook. How's school?"

Henry lifted a shoulder. "I prefer being home, but I think most of us do."

He held a branch out of her way, ducked under it, and followed her. Addy drew up short as they stepped into the small meadow where the dovecote stood. A tartan red blanket was spread out on the ground, held in place by one of the wicker picnic baskets. His horse was conspicuously absent.

Uncertain, she risked a look at him. He was watching her, and his expression sent a wave of pleasure through her. "I thought I'd bring the picnic to you today."

She followed him at a slight distance, a heady mix of excitement and nerves swirling inside her.

Henry folded himself into a cross-legged position and looked up at her expectantly. "What's wrong?"

It felt different, she realised. Perhaps she felt different. All this talk of marriage with Lucy, of finding a husband and planning a future, had made her think about life in a new way.

"N-nothing's wrong," she stammered, though her voice was husky. She cleared her throat.

Henry held up a book. *"The Adventures of Robinson Crusoe,"* he announced. "Come sit. You read and I'll pour the cider."

She approached cautiously, but, like an addict seeking the next rush of pleasure, she could no more walk away from him than she could deny herself air. Henry lifted fresh bread, cheese, and meat from the basket.

"You got all that from the kitchen?"

"I did," he said. "Told Mrs Porter I needed a feast fit for a growing man."

"Do you think she knew it was for me?"

Henry eyed her. "I doubt it," he said, his brows drawing together. "You don't have to sit if you don't want to."

Addy sighed. "Henry... I'm just a maid. We could both get into a lot of trouble if we're caught together."

He regarded her solemnly. "We're friends, aren't we?"

Slowly, she nodded, though inside she knew he was so much more to her.

The cider glugged into the glass, fizzing up to the top. Henry slurped at the overspill. When she hesitated still, he eyed her. "Addy... the last few weeks, I've thought of nothing but this moment. Please, come and read to me," he said. "Having a pretty girl read to me is the one thing missing from an all-boys school."

She felt her resolve crumble like a snowball under the summer sun.

Henry grinned at her when she sighed and settled in. He'd spread the blanket under the large oak tree, sunlight dappling the ground around them. She accepted the book and the cider he passed to her. The afternoon stretched on in quiet companionship, the air around them warm with the lazy promise of summer. She knew it was wrong, but her trepidation was soon lost in the pleasure of his company and the intoxicating buzz of the cider. He lay back on the ground, his hands stacked behind his head, as she wove the story of adventures.

Dusk settled around them, and overhead, the first stars began to wink in the darkening sky.

"It's getting too dark to read," she murmured, closing the book. "I should head back soon."

He said nothing, and when she looked across at him, his stare was fixed on her face. She should have felt nervous under such intensity, but she couldn't look away. The cider thrummed in her blood, making her feel braver under his stare. She held his gaze even as he sat up, her breath hitching as he softly murmured her name, the word laced with a longing that mirrored her own.

His hand reached out, his fingertips grazing her ear as he brushed a loose lock of hair behind it. She shivered at his touch, her mouth parting to release a pent-up breath.

In the fading light, Henry leaned forward and gently pressed his mouth to hers.

CHAPTER 28

Addy knew, even before Hopkins burst into the kitchen demanding a bowl of chicken broth and some Beecham's, that Mrs Scorby wouldn't survive the fever that had taken hold of her.

She'd heard that cough before.

She'd seen how fast a fever could snatch away a life back in the workhouse.

She also knew of Mr Scorby's explosive rage at the futility of it all.

Snow lay thick on the ground outside. Branches bowed under its weight; paths buried in the frozen earth. Longhaven was plunged into mourning, a sombre air shadowing the house.

Mrs Scorby was unlike any other mistress—kind and benevolent. She knew each servant by name, having personally chosen each one. They all had touching stories about her, which they shared on the night the doctor confirmed her passing. But more than sadness, Addy felt a familiar sense of impending change, an omen she'd often sensed in her past.

She expected shattered sobs and sadness from the staff. What she hadn't anticipated was the raw grief that ravaged Henry's face when she first saw him.

He'd returned from school early, fetched home by his grieving father.

It took her a while to slip away unnoticed to go and find him. Henry wasn't in his room, nor was he in the library. He wasn't in the dining room or the study. Chewing her lip, she glanced out of the window as she pondered where else he might be. The vast cold sky blended seamlessly with the frozen fields.

And she knew where he was.

She pulled on her woollen coat and headed out into the biting cold. The snow reached past her knees in places, soaking her to the skin. The chill cut through her layers, numbing her face. She ducked under snow-laden branches, finding drier ground in the forest where animals lay hidden in their burrows, asleep in the winter silence. Then she reached their little meadow. Snow crunched underfoot as she crossed to the dovecote, the ancient round building standing stark against the whiteness. She pushed her shoulder into the door to force it open, her breath puffing in the air.

She halted when her gaze met Henry's red-rimmed eyes. Though she hadn't heard him weeping, the signs were clear, familiar. He was sitting against the far wall, knees drawn up under his chin. He wasn't the young man who'd made her laugh and stolen kisses on lazy summer Sundays, who'd read stories to her until she'd fallen asleep in his arms or walked her back as far as he dared.

Right now, he looked like a small boy lost in misery.

"My mother is dead," he intoned dully.

She went to him, sitting beside him in quiet comfort. "I know. And I'm so sorry."

"I didn't get to say goodbye to her, Addy," he sniffed. "I didn't tell her how much I loved her."

"She knew," she murmured.

"Do you think so?"

She nodded. "I know so. She was so proud of you."

He sniffed, taking in her words.

"You know, she lives on. People are kept alive in our memories, by talking about them," she said, leaning back against the wall, soothed by the soft cooing in the nesting boxes above. "All the servants loved her. I've been listening to their stories about how she touched their lives."

"Really? Tell me some stories about her, Addy."

"I've been helping Bess, the new scullery maid, with her reading and writing. Mrs Burgess and Mrs Porter gave me the paper to help her. I tried to pay them for it, knowing how expensive paper is, but it turns out your mother was the one supplying it."

Henry tipped his head back, his eyes shining in the low light as he watched the nesting birds overhead. "She valued education above many things," he murmured.

Addy mimicked his posture, her voice low and soothing. "I don't know if you're aware, but the footman, Samuel—his brother got into some trouble and ended up in prison for theft. Your mother made sure the family solicitor helped reduce the sentence, and she arranged for Samuel to have time off to visit him, too."

In the dim light, Henry turned to her, his eyes fierce and bright.

"There was no fuss from her, even though Samuel worried about his position in the household."

"What else?" he whispered, tears slowly slipping down his cheeks.

"Mrs Porter, the cook... her sister has been sick. Your mama sent the doctor to treat her and paid the bill so Mrs Porter wouldn't have to worry about it."

Henry's swallow was audible in the silence.

"She was a kind, compassionate woman who will be sorely missed," Addy told him.

"Thank you," he replied softly.

He took her hand, and she leaned her head on his shoulder. In the quiet of the lonely dovecote, she let a son mourn his mother in peace.

~

Henry didn't return to school right away. He claimed it was because the winter holidays were near, but Addy knew all too well the depth of grief he was experiencing.

Mr Scorby had all but withdrawn from society, retreating into his work and spending long stretches away from home. His grief manifested in bursts of anger and unpredictable rages, meaning the household staff had to tread carefully so as not to disturb a man haunted by loss.

The only bright spot in the servants' hall was that Lucy had finally received her proposal, and Addy couldn't help but feel genuinely happy for her friend— even though it meant Lucy would soon be leaving her position in the household.

Christmas passed without any of the festivities of years gone by. Smale and Mrs Burgess tried their best to bring a bit of holiday cheer to the house. They decorated a tree modestly, but when Mr Scorby arrived home, he furiously knocked it over, raging that there would be no celebrations in a house of mourning. The servants had a small, quiet celebration on Christmas night in the servants' hall. Addy sat in the corner, thinking about the young man upstairs alone in his room, and didn't feel much like celebrating.

Addy understood Mr Scorby's aversion to the smallest reminder of joy. She had seen it before, in how her mother had come apart at the seams after the death of her father.

"It'll pass," she told Henry one day when they were walking along the path at the edge of the estate. "He's deeply hurting. My mama was like that too, after we lost my father. Grief is a funny thing. It can take hold of us when we least expect it and doesn't let go easily." She realised these were the words Janey had once told her, all those years ago.

Henry wore a heavy wool coat, his cheeks red from the sting of the crisp January air. "How long did it take your mother to come back from it?"

Addy hesitated, her heart sinking. She didn't have the heart to tell him the truth—that her mother had never truly recovered, and grief had hardened her into a sorrow so deep that she had spent her final year in the workhouse a shell of the vibrant woman she had once been. Her heart ached at the glimmer of hope that sparkled in his blue eyes.

"It takes time," she hedged, hoping he wouldn't press for more details. She wished she could spare him the sadness she could feel as keenly as if it were her own.

As Mr Scorby's trips grew longer, Henry would

often seek Addy out for company. They would spend time together when she wasn't working, wandering the grounds or reading side-by-side in the dovecote.

She knew the household must have noticed their companionship, although no one ever seemed to mention it. Perhaps it was common for a servant to fall in love with her employer. Or maybe it was out of loyalty to the late Mrs Scorby that the staff were glad Henry had found a companion to ease his unhappiness. Addy knew, deep down, the impossibility of their friendship. She understood that Henry's future lay elsewhere and was painfully aware of the reality that he would one day marry within his own class. The thought lingered over her heart like a shadow. Yet, while she remained aware of this unspoken truth, she cherished every laugh and every shared glance.

As March rolled on and the spring flowers returned once more, Lucy finally packed up her belongings.

She was marrying her young farm labourer and leaving to start a new life. On her last day, Addy bid goodbye to her friend with a tight hug and a promise to stay in touch through letters. Shortly after Lucy left, Mrs Burgess called Addy into her office and offered her an unexpected opportunity.

"With Lucy gone, I need another housemaid," the housekeeper said carefully. "You know the house better than anyone else here. It means a bit more pay in your wages—not much, granted, but you'll be working above stairs. I know you're capable of the work, Addy. I think it's the right step in your career."

Addy was grateful that Mrs Burgess had noticed her diligence. The promotion meant she would spend more time upstairs and have more opportunities to be in Henry's world.

She accepted gratefully.

The duties of a housemaid were different from her previous responsibilities as a kitchen maid. Now, she was responsible for all of the bedrooms, including Henry's. She quickly noticed how much he had changed. His room, once cluttered with an array of books and papers, was now meticulously tidy. His clothes were folded, his bed perfectly made. It troubled her that his desk was no longer filled with his beloved books, and she sensed a restlessness in him.

She dared to mention it on one of their Sunday afternoon walks.

"I'm not sure that I want to go back to school, Addy," Henry finally admitted. "I could simply go into business as my father wants. I don't need to be poring over dusty books or staying away from home."

"But... but studying philosophy and the law brings you joy, Henry."

"What good is it to sit in a classroom all day when no one really cares?"

She stopped walking, giving him a stern look. "It matters because it's part of your future. What would your mother think, knowing that you have so much to offer the world and yet you chose to walk away from that? Don't give up on your dreams now."

She wondered for a moment if she had overstepped the boundaries of their friendship. Henry continued to wander in silence. They were on their way back when he finally agreed to return to school for his final year and a half.

At the edge of the woods, Henry gathered her close. "Thank you, Addy. For everything. You've been like my guardian angel these past months, the only light in a dark world."

Addy hugged him back. "I'm glad I could help."

He waited until his father returned from his latest business trip, and a few days later, Charlie and Samuel packed up his trunk into the carriage. Reginald escorted him to the train station.

Addy watched him go from the line-up of the servants. She returned to the servants' hall, listening as Mr Smale and Mrs Burgess chatted about the positive outcome of Henry returning to his studies. Inside, she felt a familiar ache of loss settling over her, yet she knew she had done the right thing in encouraging him to go. Henry had a future to build, and she would not be the one to hold him back.

But now, without Henry's companionship, and without Lucy's friendship, Addy was alone once more.

CHAPTER 29

"It was bound to happen sooner or later," Mr Smale's deep voice rumbled with disapproval.

"Poor Mrs Scorby," Mrs Porter replied softly. "That poor woman barely cold in her grave."

In the corner of the kitchen, Addy exchanged a look with Bess. The very fact that the senior servants were openly discussing the family was almost as perturbing as the news of Mr Scorby's swift remarriage.

It seemed that every servant was unsettled; the unease in the below stairs was almost tangible in the air. As always, Addy remained quiet as the servants gossiped about the new mistress, Vanessa Jacobson, an exquisite young widow with a reputation for ambition and acerbity.

It wasn't just the shock of a new mistress so soon after the passing of the old one that shook them all, but the inevitable changes that would come in her wake.

The new Mrs Scorby was quick to put her mark on Longhaven Manor, arriving with an entourage of trusted servants from her former household. She was a striking woman, much younger than Mr Scorby, with dark brown hair and a beauty that commanded attention. Where the late Mrs Scorby had been gentle and compassionate, Vanessa was quick to impose her authority on the house.

The servants were in no doubt as to who was in charge.

Hopkins, the lady's maid, was the first to be let go. More upsetting for Addy, Mrs Burgess received her marching orders not long after. Vanessa was ruthless in her decisions, claiming that there were too many servants within the household and that the staff had grown complacent under Mr Scorby's leniency. Her insistence that they could manage with fewer staff and save money was quickly accepted by the master of the house.

Several maids and hallboys were dismissed within the first month, leaving the remaining staff scrambling to pick up the extra work. The added burden came without a single increase to their pay.

Vanessa's housekeeper, a severe woman named Mrs Blythe, ran things militantly. She had no patience for sentimentality or tradition and looked down her nose at the Longhaven staff as though they were lesser for their loyalty to the late Mrs Scorby.

And then there was Vanessa's son, Isaac.

He was older than Henry, a handsome young man clearly accustomed to privilege and indulgence. Just like his mother, he made his wilful, spoiled presence known immediately.

Whenever Mr Scorby was away on business, Isaac

would throw parties that rattled the walls and filled the air with drunken laughter late into the night. The next day, the house would be littered with empty bottles and glassware, leaving the servants to pick up the remnants of his revelry in addition to their daily chores. Isaac would sleep late, oblivious and unconcerned about the chaos he brought to the house.

Samuel had been among the servants to lose his job; no doubt due to his brother's sticky fingers. Charlie had been given the role of valet to the new young master, a job he did not relish. "He has two wardrobes filled with fine clothes, yet I'm constantly finding him half-dressed," he would grumble often. "Can't even step into his room without risking an eyeful—and I've yet to see him sober!"

Addy was upstairs alone when she encountered the new young master for the first time. Isaac Jacobson looked every inch the rake, with tawny brown hair and chocolate-brown eyes. He lounged on his bed, dark eyes glinting with languid interest as he watched Addy enter.

"And where have they been hiding you?" he drawled, an indolent grin sliding across his face.

"Beg pardon, sir," she murmured, bowing her head respectfully. "I thought everyone had gone down for breakfast."

Uncaring of his near-nakedness, Isaac scratched his bare stomach lazily. "Why don't you be a darling and fetch me up a tray," he said with a flick of his wrist.

Addy hesitated, knowing full well that Mrs Porter would already be preparing lunch by now and wouldn't be pleased to be interrupted in order to prepare a tray for this lazy so-and-so.

Isaac's smirk curved, his gaze lingering over her

attire in an unnerving manner that sent a blush crawling over her skin. "What's the matter?"

"Nothing, sir," she replied hurriedly.

She turned, her mind racing as she flew down the narrow back stairs to the kitchen. Sure enough, Mrs Porter was not pleased about the request, muttering under her breath about spoiled young brats who didn't deserve hard-working staff. However, when she returned to Isaac's bedroom, the bed was empty. She quickly crossed the room and set the tray down on the dressing table, assuming he had left.

Just as she turned, he slipped out from behind the door, effectively blocking her escape route. His hungry gaze raked over her, his mouth twisting with glee. He wore only a pair of breeches, partially unbuttoned, and trailed his fingers down his bare chest to the opening.

Addy quickly averted her gaze. His chuckle was throaty, and she cringed as she realised he was revelling in her discomfort.

"My, my," he murmured as he ambled towards her. "Are all the maids around here as pretty as you?"

Addy felt her face burn, a sickening heat spreading through her. She kept her head down, uncertain what to say in reply.

"What's your name?"

"Addy."

"Pretty name for a pretty girl," he purred. "I bet all the men pant after you."

Isaac came to a stop in front of her, too close for her comfort. He reached out to play with a loose length of copper hair that had slipped out from under her mob cap. He rubbed the strand between his fingers. "What a beautiful colour, Addy."

Her heart pounded in her chest as she schooled her

face to remain as neutral as she could, just as she'd learned in the workhouse. "I must be getting on, sir. I have a lot to do."

Isaac matched her sidestep, his laugh low and mocking, sending a chill down her spine. "You don't need to be in such a hurry, do you? I'm new around here. What if I need you to show me around?"

Addy attempted to sidestep him once more, but he mirrored her move. She looked up, meeting his gaze, and he grinned at the defiant tilt of her chin. A cold tremor ran through her as she saw the greedy glint in his eyes, his gaze roaming over her. In a swift motion, she darted past him, slipping through the door and slamming it shut behind her, nearly stumbling in her haste—only to collide with a stern-faced Mr Smale.

The butler's sharp gaze swept over her, moving from the door to her flushed face. "Adelaide, is everything all right?"

"Mr Smale, I–" Addy replied in a rush, close to tears. "I…"

Mr Smale's gaze shifted back to the closed door. "You've delivered his tray?"

"Yes."

Mr Smale lowered his voice so it wouldn't carry along the hallway. "You must be careful, Adelaide. You're getting older, and there are people in this world whose intentions are not as pure as yours. Do you understand my meaning?"

Addy managed a quick nod, understanding the warning all too well. She hurried along the corridor, instinctively knowing that Isaac was a dangerous man—and that she must avoid him at all costs.

CHAPTER 30

*A*voiding Isaac was easier said than done.

She tried her best, keeping her head down and quickening her step as she went about her duties as a maid, which kept her above stairs more often than not. She found herself wishing she had turned down the promotion that forced her into Isaac's presence so frequently. She would have loved nothing more than to retreat to the safety of the kitchen and be berated by a huffing Mrs Porter in the steamy atmosphere rather than feeling Isaac's stare whenever she least expected it. But with her work focused on the upper floors, she was constantly on edge.

She wasn't the only one feeling the new master's presence; Isaac was making a nuisance of himself with all the other maids, but it seemed that Addy was the one who received the majority of his thinly veiled advances and unwanted glances.

Addy learned his schedule. She learned to work faster, timing her chores to minimise the risk of running into him. He was rarely out of bed before midday, and if she worked quickly enough, she could finish her tasks before he even set foot outside his bedroom.

The new Mrs Scorby was nothing like her predecessor. Gone were the garden parties and lively gatherings that once filled the manor house with joyful laughter. Vanessa was strict with the staff, and Blythe, the housekeeper, enforced her precise wishes with pugnacious efficiency.

Time off was strictly limited, reduced to just a single half-afternoon each month instead of the weekly half-day they'd once enjoyed.

The message was clear: if you didn't like the new rules, then you could leave.

Life felt nearly as restricted as it had been in the workhouse. The sense of camaraderie and family Addy had held with the other servants was fading fast, each day becoming a relentless grind with no respite in an atmosphere of fear and discontent.

By the time summer rolled around, the household staff had been condensed to a skeleton crew, with just enough to keep the house and vast estate functioning. Mr Scorby appeared almost oblivious to the changes, clearly enchanted by his young bride, who was redecorating Longhaven in her own unique style.

For the servants who moved through the house each day, it seemed that the new Mrs Scorby was systematically erasing every trace of the woman who had come before her. Vanessa's style was cold and harsh, seeming to drain the warmth from the walls. Trinkets were sold, and each room was stripped of its former character. Any loyalty Mr Scorby once felt for the staff faded under Vanessa's influence. When Henry finally returned from school for the summer, Addy knew that Longhaven must be barely recognisable to him.

His little notes and gifts appeared in the fireplace once again, though she struggled to be able to meet him. However, she didn't dare leave a reply for fear that Mrs Blythe would discover it.

Henry had been home more than a week by the time she was able to slip out the back door with a basket filled with scraps for the goats and the chickens, though she gave the house a wide berth, hurrying to the one place that remained untouched by the changes sweeping through the manor.

The dovecote.

Henry's eyes lit up when he saw her, gathering her into his embrace without hesitation. "I've missed you, my angel," he sighed into her hair as he held her close.

Addy tried to relax in his embrace. She'd missed him so much, but the constant strain of living under perpetual worry had taken its toll.

Henry sensed it immediately. "What's wrong?"

Addy started to brush off his concern, but he caught her chin as he frowned down at her, his eyes filled with gentle insistence. "My angel, whatever is the matter?"

Addy hesitated, looking around the dovecote—their place of refuge—as the shadow of Isaac lingered on the edges of her mind.

"Out with it," Henry urged softly.

The truth spilled out.

She told him everything: the way the house had changed, the cold efficiency with which servants were dismissed, the whispers from the other maids, and the relentless reduction of staff. She described how Longhaven had become clinical and cold, stripped of all warmth and charm. Finally, she confessed her fear of Isaac—the lingering glances, the unspoken menace, and the feeling that he was intent on catching her alone.

Henry's expression darkened as he listened. "He must be stopped." He placed his hands on her shoulders, his eyes flashing with anger. "My mother wouldn't have tolerated any of this for a moment. Hopkins might have been a grouch, but she was loyal to our family. Vanessa has no right to behave like this. What she's selling is my inheritance. And Isaac... he has no right to make you feel this way."

"But what can be done?" she whispered. "She's the mistress of Longhaven now, and your father seems smitten with her every wish."

Henry's jaw tightened. "I'll speak with him. I'll make him see sense. Try not to worry; I'll set things right for all of you."

But his talk did no good.

His father dismissed his concerns as childish jealousy. This only served to widen the rift between them. Vanessa didn't care for Henry interfering. Every further attempt by Henry to reason with his father only seemed to make matters worse. The arguments it generated rattled the bricks.

Addy tried to steal moments alone with Henry, but with her added duties and Isaac's unwanted attention, it became almost impossible. So, the tension in her life continued to grow. She did her best to avoid Isaac, hurrying in and out of his increasingly messy room, but her luck soon ran out in the library.

She was scanning the spines of books she longed to read when she heard the soft click of the door closing behind her. For a moment, she'd forgotten about his presence, but when she turned and met his intense gaze, her blood ran cold.

"Well, well, well," he drawled, stalking towards her with intent in his eyes. "If it isn't my favourite maid," he crooned indolently. His movements were slow and deliberate as he approached her. "If I didn't know better, I'd think you were hiding from me."

Addy swallowed. "I'm just finishing up in here, sir. I'll be out of your way in a jiffy."

"What if I don't want you out of the way?" His mouth into a smirk. "What if I like you being in my way?"

Addy tried to edge around him, but he moved closer, his gaze roaming over her in a way that left her feeling vulnerable and exposed. "Please, sir," she whispered. "I have other rooms to attend to."

"Oh, I have needs for you to attend to," he chuckled. "Why don't you stay awhile? Let's talk. I'm sure I can find better uses for you than a bit of dusting."

Just then, the door swung open, and Henry strode into the room. He took one look at Addy's pale face and turned to Isaac, his expression thunderous. "What do you think you're doing?"

"Just conversing with our household staff," Isaac sneered.

"Addy?" Henry's voice was filled with concern.

Addy's stomach twisted with dread as she pressed a trembling hand to her lips and gave Henry a slight shake of her head.

Henry's jaw hardened as he placed himself firmly between her and Isaac. "You will leave her alone, Isaac. She's here to work, not to be harassed by you. Find someone else other than a servant to 'chat' with."

Isaac's brow rose as he divided a look between

them, his lips curving as understanding dawned. "I see," he chuckled. "You've already marked this one for yourself."

"That's enough," Henry said sharply. "You *will* leave her alone."

Isaac raised his hands in mock surrender, sneering, "Silly boy. You haven't even a whisker on your chin, and you think you're old enough to play the hero?"

Henry clenched his fists at his sides but held his ground.

Isaac let out a cruel laugh as he brushed past Henry. "You'll be off to your precious school soon, young *Master* Henry, and you won't be here to save her then. Two more terms to go—that's plenty of time for me to get better acquainted with our dear Addy."

His scornful laughter echoed down the hall as he left.

Addy locked her knees to keep from collapsing, her body trembling.

"Are you alright?" Henry asked softly, his concern evident.

"I'll be fine," she replied in a rush. "Thank you for being here, but... he's right. I don't know what I'd have done if you hadn't come, and I don't know what I'll do when you leave."

Henry cupped her cheek between his hands, his gaze fierce. "I won't let him hurt you, Addy. Somehow, I'll find a way to make this right. I promise you I'll find a way."

CHAPTER 31

The summer dragged on interminably. Isaac had been distinctly absent, and Addy had thrown herself into her work. Henry had insisted that Mrs Blythe stay out of his room. The housekeeper had reluctantly agreed. This meant that Henry was able to once again leave little notes for her in his room. This method of communicating in secret had allowed her to steal a moment here and there with Henry in the dovecote until his final day before the autumn term arrived. The little building was filled with a sombre quietness, weighed down by the knowledge that he would soon be gone, leaving her vulnerable to Isaac's ever-watchful gaze.

"Promise me you'll write," Henry murmured. In the soft light, she could see the intent and desperation in his blue eyes.

"I can't."

"Just a few lines so that I know you're okay."

Addy sighed, resigned. "It's no good, Henry. We wouldn't get away with it. And the risk is even greater now that Isaac believes something is going on between us."

"But something *is* going on between us," Henry insisted, linking their hands. "You're my guardian angel, Addy. You're the one who keeps me steady in the storm. Knowing you'll be here when I come back is the one constant in my life I can rely on," Those breathtakingly blue eyes settled on her face. "Addy, you are my angel, and I love you."

Her heart thumped, and a quiver of pleasure ran through her. To hear such eloquent words filled her with joy.

His brows knitted together as the silence drifted between them. "Do you love me?"

The uncertainty in his voice almost hurt. She did love him. He was the one bright spot in her life, too. She looked at their joined hands, realising that saying the words he longed to hear out loud would be futile. Nothing would—could—change between them. He was the master; she was a housemaid.

She looked at him with a sad smile as she gently pulled her hands from his grasp. "Your father would never allow anything to happen between us. You're his only son."

"I don't care about that."

"Your father would. He would be disgraced to know how his only son was in love with a lowly maid. You'd be disinherited."

"It doesn't matter to me," he replied fiercely, taking hold of her hands once again.

"It *should*," she insisted.

"My father would want me to be happy."

"Maybe, if your dear Mama was still alive, he might have been persuaded, but not now. We've all heard the terrific arguments, Henry. Your relationship with him is… strained."

The light in his eyes burned brighter. "I'm certain that once the shine has worn off his new marriage, he will come around. We will simply wait. Just write to me, Addy. I miss you so much when I'm not here."

"I cannot risk it, Henry," Addy insisted. "I've seen life without money, and I can't afford to lose my job." She shook her head when he tried to argue, her eyes imploring him to understand. "Your father wants what's best for you, and a maid is not it. You know what's expected of you. Everyone in this house does. You're meant to marry well. That's been the expectation for as long as I can remember."

"Addy, I'd give it all up for you. You have to know this."

Her throat tightened, her heart aching at his words. She loved him too, more than she could say, but she knew all too well what it was like to lose everything, to be left adrift with nothing and no one. She couldn't let Henry risk that for her. She couldn't bear to be the reason he lost his home, his family, and his future.

"Henry…" Her voice trailed off.

"Don't say it now," Henry said, drawing their joined hands up so he could kiss the back of her hand. "I know you love me. I feel it in my heart."

His eyes dwelt on her lips, his fingers tangling in her hair as he traced feather kisses along her cheek and then drew her into his arms. She almost capitulated, the words tumbling in her mind until her pounding pulse drowned them out and his kisses turned everything inside her to liquid gold.

He drew back, swiping the pad of his thumb across her damp mouth. "I will write to you."

"No, please don't," she whispered, trying to hold onto her sanity. "Finish school first. And then…"

He sighed. "Fine. I'll finish school next year. By then, I'll be of age and in charge of my own destiny."

For now, Addy accepted that this would have to be enough. Hesitantly, she nodded.

"I'll see you at Christmas," he whispered, drawing her in for one last kiss before he departed for school.

THE DAYS after Henry's departure were harder than she had anticipated. His absence left a hollow space she couldn't fill. She clung to her daily routines, trying to keep busy, attempting to banish the ache of missing him. But, just as she had feared, without Henry's protection, Isaac once again began to appear in places when she least expected him.

One chilly afternoon, as she hurried up to the attic floor to change her apron, she stopped short when she noticed that her bedroom door was slightly ajar.

With a frown, she approached the room cautiously, a prickle of premonition tingling across her skin. She pushed the door open, wincing as it creaked. Her heart dropped like a stone as she took in the scene before her.

Isaac was in her room, lounging casually against the bedpost, a smug grin tugging at the corner of his mouth. But, more worryingly, her belongings were spread out across the bed—the small treasures she had carefully collected over the years. Her books and notebooks, the delicate origami cranes and flowers Henry had made for her. The shiny buttons and coloured stones he had left in fireplaces—all laid bare between them.

"Quite the little collector, aren't you?" Isaac exclaimed.

She reminded herself that the servants' floor was supposed to be off-limits to the household. This was their domain, a place where they should have some privacy.

"You're not supposed to be up here," she managed to force out, despite the tightness in her throat. "Mrs Blythe doesn't like it."

Isaac's grin only widened. "I couldn't care less what that old harpy says." He bent down, picking up one of the paper flowers, turning it over in his hands. "Did you make this?"

Addy said nothing, not trusting herself to speak. She fought the urge to snatch it back, to gather up all her belongings, to protect them from his careless hands. But she dared not provoke the unpredictable anger that always seemed to lurk beneath the surface of his demeanour.

"It's clever," he said with feigned interest, "so delicate... like you." He shot her a lingering look. Her pulse spiked sickeningly as he picked up a paper crane, and she recognised it as the first one Henry had made for her. Isaac toyed with it carelessly while his gaze roamed over the belongings scattered on the bed. "And the books? There's quite a few here."

"Please," she said quietly, "I need to change my apron."

Isaac's grin turned wolfish when he looked at her, and he rolled his hand in a mocking gesture. "Don't let me stop you stripping off."

Her face burned with humiliation, but she stood

her ground, crossing her arms firmly over her chest. "You need to go downstairs, Mr Jacobson. It's not right that you're up here."

He laughed a dark, contemptuous sound that sent an icy shiver down her spine. "It's not right that a maid has all these books. Did you steal them?"

"Of course not," she snapped before she could stop herself, immediately regretting it as she saw something dangerous flash in his eyes.

His gaze narrowed, calculating. Slowly, deliberately, he held the crane in the centre of his palm, smirking cruelly as he crushed it in his fist, the delicate folds crumpling beneath his fingers. He let the balled-up paper fall to the floor.

Her lips parted in a horrified gasp. Then he reached for the lotus flower, which quickly met the same fate, joining the crushed crane on the floor.

"Please," she whispered, barely audible. "Don't."

His smile was cold as he crushed another origami figure, savouring the way she recoiled. Tears filled her eyes as she whispered hoarsely, "Stop. Stop that right now."

He looked down at the crushed paper before stepping closer to her, making sure he stepped on the papers as he did. Extending one finger, he tapped her on the nose, laughing as she flinched away from his touch. "Sweet, little Addy."

He'd reached the door before he paused and looked back at her. "You don't tell me what to do. You're just a maid. And in future, you watch your mouth, or I'll make sure you watch me burn every single thing in this room."

CHAPTER 32

*A*ddy tugged her shawl up higher around her next as she made her way back towards Longhaven. She had lingered too long, enjoying the fine, crisp October weather as she'd gone to post Lucy's letter and do a small errand for Smale. Dusk would soon settle, the blue sky beginning to deepen to shades of amber. She climbed the stile into the orchard, thinking the shortcut might save her a few minutes.

The earthy scent of fallen leaves filled the air, the evening quiet all around her except for the decaying carpet of leaves and twigs underfoot. She let herself out of the orchard, and set out across the yard, frowning when she caught the low rumble of voices somewhere to her right.

Her heart leapt into her throat when she spotted two men, shadowed under the trees in the far corner. Poachers? Mr Roberts would surely fetch his gun and see them off.

The taller of the two was handing the shorter,

stockier one what looked like a black sack. She was about to go and find the groundkeeper when she heard, "Where the hell have you been? I don't like to be kept waiting!"

Fear froze her to the spot. *Isaac*. His voice was terse with irritation.

The broader man's hulking form exuded menace, and his laughter was laced with derision. "Crime doesn't run to a clock. You want this stuff hocking; you sell it yourself."

"Just take that lot and go," Isaac snapped, "and don't stiff me on the price this time."

"You'll get what I say you get," the Neanderthal groused, "or I'll have to let slip to your new Papa where all his stuff is going."

Her stomach churned. The servants had assumed it was Vanessa stripping Longhaven of its valuables. Had it been Isaac all along?

"What do we have this time?"

"What are you *doing?*" Isaac hissed at him, as the man shook the sack and delved inside. In doing so, he dropped the sack. It hit the ground with a clatter of metal on stone.

The contents spilled out of the opening and the man drew something out of the pile and cackled. "What am I supposed to do with these?" The string of pearls gleamed softly as he swung them. "A string of pearls isn't exactly discreet, is it?"

Isaac looked around him. It was then that he spotted Addy, frozen in the centre of the yard. His usual air of arrogance slipped momentarily as he stared at her.

"These are more suited for her type," the oaf

pointed out as he calmly stuffed the contents back in the sack.

Isaac ignored him. "What are you doing out here?"

Addy had to swallow. Fear had dried her throat. "I... I was on my way back from the post office."

The oaf only chuckled. "Seems to me you're in a bit of a pickle, Jacobson. A maid sees all and knows much."

"Shut up," Isaac rounded on him. "Pick up the rest of that stuff and clear out."

He dangled something from his fingers. It spun in the light. "Give her this. You'll keep quiet about this little operation if you're paid well enough, won't you, sweetheart?"

Addy's breath hitched when she recognised the sapphire pendant that sparkled. The words were out of her mouth before she could stop them. "That's not yours. I've seen the late Mrs Scorby wearing that."

Isaac snatched the necklace out of his grip and shoved it into his pocket. He gestured at the thug. "Mind your business. Just go."

The other man was clearly enjoying this. He indicated the last remaining trinkets. "Which is it, oh, masterful one. Pick this lot up or go? Maybe I ought to be paid extra, too."

"You're forgetting who you're dealing with, John Brown," Isaac muttered, deliberately saying the man's name in order to incriminate him, too. The man's smile vanished. Isaac leaned closer, "I will see you at the end of the hangman's noose. Now, go, before I change my mind and fetch the police here. Wouldn't do to be caught with a bag of stolen property now, would it?"

The man scoffed as he straightened. He slung the

sack over his shoulder. "Suit yourself," he muttered, trudging off into the darkness.

Isaac didn't move until the man had vanished entirely. He collected up the last few objects off the ground.

"Those things," Addy croaked. "they're not yours. They belong to Henry."

Isaac stilled, his head cocking. The smile was slow, predacious, as it moved over his mouth. He approached her. "And you're hoping that they will be yours one day?"

"No," she said quickly.

Isaac's laugh was low, mocking. "Liar. I've met grasping harlots like you before. Henry is too stupid to realise that with his wealth, he can have any woman he wants. His father might turn a blind eye to his son fiddling with a servant, but he will never allow his beloved Margaret's jewels grace the neck of someone whose hands are covered in soot from cleaning the fireplace."

She knew all of this, yet his words cut her to the quick. She lifted her chin, meeting his scornful expression with defiance. "Put everything you have in your pockets back. Never sell anything else, and I won't breathe a word."

Isaac closed in on her, and danger trickled down her spine. "No." His hand shot out, and she flinched, which drew more taunting laughter from him. "Easy. It occurs to me that we could be allies, Adelaide. I could be good to you, if you'd let me." In his open palm lay a beautiful cameo brooch. "For your silence. It will fetch a pretty penny."

"They're his mother's things," Addy pleaded. "Put it all back. The sapphire pendant was her favourite. Have you no heart?"

This time, he grabbed at her, his grip bruising. "The dead have no need for baubles," he snarled in her face. "And if you open your mouth about this, you'll join your precious Mrs Scorby."

~

NOVEMBER MISTS CLUNG TO LONGHAVEN, shrouding the frozen landscape in a ghostly veil.

The unforgiving chill settled across the land as winter took a firm bite, dusting the fields with wisps of snow. Addy moved quickly between the bedrooms, keeping the fires banked and doing her best to push back the chill that seeped into every corner. The endless fetching and carrying of coal and logs kept her hands busy and her mind occupied.

Staff levels at Longhaven were leaner than ever, and it showed. Small tasks were being missed, and Mrs Blythe was quick to point out her shortcomings. Working alone meant that each room took twice as long as it should. Addy pushed on through the scoldings and the slaps, doing her best to maintain the standards at Longhaven if only to appease Mr Smale. She suspected it was Mr Scorby's need to preserve his status and his attachment to following traditions of a grand household that kept old Smale in his role.

She missed Lucy's companionship. The old maid wrote to her regularly, talking about her new life on the farm, with its steady cyclical rhythms of the seasons. Addy envied her friend's newfound freedom, but there was little time to dwell on it.

She paused outside Isaac's bedroom door, feeling an uneasy flutter as the familiar dread rolled through her.

You'll be dead, too.

His threats echoed in her head, as they always did whenever she thought about him. She reminded herself that during breakfast, one of the groomsmen had mentioned that Isaac had set out early for the day. Unusual, yes, but it had been a habit ever since the incident in the yard. His absence gave her a small sense of relief as she went about her chores. Although, she knew he was out riding for the day, she still felt a prickle of trepidation.

Taking a steadying breath, she opened the door. The embers in the hearth glowed faintly in the grate. She turned her attention to them first, stoking the fire, adding fuel and more coal from the bucket to keep it going, and arranging fresh logs to fill the room with a bit more warmth. She filled the coal scuttle as much as it would hold, hoping she wouldn't need to refill it again until tomorrow.

With the fire taken care of, she turned her attention to the bedroom. Like Henry had been when he was younger, Isaac was a messy occupant. His clothes were strewn carelessly around the room, draped over the furniture and scattered across the floor. The bed was a tangled nest of sheets and blankets. She worked swiftly, tidying as she moved, gathering up discarded clothes and folding them with practiced efficiency before returning them to drawers or hanging them in the wardrobe. She shook out the sheets, pulled the blankets tight, and smoothed out every crease.

She was just tucking in the last corner of the bed when the familiar, taunting voice broke the blessed silence.

"Well, aren't you a sight for sore eyes."

Her heart dropped to her stomach as she whirled

around just as Isaac closed the door behind him. Panic flared as she realised her only escape route was now blocked.

"S-sorry, sir," she stammered, "I thought you were out for the day."

Isaac let his gaze travel over her, drawing out the silence as he did so. He eased away from the door, tugging at his collar and loosening the stock around his neck as he approached. "My horse threw a shoe," he shrugged, dropping the stock carelessly onto the floor she'd just tidied. Standing in the middle of the room, he untucked his shirt, pulling the tails free from his breeches. His actions were unhurried and deliberate as he began to unbutton it.

Addy's hands fumbled as she grabbed the pile of bedding. Her instincts screamed at her to leave, to get out as fast as she could. "I'll fetch Charlie for you, sir," she said hastily, clutching the linens to her chest.

"Why?" He drew the shirt over his head, mussing his hair as he dropped that garment on the floor, too.

"To help you change."

His hands went to his waistband. "I don't need another man to help me undress, but I wouldn't object if you helped me, Addy."

He tugged at the ties, unconcerned. Addy tried to look anywhere but at his hands. "Surely, you've seen Henry more naked than this," he drawled. "Or maybe not, judging by how red you are."

Addy's mind raced but terror had rooted her feet to the ground.

Isaac moved closer still, pulling his waistband open, revealing the same dark hair as on his chest. "Is he too much of a dandy to handle a woman as beautiful as you? I know what a woman wants, Addy. You know my secret, and I know yours. We'd make a great team."

Heat scored her cheeks. She sidestepped. "I have other rooms to tend to. Your mother doesn't like it when the fires are too low," she pretended to take an interest in the state of the room as she turned for the door, hoping he'd take the hint and let her go.

Without warning, he lunged for her, knocking the linen from her grasp. Addy squawked as he grabbed her, filling his hands with her backside.

Addy twisted and squirmed as Isaac nuzzled her neck, his wandering hands roving over her.

"Please, Mr Jacobson, please don't. That's not – let me go," Addy struggled in vain. His hands travelled up her side, skimming her breasts. He grinned as she struggled and pressed his mouth to hers.

When she turned her face away, he gripped her chin and thrust his tongue into her mouth.

"Get off me!" She yelled and pummelled his chest though it was futile. The sheets had tangled around her feet, and she tumbled into the bed. Isaac followed her down, pressing her into the mattress. His jeering laughter filled her ears, and she heard material tear, then his hot touch was on her thigh, seeking higher.

Panicked, Addy thrashed around. She heard his breath hiss as she connected with flesh. The slap exploded on her cheek. Her pain-filled cry drove him into a frenzy.

"What is going on in here?" Smale's deep baritone lashed out.

Isaac froze then, twisting to look back over his shoulder. Addy quickly rolled out from under him, breathing heavily as she faced the butler and Charlie in the doorway. Her face throbbed, her black dress was ripped in several places. The footman's horrified expression told her all she needed to know about her state of undress.

"Adelaide?" Smale's furious gaze was on Isaac. "Are you alright?"

She could only shake her head, tears choking off her voice.

"I don't remember inviting either of you in here. This is *my* room in my *mother's* house," Isaac snapped at the butler as he touched a hand to his neck, glaring balefully at Addy when his fingers came away bloody. "You cut me, you little witch!"

"Addy, go, now," Smale's glower didn't waver from Isaac. "I shall deal with this. Leave the scuttle and the linen. I shall send Bess upstairs shortly."

Addy hurried from the room, gripping the tattered edges of her uniform. Isaac's vociferous protests faded as she darted through the door to the back stairs, up to the attic floor. By the time she reached her room. She was shaking uncontrollably. She just about made it to her bed before her boneless legs gave way.

CHAPTER 33

Addy hadn't witnessed the argument between Smale and Mrs Blythe firsthand. However, Bess assured her it had been nothing short of spectacular, with the housekeeper demanding to know why the butler was interfering in the management of the female staff. The butler refused to shed any further light on why he insisted that Addy returned to her old role as a kitchen maid. Addy's shame was spared when she understood that only Smale and Charlie were privy to what had happened to her in Isaac's bed chamber.

Addy gratefully returned to the kitchen, while Bess, pleased with her promotion, had taken her place upstairs. Addy kept a close eye on her, worried that Isaac's loathsome attentions might now shift to the new maid. Yet, it seemed that he had finally accepted her silent defiance and had decided to leave her alone.

There was no reason for their paths to cross now that she could hide away in the safety of the kitchen.

Addy threw herself into her role with as much

vigour as she could summon, and slowly, she dared to believe that things had turned a corner.

The relief was short-lived, though. Her fragile peace shattered on the day she was summoned to Mr Scorby's office.

She was thankful for Mr Smale's company as he preceded her into the room and announced her presence. Addy's eyes widened when she saw her precious books spread out across the master's cherry wood desk. Isaac lounged in the corner, legs crossed, watching her with a lazy smirk. Mr Scorby dismissed the butler, but Smale, ever loyal to his staff, stood sentinel in the corner.

"Do you see, Reginald? Do you see how defiant the staff are here? Now, do you understand why they should all be replaced?" Vanessa looked particularly stunning; her deep burgundy gown set off her rosy complexion to perfection.

Mr Scorby made a dismissive gesture, his dark gaze fixed on Addy. Her heart raced as he held up a book, and she recognised it as the one Henry had given her for Christmas all those years ago.

The cover of *Jane Eyre* was slightly worn, a testament to the countless nights she'd spent reading it by candlelight.

Without preamble, Vanessa's voice cut through the silence like a knife. "What do you have to say for yourself, you little thief?"

Addy's eyes widened, her mouth opening in surprise. "I'm not—" she began.

"And this?" Mr Scorby held up the sapphire necklace so that it flashed blue fire in the light as it twirled. "Why was this in your drawer? I've checked and there is a lot of my late wife's jewellery missing. Where is it all?"

Panic closed off her throat. Her eyes wheeled around to Isaac. He merely quirked a brow at her. "Please," she forced the words out in a strangled whisper. "I didn't take anything. I swear."

"Then how did this get into your room?" Mr Scorby raged at her. "Where is the rest of it?"

"Isaac –"

"Don't you dare lie!" Vanessa spat. "They might lie in the workhouse, but in proper society, we own up and take responsibility for our errors."

Addy's breath caught. "I d-didn't steal anything, ma'am," she stammered, her eyes turning to Smale, pleading.

"With respect, Mrs Scorby," Smale's deep voice was quietly assured, "Addy is as honest as the day is long. She has worked here for many years. Always truthful. She is a keen reader. I have loaned her many books and—"

Vanessa snorted in disbelief. "Are you going to let this insolent behaviour carry on, Reginald?" She pointed at the desk. "Books are for people with intellect, Smale, not for dirty, conniving servants with idle minds who have nothing better to do than throw themselves at eligible gentlemen in the hope of scrambling up the social ladder. Do you see what she's done to my son's neck? She ought to be flogged for what she's done to him!"

In the corner, Isaac's expression was one of gleeful satisfaction. Addy's heart sank as she caught his twisted grin, realising he hadn't retreated at all but had instead been planning this new way of torturing her.

"I didn't do any such thing," she protested.

"A thief and a liar," Vanessa crowed. "Is there no end to your brass neck? Reginald, are you going to stand for this corruption under your roof?"

Mr Scorby waved the book in his hand, drawing attention back to the matter at hand. He seemed more put out by the book than the sapphire being found. He studied Addy. "This book is mine," he said coldly. "It's part of a set I acquired from a collector in York. Did you think you could get away with taking my property, girl?"

Addy's throat went dry, her mind racing. She had no idea that Henry had taken the book from his father's library, but to tell the truth would surely betray Henry. To try and explain why the master's son had given her such an expensive gift would require further explanation, and she didn't want to break Henry's confidence. She remained silent, even as Smale rushed to her defence once more. The butler insisted again in her morality, that she was well-read, that he had loaned her books, and that she had even helped Bess learn to read and write.

"Is this true, girl?" Reginald questioned.

Addy nodded quickly. "Yes, sir."

Hope flared when she sensed Mr Scorby's hesitation. In a fit of impatient frustration, Vanessa snatched up the remaining origami shapes and notebooks and tossed everything onto the fire.

"No!" A cry tore from Addy's throat as she reached out to save her precious belongings, but Vanessa shrieked, "Don't you dare lay a hand on me! Do you see, Reginald? She went for me! When will this madness ever end?"

Addy watched helplessly as the paper twisted and blackened in the fireplace, the flames devouring them.

She ignored Isaac's mocking laughter, balling her fists at her sides as she faced Reginald Scorby. "I didn't steal a thing, sir. I swear it."

"Then why was my book in your room? What else have you taken, and probably sold, from this house?"

"Nothing!" Addy cried.

"I will not tolerate these lies, Reginald!" Vanessa shouted. "The girl is guilty. She attacked my darling son—look at his neck!"

"That's not true," Addy blurted. "He attacked me!"

"Smale?" Reginald queried, a heavy dark brow lifting, though Vanessa erupted in fury.

"Reginald, are you taking the word of a servant over your *wife?*" Vanessa squawked. "Your stepson? Is this how little we're valued in this household? Choose, Reginald. Either call the constable to have this girl thrown into prison. Or so help me, I will leave you and cause the biggest scandal this country has ever seen."

Mr Scorby's expression turned to stone. "You have violated the trust of this household, girl. No thieves, beggars, or liars. You are dismissed from your position and must leave immediately without benefit of a reference."

Stunned, Addy could only stare. Her wild eyes swung to Smale, and she opened her mouth to protest, but Reginald cut her off, raising his voice above his wife's hysterical shouts. "Leave without a fuss, or I'll be forced to call for a constable."

CHAPTER 34

The streets of Liverpool filled with the jarring din of city life, and it felt strange to be back here after the quiet, sweeping grounds of Longhaven. Choking fog hung in the air, coating the buildings with the stain of industry. Addy clutched her small valise tightly, weaving her way through the narrow streets. The cries of hawkers and the clatter of wagon wheels formed an apt backdrop to her racing thoughts.

She counted herself lucky to have spotted the advert pinned to the noticeboard in the newsagents outside the train station. Asking for directions, she made her way along the side streets as the city noise began to fade the further she walked.

The lodging house was down a narrow side street. The red brick exterior, clean stone steps, and swept porches gave it a respectable feel. But when she stepped inside, the interior told a different story. The decor was dated, with cobwebs around the windows hinting at neglect. Mrs Sharp, the landlady, was a scrawny woman with a ruddy complexion, her hair twisted and pinned into a severe knot.

She subjected Addy to several pertinent questions before even allowing her entrance, setting Addy's nerves on edge. She led her up a creaking staircase, past several damp patches, the flickering lights barely illuminating the worn carpets and peeling wallpaper. "Your room is this way," she said over one shoulder.

The room itself was bare, containing only a small bed and a cupboard that leaned drunkenly against the wall. The windowpane was cracked in one corner, condensation gathering around the edges. There was no fireplace to warm the space, only a tiny, black pot-bellied stove tucked into an alcove. The threadbare carpet was dull and stained from years of use.

Addy did a slow circle to inspect the room as perhaps was expected of her. "Washing is extra," Mrs Sharp informed her abruptly, standing in the doorway with her arms folded. "Bathing is generally done on a Sunday. And your rent is paid a week upfront," she continued pointedly, giving Addy a long, critical once-over, "and there are to be no gentleman callers."

"Oh, goodness no, Mrs Sharp," Addy shook her head as she set her valise down by her feet. "I would never do anything like that."

"Good," the woman sniffed primly. "I run a respectable house."

Addy opened her purse and placed the coins into the woman's outstretched hand, acutely aware of how much this ate into her budget after the train fare and the sandwich she'd eaten. Not since living with her mother had she needed to consider these matters. Accommodation had been included with her position at Longhaven, and she'd not had to pay her way since working in the workhouse. Her budget was extremely tight, and she needed to find work immediately. The landlady folded her fingers around the coins with a satisfied nod.

Rather than leaving, Mrs Sharp studied Addy with the same scrutiny she'd given her at the front door. "You're looking for work, you say?"

"That's right." The words caught in her throat, and she had to draw in a steadying breath.

"You don't look old enough to be out on your own," the landlady remarked with a tilt of her head. "Nineteen years old?"

"Yes, Mrs Sharp," Addy replied, managing a smile to hide the small white lie. She was still a year shy of nineteen, but she wasn't sure the woman would have accepted her if she'd known she was younger.

The landlady didn't look convinced, her lips pursing, though she didn't press the matter further.

"Would you happen to know of any jobs going locally?" Addy ventured.

"There's always folks looking for servants, of course," Mrs Sharp replied. "And I'm sure a nice girl like you, with the experience you say you have, will have no trouble finding work."

"Thank you," Addy said politely.

With that, Mrs Sharp left the room, her footsteps fading down the hallway. In the following silence, Addy stood and looked around the small, shabby room. The bed creaked as she lowered herself onto it.

For the last eight years of her life, Addy had always had company in her room. From the dormitories in the workhouse to the cramped attic room at Longhaven, she'd learned to sleep alongside the sounds of people nearby. She'd yearned for a place of her own, free from watchful eyes and chatter that interrupted her reading.

Her fingers spread across the thin blanket beneath her hands, plucking at the worn material. Tears burned at the back of her eyes, but she held them in check.

Now, she had exactly what her heart had always wanted—a room of her own.

And she'd never been more terrified in her life.

~

Lodgings for single women were not built for comfort, and at first, Addy hadn't planned to stay with Mrs Sharp for too long. She hoped her experience at Longhaven would help her find a position somewhere in the city.

She kept careful watch over her spending, foregoing fuel in the stove and meals in order to be able to stay at the lodging house for as long as she possibly could. All she needed was a job in service, and she would be fine. She had saved a little of her wages from Longhaven, though being dismissed had meant she hadn't received her quarterly funds.

Mr Smale had insisted on giving her a little extra, though she suspected it was from his own pocket rather than household funds. Every job application Addy sent was met with rejection, and it didn't take long for her to suspect that Vanessa had followed through on her promise to ruin her. It seemed Vanessa's determination to ensure she would never work again was succeeding.

Without a reference, her options were limited and dwindled with each passing day.

She had written to Mr Smale, following up on her promise to alleviate his worries by letting him know where she had landed, but she couldn't be sure if any of her letters had reached him.

She'd never received a reply.

She had been careful to word her enquiries about the family subtly, hoping that Mr Smale would let Henry know what had happened to her and where she was.

More than the absence of work and the constant gnaw of hunger, missing Henry was just as acutely painful. She was certain he would be furious when he discovered what had happened to her, and when Mr Smale and Mrs Porter hadn't written back, she'd toyed with the idea of writing directly to Henry.

At first, she had resisted, reminding herself that she was only a maid, and Henry was a gentleman.

But he had declared that he loved her, and she was certain he would be worried about her. As the colder months crept in and she realised he would soon be finishing school for Christmas, she penned a letter. It was brief and polite, and she left a forwarding address for him.

The snow fell, turning thickly to black sludge under the relentless pace of city life. Days turned into weeks, and the weeks passed in silence. Perhaps Henry had finally come to realise that her cautionary words to him last summer were true. Perhaps he had moved on, convinced by Vanessa and his father that no good could come from their friendship. After all, Vanessa seemed to be quite adept at manipulating the truth to suit her agenda.

Still, she waited, holding close the memories of their last moments together, the way he had held her hand and promised her that she mattered. But that hope, fragile as it was, dwindled away.

Just as she had done when she and her mother had first moved to Fletcher Street, Addy trudged the streets day after day, seeking work at market stalls and shops. Following a recommendation from one of the stall owners, she approached the factory gates.

Finally, after some quick thinking and lying, Addy had managed to secure herself a job. The cigar-making factory on Cornwallis Street was her new workplace. To Addy's untrained eye, the factory room was chaotic. Lines of women hunched over workstations, nimble fingers rolling cigars with practised precision. The smell of dried leaves, cedarwood, and tobacco stung the air.

The supervisor, a rotund man by the name of Hackett, wasted no time in putting her to work. She was assigned a bundle of dry tobacco leaves and tasked with stripping the veins from each leaf. She quickly picked up the work by mimicking the movements of those around her. Talking was kept to a minimum as Hackett loomed over Addy. A lector sat on a raised platform, reading aloud from the day's newspaper. Further down the row, other workers shaped the stripped leaves into cigar fillers, binding them together to create a firm but pliable core. Those with more experience worked on the wrappers, which gave the cigars their finished appearance.

The days rolled by, and Addy's stained hands grew sore, her back aching from sitting on the hard wooden bench. But it was work, and while the pay barely covered her rent, at least she was earning. Yet, as often happened during the deepening winter, Addy found herself once again out of work.

"Last in, first out," Hackett intoned as he handed her the final pay packet.

She sold what little she could—her last pair of gloves, her case, and the last of her books—in a desperate attempt to stave off eviction, until she stood with the last of her coins in her palm. Just as she had when she was a child, Addy considered hiding from Mrs Sharp, though deep down she knew that wouldn't solve anything. Mrs Sharp had a business to run and was entitled to her rent. She had already given Addy a warning about late rent when she discovered that Addy had lost her job.

She walked home on that dark winter night, passing by the scantily clad women who loitered around the public houses and in darkened doorways. The streets were filled with women like them who, having fallen on hard times, had been forced to turn to selling their bodies to make ends meet. She knew exactly how they earned their coin, their painted faces and shimmering forms lingering under the gaslights. She understood why they made the choices they had, but she couldn't do it.

Back in her freezing cold bedroom, fat flakes of snow tumbling past the window, she made her decision. With one last long look around her room, she closed the bedroom door and left the lodging house for the final time. She had no more belongings left to take with her. She stepped out into the cold and hurried along the narrow, damp cobblestones. She kept her head down as she made her way through the maze of alleys and backstreets, casting desperate looks at the ragged wretches that shuffled past her.

Through the hazy light, she recognised the familiar outline of the Liverpool workhouse. Memories of the same trip she had made long ago haunted her with each step. She understood now more than ever the despair her mother must have felt as she approached those imposing doors.

She thought she'd left this place behind for good.

She remembered the cold, barren hallways and endless toil, the hollowed faces of the poor souls who had given up. The high walls and heavy wooden door were just as she remembered. She knocked sharply, the sound echoing beyond.

She listened and waited, hearing the shuffling of footsteps approaching from behind the door. It rattled and then creaked open, revealing a familiar face. Rheumy eyes narrowed as Mr Scott studied her. Slowly, he pulled the door open further.

"Miss Hill, what brings you back to our establishment?"

"Hello, Mr Scott," Addy said quietly. "I'm here to seek indoor relief."

CHAPTER 35

"What happened?" the old porter asked, lowering himself into the desk chair with a resounding groan. Addy stood before him, her heart pounding as memories of standing in this very room years ago flooded her mind. The receiving office was just as she remembered it, and a torrent of emotions surged through her, making it difficult to breathe. The dim light, the same worn wooden desk, and the heavy air filled with despair—it all pulled her back to the day she arrived here as a child.

"Addy?" Mr Scott prompted.

She took a moment to steady herself before she could trust her voice. Slowly, she began, "I lost my position, sir."

She carefully recounted the series of events that had led her here, right up until losing her job at the factory. She was cautious to omit any mention of her friendship with Henry, keeping her words to the verifiable facts that couldn't be misconstrued.

Mr Scott grunted, leaning back in his chair as he studied her with an inscrutable expression. "It's been a hard year," he muttered. "We've had a high intake with so much work drying up. Times are hard for everyone. Factories can't keep people on during the cold months." He scratched his chin thoughtfully, the whiskers rasping beneath his fingers. "The old Mrs Scorby passing was sudden, I'll admit. She was always pleasant enough whenever I met her at one of the board meetings." He shifted in his seat, his eyes narrowing slightly. "The new wife... she doesn't sound much like the sort I'd have thought he'd bring into the family, nor one I'd expect to see join the board of governors."

Addy kept her own counsel about her previous employer, not wanting to appear bitter. Complaints wouldn't change her circumstances and would only make her seem ungrateful.

Mr Scott drummed his fingers briefly on the desk-top. "You didn't steal those jewels, did you? Or that book?"

"I've never stolen anything in my life, Mr Scott," she replied evenly.

His brow flickered, acknowledging her honesty. "It doesn't sound like something you'd do, Addy. Lord knows, you were always a trustworthy girl."

He pulled a ledger towards him, flipped open the lid of the inkwell, and scratched her name into its pages with deliberate strokes. The admission process was long and drawn-out, involving paperwork, questions, and formalities that stretched late into the evening. By the time Mr Scott rose from his chair, the light outside had faded into night.

"I can grant you temporary leave until the meeting; you might remember that they're always held on Wednesdays," he rasped, steadying himself against the desk as he rose. "You know the drill. Let's get you through to the receiving ward," he said, motioning for her to follow him.

The long hallway stretched ahead of her, its familiarity tightening her chest. Each door she passed stirred memories. The porter's steps were slow and measured—he had once been sprightlier.

The medical officer was already present—a stroke of luck, as sometimes inmates had to wait in a holding pattern until a medical officer became available. The man was frail, appearing barely strong enough to stand upright in a stiff breeze. His examination was perfunctory, declaring her healthy enough with a distracted nod. She was allowed to bathe and issued the scratchy uniform she remembered all too well.

Addy was then led to the receiving ward. "You'll stay in here until the board meeting," the medical officer explained. "Mrs Fishman will be along to see to you shortly."

Standing just inside the doorway of the ward, Addy thanked him quietly. She wondered if Mrs Fishman would remember her after all these years. The matron had been a firm but fair woman—never cruel, though never overly kind, either.

The receiving ward was warm enough, with several people already bedding down for the night. A small stove in the corner emitted a modicum of heat, and a couple of women stood beside it, hands outstretched towards the warmth.

Addy looked around the room, largely ignored by

the others. She wondered if her face bore the same weary lines of despair etched into those around her. One inmate, a rail-thin woman with wild hair, muttered incessantly to herself, her words unintelligible. Every now and then, her voice would rise in a shriek, her arms flailing at unseen spectres.

Addy spotted a seat and sat with her head bowed, hoping to go unnoticed.

The muttering grew louder, the poor woman's voice rising into a crescendo of incomprehensible gibberish.

"Pack it in!" another woman snapped, her patience breaking. "You're driving us all mad!"

The madwoman responded with an ear-piercing wail, raw and animalistic in its pain. Addy stood, unsure of what to do, when the door swung open and a tall woman in a crisp black uniform stormed into the room.

Her voice cut through the chaos like a gunshot. "What is the meaning of this noise?" she demanded. "I can hear you all down the hallway! Cease this instant —all of you!"

"Mrs Fishman!" the madwoman sobbed desperately. "Oh, the cat! Save the cat!"

"I know, I know," the matron said hurriedly, moving towards the woman and patting her shoulder gently. "The cat is fine now, Alice. Thank you for letting me know."

The madwoman wrapped her arms around herself, quieting instantly under Mrs Fishman's calming touch. "Oh, thank you, Mrs Fishman. Thank you," she murmured as she was guided to an empty cot.

Addy stood frozen, her mouth slightly open, as the matron turned and swept her gaze around the room.

The matron's stern expression softened when her startled gaze landed on Addy.

"Addy?" Mrs Fishman's brow furrowed in recognition.

"Janey?" Addy breathed.

CHAPTER 36

The matron's sitting room was practical enough, furnished with everything Janey would need to manage the women in the workhouse. It contained a plain wooden table with two chairs, a desk cluttered with papers and ledgers, and two worn armchairs flanking a small hearth, where a fire crackled pleasantly.

Addy sat across the table from Janey, cradling a chipped, dainty teacup. The entire experience felt surreal, as though she were caught between her memories and the present. She sipped her tea, the warmth seeping through her hands.

Janey listened as she shared the story of life at Longhaven, dismissing the profuse apologies her old friend made for leaving the workhouse all those years ago.

"You should've fought the accusations," Janey said sharply. "You should've let them call the constable and shown that rotten stepson who he was messing with."

Addy shook her head, a wistful smile tugging at her lips.

It warmed her more than the tea to see flashes of the fiery, loyal girl Janey had once been, the same fierce glimmer in her eyes. "You of all people know what it's like to try and fight the system, Janey. You know as well as I do how these things work. Me, against someone like Isaac Jacobson? I'm just a lowly maid. It wouldn't have mattered how many times I told my side. Yes, I had the truth, but that doesn't count for much when you're up against people like him and Vanessa Scorby."

Janey's lips pressed into a thin, indignant line. "He's despicable," she muttered angrily.

Addy couldn't help but laugh, her friend's unchanging forthrightness lifting her spirits. "Oh, he is."

Her gaze fell to the teacup in her hands. Sitting here, drinking tea with her old comrade, felt surreal. Her eyes travelled around the plain room. Only now did she notice the homey touches: a vase of dried flowers on the windowsill, a small, crocheted doily draped over the back of one of the chairs, and two books stacked neatly beside the hearth.

It was hard to imagine her fierce friend finding time for pleasures like reading.

Janey sighed and gestured impatiently at Addy. "Come on, out with it."

Addy tilted her head, the faintest grin teasing her mouth. "Of all the things I imagined for you, Janey, 'Matron of a workhouse' certainly wasn't one of them."

It seemed her friend was used to such comments, as she didn't take offence. Instead, amusement rippled across her face. "I dare say it set the cat among the pigeons for more than a few people," she said, pouring more tea into cups. She added a sugar cube to hers and leaned back, letting the steam waft up before taking a careful sip. "Mrs Fishman passed not two years after you left. And Mr Fishman... well, he was a devastated man."

Addy pictured how Mr Scorby had been after losing his wife and nodded in understanding.

Janey lifted her cup, wincing slightly at the heat of the tea, and set it back down to let it cool. "Gordon needed help with the paperwork—running a place this size isn't easy, not alone. It was Mr Nelson who suggested I help him. He was busy carrying on the work you'd started with the younger ones, taking the extra time to teach them their letters and such. I suppose he saw the difference it had made to me and was... inspired, I suppose you'd call it."

Addy blinked in surprise, touched by the compliment and warmed by the memory.

"At first, I was hopeless," Janey confessed with a light laugh. "All fingers and thumbs, about ready to give up. Of course, it was Mr Nelson who gave me the stern talking-to I needed, reminding me of all I'd learned from you. Still, I was slow, struggling to keep up with the paperwork.

"But Gordon... that is, Mr Fishman, he was patient. We spent a lot of time together. He's... he's a kind man, Addy." Janey's cheeks flushed faintly as she traced the grain of the table with her thumbnail, glancing at Addy shyly.

"When he kissed me, he was mortified. He said he'd crossed a line, being in a position of care over me, that he'd broken the rules. But I reminded him—I'm a grown woman."

Addy saw the discomfort in her friend's expression and reached across the table, resting her hand over Janey's. "You don't need to explain yourself to me."

Janey smiled gratefully but continued, nonetheless. "He's sweet and generous, and he's a good master here. Fair and just, though there are always some who try to take advantage of his nature."

"And you're there to protect him," Addy said playfully.

Janey laughed self-deprecatingly. "Some bad habits die hard."

The room fell into a comfortable silence, broken only by the rhythmic ticking of the mantle clock. Addy was glad her friend had found happiness. As she sipped her tea, her thoughts wandered to the past.

"And now I've confessed everything," Janey said, tilting her head as her gaze pinned Addy's. "What about this young Master Scorby? Henry, wasn't it?"

"That's right," Addy said, her cheeks flushing before she could stop them.

Janey's eyes lit with mischief. "Adelaide Hill," she teased, leaning forward. "Did you fall in love with the master's son?"

"No, no," Addy replied quickly, though it felt wrong to deny the truth.

Janey leaned back, folding her arms as her eyes sparkled with interest. "You should write to him," she suggested. "Let him know where you are."

"I have," Addy admitted sadly. "But I've heard nothing back. I think now... it's probably for the best."

"Why would you think such a thing?"

"Mr Scorby was set on doing things the proper way. Henry's a gentleman, and I'm—"

"The daughter of a gentleman," Janey interjected firmly.

"Not anymore," Addy sighed. "Now I'm the same as everyone else here. I tried to make it out there on my own, but I can't work without a reference. Mrs Scorby had her wish, and here I am. I've failed, Janey."

"This is temporary, Addy. Everyone knows work dries up in the winter, but spring always brings change. People leave when the days grow longer, and the work returns. We see the same faces come and go with the seasons." Janey patted her hand, her eyes earnest. "This isn't forever. You'll see."

CHAPTER 37

Christmas Day dawned bright and crisp, the light frost glinting on the windows as the bell called for the inmates to rise. It was a peculiar mix of traditional formality, but this year, there seemed to be an unfamiliar cheer that had been absent in Addy's previous experiences.

She dressed quickly, the cold air chasing gooseflesh over her skin in the bitter morning. She set to work, emptying the ashes from the fire as other inmates took advantage of one of the only days off that they were allowed each year.

Essential chores to keep the workhouse functioning were still required on Christmas Day, but they were kept to a minimum.

The day began early with a chapel service. Addy filed in with the other women, her eyes drawn to their exclamations over the pretty decorations.

A communal table stood with a cross made from bright Christmas berries. Holly and laurel draped the pews and altar. As if sensing the festive spirit, the air filled with the joyous sound of women singing familiar carols, their voices lifting hearts and spirits alike.

For Addy, it was a reminder that even in the harshness of a place like this, there could still be beauty, warmth, and celebration.

After the service, the inmates moved to the dining hall, which had been transformed for the occasion. Evergreens adorned the walls, and gilded stars hung from the ceiling, catching the winter light filtering through the high windows. The Prince of Wales' plumes were prominently displayed alongside festive banners, one proclaiming: *Long life to Mr and Mrs Fishman.* The sentiment touched Addy, showing her just how much love that the inmates had for the couple who had done all they could to brighten this day.

Tables were arranged in neat rows, each one laid with the promise of a feast. Even the guardians of the workhouse had joined, mingling with the inmates and exchanging Christmas greetings and kind words. The guardians themselves served the food, and at two o'clock, dinner was served. The air was rich with the aroma of roast beef, accompanied by baked and boiled potatoes. Each adult received a pint of beer to enjoy with their meal. Addy chatted with her fellow inmates, laughing and marvelling at the richness of the food spread before them.

The men received an ounce of tobacco as a Christmas gift, while some of the elder women were given a pinch of snuff. Children squealed with delight as they were handed jellied sweets and oranges. After dinner, there was cake and fresh bread served with salty butter, which Addy savoured alongside the other women.

As Christmas night descended, the sound of

laughter and chatter was broken by bursts of song. A magic lantern display was set up, its flickering candlelight casting whimsical images that captivated both young and old. Laughter and gasps filled the air as fantastical scenes of dancing pixies and charming animals transported everyone to a world far removed from the bleak halls of the workhouse. Addy clapped and laughed along with the others; her heart lifted by the joy surrounding her.

Following the show, the room was filled with the sound of music and more singing—ancient ditties sung by the elderly and hearty carols led by Janey and Mr Fishman. Feet tapped merrily as the strains of a fiddle drifted through the air. For just a few precious hours, the workhouse had been swept along by the magic of Christmas. Worries were forgotten, the daily drudgery set aside, and burdens momentarily lifted.

Cheers erupted as the evening came to a close, with the inmates offering their heartfelt gratitude to those who had worked so hard to make the day special. Addy knew that many other workhouses did not allow for such festivities, and the gratitude that filled the room was something almost foreign to her—hope.

As the festivities wound down, the inmates shuffled back to their respective wards. Warmed by beer and full bellies, the dormitory was soon filled with the sounds of snuffles and inebriated snores.

Addy climbed into her narrow cot, pulling the thin blanket tightly around her. She lay on her back, her eyes tracing the arc of the silvery moon as it moved across the window. Her thoughts turned to Henry, as they often did in quiet moments like this. She wondered if his day had been as merry and warm as hers. She hoped he had been surrounded by friends and family and that his Christmas had been as pleasant as it could be.

With all her heart, she wished him happiness. She also wanted him to know that she understood why he hadn't replied to her letter. In the silvery moonlight, Addy finally closed her eyes. Before sleep claimed her, her thoughts lingered on Henry, on herself, and on the faint but certain promise of better days ahead.

CHAPTER 38

"What if I can't do it?" Addy said, her voice quivering.

Janey sighed, the sound full of frustration. "Of course, you can do it," she replied flatly. "You have extensive training from your time at Longhaven, and you've picked up all the necessary skills from others here in the dormitory. I've seen what you can do with a dress these days—you'll be perfect for this position."

Still, Addy hesitated. It wasn't that she wanted to seem ungrateful for the efforts Janey had made to secure this new role, but the last six months in the workhouse had become... comfortable for her. Janey's understanding of how a workhouse operated meant she had been able to make helpful suggestions to her husband, which streamlined the efforts of everyone within its walls. Addy had found a certain rhythm in this predictability, a sense of safety that now felt hard to leave behind.

"What is it?" Janey's patience was wearing thin, her

tone sharp. "You've already turned down two roles that would have been similar to this one."

"A lady's maid is a lofty position to aspire to," Addy said quickly. "You forget I've worked with two of them. They're highly skilled and... well, not very pleasant. My skills as a maid might not be adequate enough."

"Mrs Glover is not a woman to be trifled with," Janey explained slowly. "When I presented your skills to her, she was more concerned about whether you would fit into her household. It's not a large team—just a butler, a cook, and one other maid, plus someone who tends to the grounds, of course. I've never had any issues with her, but I get the impression she doesn't suffer fools gladly. If she's not happy with you, she'll have no qualms about saying so," Janey added with a slight shake of her head. "But if that happens, at least you'll have the benefit of a reference, and you'll be able to find another position elsewhere."

Addy twisted the material of her skirt between her fingers nervously. Over the last six months, the predictable routine of the workhouse had been her salvation. Each day had been a mirror of the last, a steady rhythm of chores and responsibilities that kept her grounded.

She was safe here.

"The workhouse doors will always be open to you, Addy," Janey pointed out, her voice softening, "but you're so much better than these cold walls. This place —it's not meant for someone like you. And a small household on the outskirts of Manchester is a perfect fit."

Reluctantly, Addy agreed, and the following morning Janey was waiting for her in the receiving hall. She held a small parcel in her hands. When Addy opened it, a soft woollen scarf and a pair of black leather gloves tumbled free.

"These must have cost you a fortune," Addy said, her eyes wide. "And you've already given me a dress—it's too much, Janey."

"Stuff and nonsense," Janey said. "It's no less than you deserve, Adelaide Hill. You helped change my life, and many others here, too. Look at Rosie. She has a job in service, thanks to your help. You're an angel, Addy."

The endearment, so reminiscent of what Henry used to call her, caused a shaft of pain to lance through her. Her face crumpled and Janey gathered her closer. "Now, there's no need for all that, is there? You deserve a bit of luck and I'm glad I could help you somehow. I'm going to miss you, my friend," she added softly.

Addy hugged her tightly. "I shall miss you, too. Thank you, Janey, from the bottom of my heart."

With her carpet bag in hand, containing her old dress and the book Janey had gifted her last Christmas, and wearing the altered dress she had repaired herself, Addy left Liverpool Workhouse for the second time.

She climbed onto the omnibus headed out of the city, bound for Manchester.

She watched the clock tower of the Victoria building fading in the distance as Liverpool was left behind. The bus rattled along the wide roads and the city soon gave way to countryside. Through the window, Addy watched fields of wheat waving in the sun. Hedgerows were dotted with wildflowers. Overhead, blackbirds winged majestically on warm breezes. The vibrant greens and yellows were a soothing sight, though her thoughts turned to Henry.

By now, he would have left school and begun a life filled with opportunity and privilege. She pictured him tall and confident, ready to take on the world. The ache of longing tugged at her heart, as it always did when thoughts of him snuck into her mind. With effort, she pushed the images away. Dwelling on the impossible would serve no purpose.

The conductor's voice jolted her from her reverie. "Langmere! Next stop! All off for Langmere!"

The omnibus trundled to a stop in a small square. Its cobbled corners bustled with activity.

Langmere was caught somewhere between the charm of a village and the bustle of a small town. Red-brick and sandstone buildings framed the square, busy with carts and pedestrians. A greengrocer, a butcher, and a post office made up some of the shops clustered around the square, with a sprawling oak tree at its centre. Smartly dressed servants and well-heeled townsfolk moved about with purpose, their friendly greetings to one another reaching her ears as Addy alighted the omnibus.

Clutching her carpet bag in one hand and Janey's handwritten note in the other, Addy walked across the square. She passed the church and the black-and-white framed houses leaning over the streets, taking the first left past the vicarage. The houses were quiet, their gardens bursting with vibrant blooms. The air perfumed by the sweet scent of flowers. The sun warmed her back as she walked, the gentle hum of bees and chirping of birds creating a melody that sang to her soul.

She continued along the winding country lanes, passing cottages hidden behind thickets of trees and lush verges.

At the end of a long, shaded lane, Rose Villa came into view. On the fringe of the nearby village, it was far grander than Janey had implied. A graceful Georgian house of grey stone sat in the centre of an ornate garden, its entrance framed by elegant Ionic and Doric columns. Roses in every shade spilt from trellises and over the stone walls, the blossoms bursting in a riot of colour.

Addy let herself in through the wooden gate, her boots crunching along the gravelled path as she approached. Nerves nibbled at her stomach, and she pressed a hand to the fluttering. She reminded herself that she had ventured into pastures new before.

And if all else failed, she could always return to Janey.

She stood before the heavy oak door and gave herself a moment to steady her breath. Then, reaching for the brass knocker, she struck the door three times, whispering a silent prayer that this time, she had made the right choice.

CHAPTER 39

Mrs Prudence Glover was unlike any woman Addy had ever known. Widowed at a young age when her aristocratic husband fell from his horse and broke his neck, she was left with a modest inheritance. While most women in her position might have limped along, making the best of life or seeking the support of another man, Mrs Glover defied expectations and societal norms with a determination that Addy couldn't help but admire. Prudence turned her attention to investments in railways and steel, and over the decades, she had amassed a fortune that dwarfed her late husband's.

Now, in her autumn years, her empire was managed by a board of directors she referred to as "stuffy." Yet, despite her vast wealth and influence, Mrs Glover was unassuming, kind, and fiercely independent. She was a fine employer, although very particular in how her household was run. She was a stickler for manners and for things being done in the right way, not just in terms of politeness but also in how things were organised: her household, her clothes, her social schedule. She possessed a quiet strength that was both inspiring and intimidating.

Mrs Glover's decision to hire a young woman straight out of the workhouse was nothing short of remarkable. A lady's maid was typically expected to come from a background of strict training, never a workhouse, and certainly never someone with Addy's lack of experience. Addy had worried that her inexperience might prove a hindrance, but Mrs Glover delighted in how quickly she picked things up. Mrs Glover was thrilled to discover Addy's love for reading and learning.

Quite often, Addy found herself in a verbal sparring match with an equally sharp mind as they debated subjects.

A lady's maid had no set working hours, as all her attention was devoted to her mistress's comfort and whims. This left little time for much else, though Addy didn't mind. Her schedule was erratic and could change at a moment's notice to accommodate unexpected houseguests or sudden travel plans.

The household staff was small but efficient. Mrs Thomas, the cook, ruled the kitchen with a firm hand, much like the cooks Addy had worked with before. Harper, the dithering but well-meaning butler, drifted through the house, polishing silver and answering the door with the utmost formality. Gert, the young and eager housemaid, was still learning but brought enthusiastic energy to the household. The most excitement came when Harper and Mrs Thomas clashed over the day's arrangements. Their spirited debates amused Addy, reminding her of the camaraderie she had once enjoyed in the kitchen at Longhaven.

The day always began the same way, with Addy ensuring that Gert had banked the fire and prepared Mrs Glover's dressing room. The house, situated at the edge of Langmere, was always quiet.

Her duties were exhaustive—hairstyling, dressing, arranging jewellery, and ensuring Mrs Glover's wardrobe remained immaculate. Despite her rigorous schedule and advancing years, Mrs Glover still attended many luncheons and meetings with her board.

The bell jangled in the kitchen, signalling that Mrs Glover was awake.

"There you go," Mrs Thomas said, indicating the omelette and pot of tea on the counter. "Make sure you get that up to her quick as you like."

"Thank you, Mrs Thomas," Addy replied as she carried the tray up the stairs and let herself into her mistress's room.

Morning light filtered through the curtains, warming the space gently despite the chill in the air. The room was meticulously arranged, a reflection of the widow's character. An array of silver brushes and crystal bottles were perfectly aligned on her dressing table.

Mrs Glover sat up in bed, her grey hair neatly plaited and draped over one shoulder.

"Good morning, Mrs Glover," Addy murmured as she carried the tray across the room and set it carefully over her mistress's lap.

"Hello, Addy," Mrs Glover said, her tone brisk yet warm. "How is everything this morning?"

"Shipshape and running like clockwork," Addy

quipped as she did every day, drawing back the heavy velvet curtains to flood the room with light. "I've set out the blue dress as you requested," she added.

Mrs Glover clicked her tongue in mild disapproval. "Yes, that's right. I have that wretched meeting this morning with that boorish man."

Addy's lips twitched. The "boorish man" was Mrs Glover's legal representative, and Addy was almost certain he was petrified of her mistress. He stammered and flustered in Mrs Glover's presence until her patience invariably ran out.

"It shouldn't take too long," Addy offered.

Mrs Glover pursed her lips. "No, and Beatrice will be calling around. She wrote yesterday to ask if she could stop by for coffee."

"Yes, that's right."

"No doubt she'll be after more money for the charity," Mrs Glover added, her tone resigned.

Addy set about her tasks as Mrs Glover griped about her friend's visit. She fetched and carried hot water for washing and assisted her mistress with dressing. She styled Mrs Glover's soft silver waves into an elegant yet practical style for the day. Once her mistress was settled in her morning chair in the drawing room with her newspaper and post, Addy hurried upstairs to tidy away her nightclothes and air the outfit for the next day. She cleaned Mrs Glover's combs and brushes, tucked away the jug and bowl, and then returned below stairs.

She devoured her own breakfast quickly and spent the remainder of her morning tending to Mrs Glover's wardrobe—removing marks, ironing garments, and repairing a loose hem.

After Beatrice's visit, Addy was summoned to

accompany Mrs Glover into the village. Although the walk wasn't far, Mrs Glover called for the carriage.

"This cold air pains my bones," Mrs Glover grumbled as the carriage rolled around the side of the house and out along the lane towards Langmere.

"It's a cold one today," Addy agreed.

"It won't be long before the holly berries ripen and the robins dance in the snow," Mrs Glover mused, a soft smile touching her lips. "My husband used to love this time of year."

Addy returned her mistress's smile, a warmth filling her chest. Mrs Glover rarely spoke of her husband, but when she did, there was a wistfulness in her voice that made Addy ache for a love that could bridge both time and death. "I do so wish I could have met him," Addy said softly.

Startled, Mrs Glover's gaze swung to her. For a moment, Addy wondered if she'd crossed a line, but her mistress's expression softened.

"I dare say he would've had a thing or two to say about me hiring a girl from the workhouse. One without references and so young for a position as a lady's maid," Mrs Glover said, arching a brow as her gaze moved back to the window. "Of course, I would have smiled sweetly and had my way regardless. Poor Archibald never could say no to me."

Addy looked out at the passing fields, amusement flickering across her lips, until Mrs Glover's question drew her back.

"Do you like it here? The job, I mean. I know the work can be demanding, and I can be... particular at times."

"I'm grateful for the opportunity, Mrs Glover," Addy replied quickly.

"That wasn't my question," Mrs Glover pointed out.

Addy smiled. "Yes, I like it here very much. I enjoy the work and... I enjoy your company."

Mrs Glover's smile widened. "Some might take that as sycophancy, but I know you mean it genuinely. Although, when you meet Georgia, you might change your mind."

Mrs Glover's daughter-in-law already had a reputation that preceded her, and the thought of meeting her filled Addy with dread. Harper and Mrs Thomas had made comments that hinted Georgia might be cut from the same cloth as Vanessa. Addy's stomach tightened as she listened to Mrs Glover speak. She could only guess at the depths of pain the widow carried over the recent loss of her son at such a young age. The one light in her life was her granddaughter, Charlotte.

After running errands in the village, they returned home. Addy prepared Mrs Glover's nightclothes and ensured her room was warm with a glowing fire. She helped her mistress retire for the evening, dressing her down and ensuring she was comfortable.

On the nights when Mrs Glover had evening engagements, Addy's work stretched late into the night. She would wait up for her mistress to return, help her out of elaborate gowns and jewellery, and prepare her for bed. Once Mrs Glover was safely tucked away, Addy's duties continued. She set out the breakfast tray for the morning, folded garments with care, and tidied the room.

The work was demanding, and her time was no longer her own, but there was a deep satisfaction in the order and purpose of her days.

As a lady's maid, she was granted a generously

sized room of her own on the attic floor. She slipped out of her stiff black uniform, hanging it carefully on the back of the door, and crawled between the cool, clean sheets. The exhaustion of the day weighed heavily on her.

Tomorrow, she would write to Janey and update her on the latest. As sleep claimed her, smiling blue eyes teased the edges of her memory, a bittersweet comfort before her dreams carried her away.

CHAPTER 40

Five Years Later.

"I'm sorry you've had to come all this way," said Mrs Drury, the stout and cheery shopkeeper, as she set out the paper parcels on the countertop. "What with my Tommy laid up in bed, I've not been able to get the deliveries out."

"Think nothing of it," Addy replied as she added a packet of gelatine and some nutmeg to her basket. "I only wish I could do more for you."

"You've got a good heart, Addy," Mrs Drury said warmly, jotting the items into her ledger book. "You'll make a fine wife one of these days."

"So, I keep hearing," Addy said with a small laugh. "But I've yet to find an offer better than working for Mrs Glover."

"I hope the old widow knows what she's got in you,

Addy. There's not a bad word against you in these parts, that's for sure."

"That's nice to hear," Addy adjusted the handle of her basket. "Is that everything?"

"For now, yes," Mrs Drury replied. "Though you'll have to let Mrs Thomas know I'm still waiting on the ginger. Why she needs such a thing, I've no idea."

"It's for the biscuits—Charlotte's favourites."

"Ah, and when is she visiting us?"

"She should be here for Christmas, no doubt," Addy said. "Perhaps even until the New Year this time, if she doesn't get too bored of the slower pace."

"I can't see myself ever wanting to live in a big, stinking city like London," the grimace conveyed just how horrifying a thought it was. "And how is Mrs Glover doing?"

"She's getting there," Addy said, lifting her basket onto her arm. "A little less active perhaps, but her mind is still as sharp as a tack. That last bout of flu really took it out of her."

"No doubt Charlotte's visit will brighten her spirits. That granddaughter of hers is the apple of her eye. It's just a shame she doesn't visit more often."

Addy couldn't suppress a fond smile. "Charlotte's a lively one, that's for sure. I daresay Mrs Glover doesn't mind spoiling her if it means having her close." Addy remembered how upset Mrs Glover had been in the early days after Georgia had moved to London, taking her daughter with her. Mrs Glover felt the loss keenly, though she'd never admit it aloud. "She dotes on her, and Charlotte lights up the house whenever she's here."

With the order packed—fine tea leaves, sugar lumps, canned fruit, and a tin of cocoa, all luxurious items ordered especially for Charlotte's visit—Addy stepped out into the sunshine.

The remnants of the May Day celebrations still fluttered from lampposts and trees, brightening the cobbled streets with pops of colour. Addy left the grocer's and made her way across the square, pausing when someone called her name.

"Addy! Oh, Addy!"

She turned to see Billy Baker, so-called because his father owned the local bakery, a silly grin plastered across his face as he stood beside his bakery cart.

"Hello, Billy," Addy greeted.

"Well, isn't this a grand sight—seeing my favourite girl on such a fine day."

Addy smiled politely as Billy hefted a tray of fresh bread into his cart.

"When are you going to dance with me again?" he asked.

The May Day tea party had been well attended by local servants. Addy had given in to Gert's pestering and accompanied her, if only for the chance to ride the carousel. Billy Baker had made his intentions clear that day, but Addy's work left her with little free time—and she couldn't say she was much interested in courting, anyway.

"I told you, Billy, the other night was a one-off. You know how busy my work is."

Billy leaned forward, steadfastly undeterred by another of her polite rebuffs. "All work and no play makes Jack a dull boy."

Addy leaned forward, too, meeting his playful look with a steady one. "Then it's a good job I'm not Jack. Good day, Billy."

Billy clutched his chest in mock horror. "Addy, you're breaking my heart."

"I'm sorry about that," she tossed over her shoulder, hurrying along the pavement.

"I look forward to seeing you tomorrow when I fetch Mrs Thomas's bread order to you!"

Amused, Addy waved at him. Langmere was a busy place. The focal point of several outlying hamlets, the square was a throng of visitors. The butcher's, greengrocers and the general store did a brisk trade. The inn provided a rest for weary travellers. The huge oak tree cast a welcome shade, the sunlight dappling the cobbles.

Addy hurried on home, past the neat cottages and tidy gardens. Carts and wagons that rolled past greeted her by name. She walked back to Rose Villa, thinking about the latest letter from Janey. As the familiar grey façade of the house came into view, she wondered if Janey was truly aware of the depth of her gratitude. Her life in Langmere was a contented and fulfilling one. She had accompanied Mrs Glover on her travels to the continent, enriching her experienccs, and she enjoyed the quiet satisfaction of a well-ordered and purposeful existence.

She'd meant what she'd said to Mrs Drury.

Billy Baker wasn't the first man to flirt with her and encourage her to leave a life in service to become a wife. Mrs Glover's calendar might not be as varied and busy as it had been when she'd first arrived at Rose Villa. These days, she declined more invites than she accepted. She also tended to retire to bed early, leaving Addy's evenings free to read to her heart's content.

She would be forever grateful to Janey for urging her into the role.

She made her way around to the side of the house, pausing to smell the climbing roses. Each year, she looked forward to the blooms.

"You'd best go to her," Mrs Thomas called out when Addy walked into the kitchen. "She's got a right bee in her bonnet."

Addy took in Gert's tear-stained face and knew instantly what had happened. She set the basket on the table and grabbed her mob cap off the hook in the hallway on the way through.

Upstairs in the drawing room, Mrs Glover sat in her winged-back chair, looking regal in her purple dress. She eyed Addy belligerently. "Where have you been? That wretched girl brought my tea tray in. The tea was cold and the biscuits soft."

"I was at the greengrocers. Tommy Drury is sick, and Mrs Thomas needed the powdered gelatine for Saturday," Addy wasn't fazed by the waspish tone of her mistress. She spread a blanket across her lap and tucked it in. "Shall I fetch some fresh tea?"

"No. You can open the window," Mrs Glover ordered. "Let these bad vapours out."

Addy did so. "There now. You can smell your beautiful roses."

Mrs Glover smoothed her lap blanket. "Thank you."

Addy pottered about the room, straightening a cushion, swiping at a piece of lint. "They still have those flags up in the square."

Mrs Glover harumphed.

Addy turned to her. "Would you mind if I read a little more of our book? I thought about it the whole walk back."

A papery hand gestured. "If you like."

Mrs Glover's failing eyesight was a bone of contention for her. Unable to work on her cherished embroidery or read anymore, the widow found solace in a new habit. One evening, as Addy recounted a passage from the book she was reading, she read it aloud to the widow. That simple gesture blossomed into a daily ritual. Addy resumed reading the book. The bad mood faded and soon, Mrs Glover was dozing peacefully in her chair.

Quietly, worried that she might catch another cold, Addy closed the window and tugged the blanket a little higher. She carried the tea tray down the stairs and into the kitchen.

"All sorted," Addy placed the tray on the table.

Gert cast a mournful look over her shoulder.

Mrs Thomas's mouth moved in sympathy. "Poor girl had a flea in her ear. Those biscuits are the same ones you take up, yet she always manages to find a fault with young Gertie."

Addy poured out the cold tea, swilled the tea pot of the leaves and set it to dry. "She doesn't mean it."

"You deserve a medal for putting up with her," Gert muttered mutinously.

Addy remained silent. Mrs Glover could be sharp with others, but when compared to the harsh personalities Addy had encountered in her life, Mrs Glover's temper was as mild as a kitten's.

"Any news from your friend? The matron?"

Addy patted her pocket so the cook could see. "Had a letter from her this morning. She writes with news of another charity she's helping."

"Heart of gold, that one," Mrs Thomas acknowledged.

Addy wiped up the droplets around the Belfast

sink. "She also writes about how she's getting hot under the collar about women's rights. You know, the vote and such."

The cook looked at her with such horror that Addy couldn't stop her grin.

"What do women know about the vote? Just the same as a man shouldn't be in the kitchen, a woman shouldn't get involved in such matters." She banged the copper pots with vigour. "It's not our place. As it goes, men know more than we do about politics."

She could remind Mrs Thomas about the chefs in the hotels they'd visited in Paris all being men, but Addy knew better than to argue with the cook. The woman took umbrage with the slightest infraction and so Addy kept any argumentative remarks to herself. Instead, she turned the conversation subject to Charlotte's imminent arrival.

CHAPTER 41

Charlotte's appearance brought a flurry of activity, although Addy took it all in her stride.

A dinner party had been planned for the occasion, and Mrs Glover had taken great care to ensure that the guest list was perfectly balanced. Charlotte, a petite young woman with golden curls and an infectious smile, greeted her grandmother with boundless enthusiasm, her energy filling the house with charm.

As Charlotte had not travelled with a maid, Addy was tasked with helping her dress as well. Charlotte's visits were always lively affairs, and this one was no exception. She flitted about the house, doting on her grandmother and filling the space with her laughter.

Given Mrs Glover's age and the quiet nature of the household, it had been some time since a dinner party had been held at Rose Villa. Two local men had been drafted in to serve as footmen for the evening.

During the dinner, Addy stayed downstairs with

Mrs Thomas, helping where she could, while Harper oversaw the formalities of the dinner.

The dining table was laden with roast chicken, roast beef, buttery potatoes, green beans tossed with almonds, and a baked custard for dessert. Charlotte's enthusiasm was contagious, and even Mrs Glover seemed rejuvenated by her presence. By the time Mrs Glover was ready to retire for the evening, she waved Addy away.

"Go and help Charlotte," Mrs Glover instructed. "I'll be fine for the rest of the evening."

"Very well," Addy replied, gathering Mrs Glover's gown over her arm before leaving the bedroom.

She knocked gently on Charlotte's bedroom door and waited until she heard Charlotte's cheerful voice bid her enter. Inside, Charlotte sat at the vanity mirror, a wistful smile playing across her lips.

"Hello, Addy. How is my grandmother now?"

"She's doing well," Addy said, crossing the floor to pull out the pins securing Charlotte's golden curls. "It's so nice to see her almost back to her old self. She always looks forward to your visits."

"You must tell Mrs Thomas she's outdone herself. Dinner was delicious," Charlotte added with a smile.

"I'll be sure to pass along the compliments," Addy replied as she began brushing out the shining locks.

Charlotte sighed softly, a smile tugging at the corners of her mouth.

"It's nice to see you so happy," Addy remarked. "Your last visit was fraught with news of—"

"Let's not talk about him," Charlotte interrupted with a mutter. "The less said about Carroll, the better."

Charlotte picked up a small jar of cream and slowly unscrewed the lid. Addy met her gaze in the mirror.

"I've met someone else," Charlotte confided, her cheeks glowing. "He's quite perfect. Mama loves him already."

"Well, that's a good start," Addy said. "As I recall, your mother couldn't stand Mr Carroll."

"She couldn't," Charlotte admitted, "but this one has her seal of approval. He comes from a good family."

Addy carefully placed Charlotte's jet beads into a drawer and set her earrings neatly beside them. "That's exciting."

"He's something to do with shipping," Charlotte said dreamily, applying cream to her hands and arms. Addy quelled the little tremors inside. Fred Latchford had been in shipping. She hoped that this new admirer had better morals than Fred. Charlotte continued, "He works in London. We met at this frightful bore of a house party, but meeting him made it worthwhile."

She smoothed more cream onto her neck as Addy listened absently, her thoughts racing ahead to the remaining tasks of the evening.

"I think he's going to propose soon. In fact, I just know it," Charlotte said with certainty, catching Addy's reflection in the mirror. "You know when you just *know* these things?"

"I've heard that's how it happens, though I wouldn't know from experience," Addy replied.

"He's funny, ever so handsome... and clever," Charlotte gushed. "I just know Papa would've adored him if he'd lived."

Addy bent to pick up a ribbon that had fallen to the floor. "You'll make a beautiful bride. Will you marry here, or will it be in London?"

"Oh, goodness!" Charlotte exclaimed with a laugh. "As much as I love Granny, London simply doesn't compare to Langmere. So, London it will be. Of course, he has to pass muster with Granny, too."

"Any man who will love and care for you in the right way will be alright with Mrs Glover," Addy assured the young girl with a knowing smile. "She just wants you to be happy."

Charlotte sighed happily. "She simply must adore him. Everyone who meets him does."

"And when do you think he'll propose?"

"Sooner rather than later, if I have my way," Charlotte said with a twinkle in her eye. She clasped her hands together and beamed. "Oh, Addy, I cannot wait to be Mrs Henry Scorby."

CHAPTER 42

It felt like a blow to the stomach. Charlotte prattled on, oblivious to anything else.

Henry Scorby? Could she mean *her* Henry?

Charlotte stared dreamily at her reflection and a sharp, fierce jealousy carved a hot streak through Addy.

She cleared her throat, her heart pounding. She dared not ask the question if it was him – it would sound too impertinent. A good lady's maid had to listen but never share her opinion unless directly asked. And she was always discreet. "Will that be all this evening, Miss?"

"It will, Addy."

"Very well, miss." Addy scurried from the room on legs that felt like jelly. In the quiet low light of the corridor, Addy braced a hand against the wall, her breath sawing in and out like bellows.

London? What was Henry doing down there? Shipping? Her Henry was set to work alongside his father in the family business. She wracked her memory. Came up blank. Was Reginald in shipping?

Surely, Charlotte's Henry must be another of the same name. Addy straightened, dragging her mind back to her duties. But as she climbed up to the attic floor and quietly let herself into her room, she knew that she wouldn't sleep tonight as Henry's name echoed in her thoughts once again.

∼

THE DAY HAD STARTED POORLY, and no matter what Addy did, it felt like she was one step behind. She had forgotten about two visitors and neglected to set out the correct tea service and accessories for the afternoon guests. Mrs Glover hadn't minced her words about Addy being so distracted, leaving her feeling thoroughly out of sorts.

By late afternoon, Addy sought refuge in the servants' hall. She had several garments spread across the long wooden table, meant to be checking hems for mending, but the items lay untouched. She was staring into space when Mrs Thomas appeared in the doorway.

"You look like you've lost a gold crown and found a penny," the cook remarked, setting down a tray with a teapot and two cups. "There's nothing in this life that can't be fixed with a good brew. So, let's have one, and you can tell me all about it."

"I'm fine, Mrs Thomas," Addy said, dragging her attention back to the garments.

"You're most certainly not fine," Mrs Thomas replied matter-of-factly, sitting down and narrowing her eyes. "You say you're not sick, but you look pale, and it doesn't look like you've been sleeping well. Shall I fetch the doctor?"

"I'm fine," Addy repeated more forcefully, though she softened her tone when Mrs Thomas shot her a sharp look. "Thank you, though."

Mrs Thomas poured tea into two cups and pushed one toward Addy. "What's all this?" she asked, scanning the pile of clothes.

"Checking hems," Addy murmured, lifting a sleeve absently. "Mrs Glover has been out more than usual, and I didn't have time to go over everything properly while Charlotte was here. Now that she's gone back to London, I do."

Mrs Thomas grunted. "She was as happy as a roosting hen while she was here. Must be all that mooning about that young Charlotte was doing."

"You saw that?"

Mrs Thomas rolled her eyes. "We all saw it."

Addy toyed with her teacup, her thoughts racing. Charlotte certainly seemed like a young woman in love. Yet, Addy was no closer to confirming whether the man Charlotte had been talking about belonged to the Scorby family. She'd tried to extract details from Harper without raising suspicion, but he'd been frustratingly tight-lipped.

"You should ask the old lady if you can take a few days off now that Miss Charlotte's gone?" Mrs Thomas offered.

"There's no need," Addy assured her, though her voice lacked conviction.

Mrs Thomas sighed, the quiet of the room stretching between them. "You play your cards close to your chest, but we all see when you're not yourself, Addy. This isn't like you."

Addy gave the woman a watery smile, which wobbled under the unusual kindness in her tone.

"Why don't you visit Janey? It's been months since you last saw her."

Addy longed to see her friend. She hadn't been able to share with anyone the turmoil stirred by hearing Henry's name.

The possibility that Charlotte's beau could be her Henry had thrown her world into disarray.

But why? Henry had never been hers, not really. Perhaps it was hearing the Scorby name after so long that had done it, though there was an ugly envy that pinched whenever she thought of Henry and Charlotte.

It wasn't her Henry.

Of course, he would marry someone more suitable to the Scorby name, and Charlotte Glover was a fine match for someone like him—if it even was him. And round and round her thoughts went.

"It's too far to go there and back in an afternoon," she hedged.

"Ask her to meet you halfway, then," Mrs Thomas suggested.

"Perhaps," Addy said, conceding just enough to satisfy the cook's desire to help.

The idea took root, and arrangements were made for her and Janey to meet in Warrington, a small industrial town on the banks of the River Mersey.

The tearoom on the High Street was modest, with lace curtains framing the windows and simple tables adorned with fresh flowers. It was quiet on a Thursday afternoon. They chose a table by the window, and as Janey studied her old friend, she immediately sensed that something was troubling her. She listened intently, her hands folded in her lap.

"It might not be him," Janey said when Addy had finished speaking.

"I know," Addy replied. "But what am I to do if it is?"

Janey leaned forward, her practicality cutting through Addy's anxious thoughts. "You're working yourself up over things that haven't even happened yet. He hasn't proposed to her. And if he does, and it is him—which I'm not convinced it is—you won't see him. Charlotte says he lives in London, right?"

"I didn't ask," Addy shrugged, misery pulling at the edges of her mouth. "My mind is swimming with unanswered questions."

Janey sighed heavily. "Well, even if it is him, there's nothing you can do about it. He's moved on, and so have you. Your friendship with him was what—five years ago? Do you think he'll even remember a maid from his childhood?"

The words stung deeply, and Addy tried not to flinch. But her friend was right. Perhaps she had romanticised what had happened between them. She'd convinced herself that her connection with Henry had been real, but had it been strong enough for him to remember her? His unanswered letter spoke volumes.

"I know this isn't what you want to hear," Janey added gently. "But if it *is* him, and he *does* marry her, how often will you see him? You're up in Lancashire, and he'll be down in London with his bride."

"Not that often," Addy admitted, feeling slightly better.

"You've spent too much time with your nose in those romantic novels," Janey teased.

Addy laughed, the tension in her chest easing a little.

Janey was right—Henry had moved on. Just as she had changed, he wouldn't be different, too.

Addy liked her life with Mrs Glover. Charlotte's visits were already infrequent enough, and they'd likely become even rarer once she married and had a household of her own.

A house with Henry, the mocking voice in her head whispered. She shook the thought away.

"Let's change the subject. I've been driving myself mad. Tell me—what's new with you?"

By the time Addy was walking back along the lane toward Rose Villa, the sun was melting into the horizon. She acknowledged that she felt much better.

Mrs Thomas had been right. Laughter with a good friend was indeed the best medicine.

CHAPTER 43

The platform at London St Pancras station was a cacophony of noise and movement. Trains groaned and belched thick smoke onto the platforms, spilling passengers into the chaos. Wheel-tappers banged at the wheels, their sounds competing with the shrill whistles of platform guards.

Addy stood guard over the mound of luggage Mrs Glover had insisted on bringing. There was an intimidating number of trunks and cases, and Addy was terrified that one might be whisked away by one of the unseen thieves lurking in the ebb and flow of the crowd. She flagged down a porter in a dark green frock coat, a gold waistcoat, and a peaked cap bearing the company logo.

Mrs Glover walked ahead with an agility that belied her years. One porter waited with the pile of luggage while another hailed a black cabbie, who pulled up to the kerb. They managed to transfer everything into the interior without losing a single item to street thieves.

Mrs Glover settled back with a groan, her displeasure evident as she surveyed the bustling scene beyond the window. "Honestly, Adelaide, it's like running a gauntlet out there," she complained.

Addy smiled. "We made it in one piece."

Mrs Glover's incisive gaze swept over her. "Are you quite alright? You seem... peaky. Are you feeling unwell?"

"Oh no, nothing like that," Addy said quickly. "Perhaps I'm just out of the habit of travelling. It's been quite a while since we've left Rose Villa."

Mrs Glover seemed satisfied with this answer. She leaned back against the velvet-covered bench, watching the blurring scenery rush past. "I used to love travelling," she mused. "London is one of the greatest cities in the world, despite its reputation for being filthy and dangerous. It's rich in history, and there's a thrill to it. But as we age, we grow weary of leaving home comforts." She turned to Addy, her eyes twinkling with pleasure. "Still, I wouldn't miss meeting this mysterious chap of Charlotte's for all the world."

The indulgent smile she gave set Addy's heart racing. Mrs Glover had been ecstatic upon hearing of the proposal and had gleaned all the exciting details from Charlotte. Though outwardly composed, Addy had kept her turmoil carefully hidden. For months, she had both dreaded and anticipated this visit. It might finally answer the question that had haunted her since first hearing the name of Charlotte's fiancé.

Was it truly Henry Scorby, the boy she had once known?

"I'm sure you'll have the measure of him within minutes of meeting him, Mrs Glover," Addy said.

Mrs Glover laughed, clearly delighted by Addy's assessment. "I have the measure of him already, Addy."

Beyond the window, London sprawled in smoky grandeur, a hodgepodge of life shrouded in damp, acrid fog that blackened the buildings. Through the gloom came the cries of hawkers and the clatter of carriages. Sparks flew from the hooves of horses on the damp cobblestones.

"When we arrive, I think I'll lie down before supper. I'll wear the pale blue dress this evening," Mrs Glover said.

Addy nodded absently, filing away the instructions as the cab trundled into the newer part of the city. The roads smoothed out, and the streets widened. Holland Park unfolded with a pristine orderliness. Newly built homes lined the avenues, their facades standing out against the surrounding gloom.

"My son invested in these developments before his passing," Mrs Glover mused. "He had an eye for potential—a wise decision, as it turns out."

Addy nodded, though she had heard this story many times before. Her son had kept one of the houses as an extension of Rose Villa. But the grand townhouse where the cab pulled up was far from a cosy country cottage. There were no trellised roses or curated gardens, just a pristine black iron fence leading up to a polished front door.

Two footmen hurried out to assist Mrs Glover, joined by a tall butler who appeared at the top of the steps. Behind him stood Georgia, her pale blonde hair swept back to reveal a beautiful face. Charlotte, however, burst out of the house with exuberance, her chatter dancing along the street as she steered her grandmother inside. Addy tried to catch snippets of the conversation, but the housekeeper, Mrs Martin, was already beckoning her towards the steps that led to the servants' entrance.

A swarm of staff descended upon the trunks and cases. *No penny-pinching for the younger Mrs Glover,* Addy thought, trying to keep an eye on things. Many of these people had likely been hired just for the celebratory weekend. Mrs Martin issued instructions, assigning rooms for the guests and detailing arrangements for supper.

"We have a mix of guests joining us this evening," Mrs Martin said as the staff bustled about. "I'm afraid you'll have to share a room with one of the maids. We have extra guests who've brought along their own valets and maids, so we're full to the rafters."

"That's not a problem," Addy said quickly, trying to reassure her.

Mrs Martin gave her a look as though Addy's opinion hadn't been sought in the first place.

Addy quickly changed out of her travel clothes and into her uniform before emptying the cases and laying out Mrs Glover's chosen outfit for the evening.

As was tradition, the servants dined before the rest of the household. The cook had prepared a sumptuous stew, and its rich aroma filled the air. Addy sat at the end of the table, listening as snippets of conversation floated around her. She strained to catch details about the fiancé, but the chatter was full of half-tales and conjecture.

After finishing her meal, she helped Mrs Glover prepare for the evening, re-styling her hair and carefully pinning a pearl and ruby brooch onto the pale blue dress. She tidied the room and ensured everything was ready for bedtime before retreating to the servants' hall for a few minutes of quiet. The hallway bustled with activity—barked instructions from the kitchen, the butler and footmen darting in and out with laden trays, and gossip exchanged in passing about the dinner table conversation. The evening seemed buoyant, filled with the promise of celebration.

Later, when the butler, Colefax, announced the end of the evening's festivities, Addy found Mrs Glover already in her room. The soft glow of the oil lamp bathed the older woman in a gentle light, giving her an ethereal quality. A dreamy smile played across her face.

"Henry is everything Charlotte deserves," she murmured sleepily. "Charming, clever, and well-respected in his field."

Mrs Glover's words offered little new information beyond what Addy had already surmised. This particular Henry Scorby worked in shipping and specialised in commercial law. There was no mention of his family, though it was clear he held good social standing.

Addy forced herself to remain composed, murmuring words of agreement as she tucked the blanket around Mrs Glover. Once dismissed, she draped the blue dress over her arm and quietly left the room.

As she walked along the landing towards the servants' stairs, Addy felt the weight of inevitability settle over her.

At last, she had her answer.

At the top of the main staircase, Charlotte stood gazing up into the face of a tall man with jet-black hair. Their hands were entwined, and Charlotte's face was alit with adoration.

Charlotte noticed her first, but Addy didn't hear the words she spoke. She couldn't hear anything over the pounding of her pulse in her ears when those achingly familiar blue eyes turned to meet hers.

CHAPTER 44

Her steps faltered. Her breath hitched in her chest and just for that moment, she was standing back in the dovecote, laughing along with him. Just the two of them. Sharing dreams and hopes.

Henry stared right back at her.

Somewhere deep in the recesses of her mind, she noticed the changes in him. The boy had grown into a man. His face was more angular. He was taller and seemed broader. His black curls tamed into a more fashionable style. He looked dashing in his dark tailcoat, the white shirt and winged collar showing against the shadow of stubble that peppered his jaw.

"Addy! Please, you must come and meet Henry," Charlotte beckoned her when all Addy wanted to do was race by them both.

Addy was the first to recover. She offered him a courteous smile and dipped respectfully. "Nice to meet you, sir."

"L-likewise," Henry husked.

"Addy is Granny's right hand, Henry. A true blessing," Charlotte gushed.

Henry cleared his throat. "I-is that right? How... how long...?"

Addy kept her head bowed. "Five years or more, Mr Scorby."

"I see."

"Of course, after we're married, I'll be looking for a maid all of my own," Charlotte said. "My maid at home does well though she lacks your...finesse, Addy. I do hope that you'll help me vet them."

Her stomach clenched over the thought of Charlotte being Henry's wife."I-I'd be happy to, miss."

There was a beat of silence as Addy waited for more questions. But none came.

Charlotte's attention was already back on Henry and just like that, the maid was dismissed. "Now then, darling, where were we?"

Addy risked a glance under her lashes as she moved by them.

Henry was still staring at her.

She felt the weight of his gaze long after she'd returned Mrs Glover's items to the dressing room and climbed into her bed.

~

EYES GRITTY from lack of sleep, Addy rose early the next day. Years of habit ensured she was up with the lark. The servants' hall was already alive with chatter when she entered. The scent of fresh bread and roasted meats filled the air as maids busied themselves keeping the house running like clockwork.

Addy sat on the periphery with her drink. The

scullery maid giggled as a footman regaled her with tales of the previous night's party, while two more footmen planned an evening at a local dance hall, boasting of promised dances with maids from another house.

Mrs Martin's clipped voice sliced through the din like a blade. "Hill, Mr Scorby wishes to speak with you."

Addy froze. "M-me?"

"Is there anyone else here by the name of Hill?" Mrs Martin's arched brow quelled any further questions.

The housekeeper turned on her heel and swept from the room, leaving Addy painfully aware of the curious stares now fixed on her.

"What does he want with you?" one of the footmen speculated, leaning back in his chair with a teasing grin.

Addy didn't answer, silently praying her legs would carry her as she hurried from the room. Further along the hallway, Henry stood awkwardly. The sight of him in such humble surroundings was just as jarring as it had been the previous night. A quick glance back at the servants' hall revealed the curious faces of her colleagues peering around the edge of the wall.

She lifted her chin, her voice steadier than she felt as she addressed him. "How can I help you, Mr Scorby?" she asked, her tone deliberately louder than necessary, hoping it carried along the corridor.

Henry's eyes flicked to the onlookers before returning to her. He pulled a folded note from his pocket. "I wanted to make sure you got this, Miss Hill."

Addy automatically reached for the note, her heart pounding as she stared up at his face. Before she could say a word, he nodded stiffly, turned sharply, and ascended the staircase two steps at a time.

The paper crinkled in her hand; her mouth dry. She returned to the hall, doing her best to ignore the attention heating her cheeks.

"What's that, then?" the footman called out and jerking his chin at the letter in her hand.

"Never you mind," Addy replied, shoving the note into her pocket.

The rolling sniggers around her only deepened her blush. Relief flooded her as the jangling service bell signalled a summons from Mrs Glover's room. Grabbing the breakfast tray, she fled the servants' hall.

The previous evening, she had barely been able to croak out a greeting to Henry before Charlotte dismissed her. She hadn't dared look back as she hurried along the corridor, too unsettled to fully process his presence. All night, she had lain awake trying to decipher the strange expression that had crossed his face.

As much as she longed to know if he was all right, being near him now felt torturous. Perhaps his shock stemmed from seeing her again. After all, she had known about him, but he clearly hadn't known about her—and that realisation had been written on his face.

What could possibly have compelled him to come down to the servants' hall?

She didn't know the staff well enough to trust them; surely their loyalties lay with Georgia and Charlotte. Why would Henry, the new fiancé, seek out a maid he didn't know—and downstairs, of all places?

Her mind raced as she hurried up the back stairs, the paper crackling in her pocket with every movement, like a reminder that she couldn't ignore. Forcing herself to focus, she dragged her thoughts away from Henry.

She liked working for Mrs Glover. The widow was kind, and the work at Langmere had restored a sense of dignity she had fought hard to reclaim. All she wanted was for the engagement celebration to be over, so she could retreat back to Langmere and hide away.

"Good morning, Mrs Glover," she called, injecting forced cheerfulness into her voice as she stepped into the room.

Her greeting was met with a harsh, racking cough that drowned out the clink of the breakfast tray. Addy froze in the doorway, her smile fading as she stared at her employer. Even in the dim morning light, Mrs Glover's pallor was unmistakable.

"Oh, Addy," the old woman croaked. "I feel like I've been run over by a hundred galloping horses."

"Shall I fetch the doctor?"

"Yes," Mrs Glover panted. "Yes, please."

CHAPTER 45

This time, Mrs Glover's bout of sickness lasted more than a week, the worst of it punctuated by moments of delirium that sent chills down Addy's spine. The frail woman would mumble incoherently, mistaking Addy for her late husband as she grasped her wrists, anchoring herself in the fever. The resemblance to her own father's final days unsettled Addy deeply. Still, she hadn't left her side. The lingering shadows of painful memories haunted her as she bathed and nursed Mrs Glover through the worst of the illness, but she refused to be undone by grief or fear.

On the first lucid morning, Addy finally heaved a sigh of relief when the doctor declared Mrs Glover over the worst of it. Relieved of duty for a short while, she went upstairs to her room, intending to take an hour to herself. It was only then she remembered the crumpled note tucked away in her apron pocket—the letter Henry had handed her, demanding that they meet. She had ignored it, and then forgotten about it entirely until another note addressed to her had arrived at the house that morning.

She recognised the handwriting immediately. It simply stated a time and place, and Addy realised she could make the meeting if she hurried. Her resolve wavered.

What purpose could meeting with him possibly serve?

Part of her wanted to discard the note, to push it aside again. He was engaged to another and meeting him felt selfish. Yet curiosity gnawed at her, compelling her to weave through the throng of people bustling about in the damp, foggy September morning.

The park he mentioned was far enough from Portobello Road that Addy was huffing by the time she passed through the gates. The green space was adorned with carefully trimmed hedges, winding paths, and ornate iron benches where people sat to enjoy the fresh air. Nannies strolled by, pushing prams. The trees were beginning to shed their leaves, and Addy swished through the damp foliage towards the fountain at the park's centre, where water trickled steadily despite the chill in the air.

She didn't see him at first, but she felt his gaze before she saw him. It drew her in, like a moth to a flame.

Slowly, she turned.

Henry stood nearby, dapper in his top hat and fine black wool coat, a burgundy scarf wrapped around his throat against the damp air. He came to a halt before her, his eyes piercing.

Delight thrummed through her blood, her heart pounding wildly in her chest. Her cheeks, rosy from the cold air, burned under his stare. But she wasn't prepared for the irritation that flashed in his eyes.

"I've been waiting a week," he said tersely, his voice sharp. "At least you came today, instead of leaving me standing here like a lemon."

"Mrs Glover has been unwell," she explained, startled by his tone. "I haven't been able to leave her side."

His jaw tightened, anger rippling off him in waves.

"H-HOW HAVE YOU BEEN?" she managed feebly.

His bark of laughter was harsh and derisive. "Don't act like we're friends."

Her mouth parted in shock. "What—"

"You left, Addy. Without a goodbye, without a backward glance. I don't even know why I wanted to see you today, except to tell you how bitterly disappointed I am."

"I told you, Mrs Glover—"

"I'm not talking about this week," he snarled. "You didn't even bother to write. You left Longhaven without a word."

Addy blinked, taken aback as her mind raced to catch up. "I did write," she said defensively, her voice rising. "I sent a letter to Longhaven, but I... I never heard back. I assumed you'd finally come to the realisation that I was just a maid, and things were better off that way."

He snorted. "Unbelievable," he scoffed. "More lies to cover up what you did."

Hurt raced through her, sharp and biting. This man before her was nothing like the boy she'd once loved. The angry tone, the haughty derision—it was as though she were seeing the Scorby in him for the first time.

"This was a mistake," she said thickly, her throat constricting with emotion.

"I never really knew you, did I?" he called after her as she turned to leave, his voice cutting through her like a whip. "After everything my mother did for you, this is how you repay her memory, Addy?"

Addy froze, her breath catching in her throat. Slowly, she turned back to face him, her eyes searching his.

"What are you talking about?" she whispered.

"You stole my mother's things," he accused, his voice cold and bitter. "And you sold them."

CHAPTER 46

Her breath caught in her throat.

She stared at him, the delight she had felt moments ago turning to dust on her tongue. He couldn't have hurt her more if he'd struck her across the face.

It wasn't just the accusation that stung. It was the righteous anger, the certainty of her guilt.

"Mama's jewels. My grandmother's sapphire. My father's books. Right there for the taking, and then you disappear without a word," Blue eyes fired ice at her.

In the silence, Addy grew aware of the curious looks that they were drawing. The maid in the worn coat. The finely dressed gentleman berating her in public. A fine spectacle they must make. And another stark reminder of the chasm that forever divided them.

Addy tilted her chin up, a struggle under the fury that rolled off him. "If you believe this, Henry, why did you seek me out?"

"Because I want to know *why*," he ground out

through gritted teeth, his fist balled tightly. "I would have given you the world, Addy. I trusted everything about you, and you played me for a fool, didn't you?"

Addy couldn't speak. Her throat painfully constricted as the wave of tears engulfed her. It took all her might to hold them back.

"You took her things, Addy. Everything that she wore... all those memories, sold to some cheap back-street pawn broker, no doubt."

Beneath his fury, she heard his hurt. And that was the bit that broke her. She couldn't defend herself when he'd already condemned her. Henry would believe what he believed; Vanessa's venomous lies had wormed their way into his mind, tainting everything between them.

Hopelessness and futility closed off any defence she could muster. Without another word, she turned and walked away.

"That's right, skulk off," his voice followed her. "I'm certain Mrs Glover would be most interested to know your history, Adelaide. I'll be only too glad to tell her about the kind of vermin she has under her roof."

She froze.

Anger; blissful, furious anger, drove her back towards him. He took a hesitant step back as she swung a finger at him. "I am not what you think!" She seethed. "I don't know what piffle you've been told about me, but you are wrong! Dead wrong!"

"Then explain –"

"What good will it do?" She flung her arms wide, frustration and tears mingling in her voice. "But I have never stolen a thing in my life!"

Henry considered her warily, a flicker of unease in his expression.

"You want to know what happened to poor Mrs Scorby's items?"

"Yes."

Addy leaned forward, eyes flashing. "Then ask your stepbrother."

Henry's brows met. "Isaac?"

"Yes," Addy hissed. "Right after he'd torn my dress to shreds trying to have his way with me, he must have planted whatever he could in my room to have me dismissed. If you don't believe me, ask Mr Smale. He was there that day. The poor man didn't know where to look when he saw the rags Isaac had made of my uniform!"

Henry only stared at her. His mouth opened but he did not make a sound.

Addy threw up her hands, anguish pressing in on her as her anger slid away, leaving only sorrow. She shook her head, searching his face. "You promised," she said thickly. "You promised me you'd save me from him. A fat lot of good that did," she finished. Then she walked away, not stopping even when he called her name.

～

"Addy?"

The voice startled her. The courtyard of the Holland Park house was more of a functional backyard, storing coal and apparatus used in the house. She hung the sheets in the outhouse that was close to the furnace, which meant that it was warm all year round. She brushed the hanging laundry aside and peered around the edge of the door.

Henry stood at the long, narrow back gate. The

morning's fine misty rain had formed beads on his coat.

He took off his hat, a hesitant smile on his face. "Hello."

"Henry? What are you doing out here?"

He flicked a glance towards the house, as if weighing a decision, then stepped forward and nudged her gently into the warm outhouse. He closed the door behind them.

"I need to speak with you," he began, his voice low.

Addy frowned up at him, disconcerted by his proximity. It had been so long since she'd been this close to him, and the years had done nothing to diminish the effect he had on her.

"Make it quick, please. I have much work to do today."

"I owe you an apology," he said, his tone contrite. "The other day, I was cross, and I... I shouldn't have behaved that way towards you."

It was the tenderness in his eyes that undid her more than his words.

"You have no need to—"

"Yes, I do," he insisted, his gaze unwavering. "You reminded me of something the other day. My father led me to believe that all the stolen property had been taken by you, and that you'd vanished in the night. But I made a promise to you, one I didn't keep."

Her breath hitched in her chest. His gentle expression softened her resolve.

"What does it matter now, Henry? It's the past."

"It matters, Addy. It matters to me." He moved as if to touch her, but then lowered his hands. "Did Isaac... did he hurt you?"

The question sent a pang through her chest. She bit

down hard on her lip, struggling to hold back tears. Slowly, she nodded.

His jaw tightened, a sharp intake of breath betraying his anger as his hands balled into fists.

"He didn't... that is, he was interrupted by Smale before he could..." Her voice trailed off. She swallowed audibly. "There was no doubt of his intentions, though," Addy explained quietly. A thought occurred to her. "Have you spoken to Mr Smale?"

"No. Smale was gone by the time I returned home for Christmas. A younger man by the name of Dockery is in charge of Longhaven now."

"Smale left?" she echoed, her voice trembling.

"Vanessa said he was too infirm for the job and put him out to pasture."

Her heart sank at the thought of the loyal butler being dismissed. She prayed his departure hadn't been her fault.

"He loved Longhaven," she murmured. "That must have been a wrench for him. He saved me more than once from Isaac."

Henry stepped closer, his eyes pleading. "What happened? I need to know the truth, Addy."

She deliberated, shaking her head cautiously. She couldn't see what purpose it would serve. Too many years had passed, and it was better left in the past where it belonged.

"Henry..."

"Please, Addy. I've been lied to for so many years. At least let me know the truth."

She sighed, the memories flooding back against her will.

"I discovered Isaac out in the yard," she began softly. "It was dusk, and at first, I wondered if it might be poachers." The dim light, the worry—it was all too easy to recall. "He was handing a bag to someone, muttering quietly. The other man dropped the bag, and whatever was inside spilt out. I heard the tinkle and clink of metal."

She sighed again, wishing with all her heart that she had turned back inside and ignored them. Perhaps things would have turned out differently.

"At first, I couldn't see what it was, but the man picked something up and laughed, asking Isaac where he expected to sell a string of pearls."

Henry's face tightened, his eyes flashing with icy fury.

"Go on," he urged.

"Isaac grew cross with the man, ordering him to pick everything up. But the man wasn't fazed at all. That's when Isaac spotted me. I suppose, looking back, he was nervous, but at the time, he just seemed angry. He ordered me inside, but the other man laughed and said I'd need to be paid off to keep silent. That's when he held up your mother's sapphire pendant."

Her voice wavered as she continued.

"I spoke up then. I told Isaac none of the items were his to sell. He dismissed the other man, then… then he offered me a cameo for my silence. I told him he should return everything—especially the pendant. It was Mrs Scorby's favourite." Her voice grew husky with memory. "The next time I saw the necklace, it was amongst my belongings on your father's desk. It looked incriminating enough on its own, but there was also the book you gave me for Christmas—the one that belonged to your father. I couldn't…"

Henry pressed his thumbs against his eyes, his frustration palpable. "You couldn't explain the book without giving away our friendship."

"Yes," she whispered.

"Addy, you should have told him."

"And betray you? No, Henry, I couldn't do that. Besides, I'd already blotted my copybook with Vanessa. I'd marked her precious son, you see."

"Marked him?" Henry's brow furrowed. "What do you mean?"

"He had scratches on his neck and cheek. He claimed I'd thrown myself at him and in trying to escape my clutches, I'd injured him. But it happened in his room—he had me trapped. He was tearing at my clothes, and I..." Her voice faltered as tears came, the terror of that moment washing over her anew.

"Please, you don't have to say any more," Henry muttered tightly.

He paused, visibly reining in his anger.

Addy sniffed, swiping at the tears with the back of her hand. "I could've tried to argue. Smale stood up for me, even as Vanessa raged at both of us. I was dismissed under the threat of the constable if I protested. And, well, it wouldn't have looked good with the property in my room. I had access to the house. Other property was already missing. Candelabra, vases, and a few frames. The servants had assumed it was Vanessa, though none of us knew that your mother's jewellery had gone. Then there was the book—a book that had been in my room for many years. Looking back, your father seemed more upset about that."

Henry ran a hand through his hair, the gesture so reminiscent of the boy she'd once known that her heart ached all the more.

"My stepbrother is quite the manipulator," he said bitterly. "I haven't set foot in Longhaven for quite a while now. I work from the office in London, managing the international shipping side of the business. It's best this way; my father and I can't be in the same room for long without arguing.

"Longhaven is not the place it once was. Isaac has my father's ear and runs things alongside him. My father is blinded by his infatuation with his young wife."

"I promise I wrote to you," she said softly as Henry clearly wrestled with this information.

Henry's brow flickered irritably. "I suspect the letter I wrote was intercepted by one of the staff there. Which makes it all the more infuriating, doesn't it?" His tone sharp with frustration. "I believed you'd left without a word. I thought our friendship had meant nothing to you and that you'd lied to me. I believed if you had left, you'd at least want me to know what had happened. My life is different from the one I was meant to have," he added, his voice dropping.

She noticed the pain behind his anger then, and her heart broke all over again for him. She ached to step into his arms, to offer comfort, knowing his life had changed as much as hers.

"Still, you seem to have done very well for yourself," he said after a pause. "The Glovers speak very highly of you."

The name halted her fanciful thoughts and sobered her instantly. She offered him a watery smile. "They're a kind family."

In the warmth of the outhouse, the gentle rumble of the furnace filling the silence, the air seemed to shift as they stared at one another.

"I never forgot about you, Addy," he whispered fiercely. "Not once."

Her heart lifted at his admission as she met his intense gaze. But a sing-song voice calling his name shattered the moment like a bucket of ice-cold water. Henry jolted, stepping back just as the door creaked open.

"Henry, what are you...? Addy?" Charlotte's bright voice filled the small space as she appeared in the doorway.

Henry recovered first, smiling warmly. "Hello, darling."

Charlotte's gaze flitted curiously between them. "What are you doing in here?"

"Unless you've noticed, it's raining out there," he teased lightly.

Charlotte's eyes narrowed as they landed on Addy. "Addy?"

"I don't know if you're aware," Henry interjected quickly, "but Addy here once worked for my father."

"No, I didn't know that," Charlotte said, her voice thick with suspicion. "What a coincidence."

"Isn't it?" Henry replied smoothly. He inclined his head towards Addy. "You must forgive my ignorance, Miss Hill."

"There's no need for that, Mr Scorby," Addy responded automatically.

Charlotte waved a dismissive hand, laughing lightly. "Who can remember all the names of the servants these days? But, my beloved, you shouldn't be loitering about out here—it's freezing. If Betty hadn't mentioned that she'd seen your driver warming himself by the fire in the service hall, I wouldn't have known you were even here. Come now," she urged, guiding Henry out of the outhouse without so much as a backward glance.

Addy watched them go.

She felt better knowing he at least appeared to believe her now, though it did little to ease the ache of loss.

She had missed her friend Henry for years.

She knew there could never have been a future for them, but knowing he was promised to another woman and realising she would soon return north and no longer be a part of his life at all, left her feeling hollow.

CHAPTER 47

That evening, Addy was summoned to Charlotte's room.

The fire crackled pleasantly, and the gaslight flickered shadows on the walls. The room was softly feminine, with rose hues perfectly complementing sage greens—a bedroom befitting a young woman whose life was on an upward trajectory.

"You wished to see me, Miss Charlotte?"

"Oh good, I'm glad you're here," Charlotte replied, flapping a hand dismissively at Betty. "That will be all. You can help if I need any further assistance, can't you?" Her saccharine tone masked the pointed comment.

"Of course," Addy offered the other maid a conciliatory smile, but Betty shot her a stony glare as she sailed past, her resentment palpable. She shut the door behind her, leaving them alone.

Charlotte took a seat at the dressing table, looking resplendent in a deep green dress. Pearls and diamonds winked around her throat and ears.

She pursed her lips as she studied Addy. "Why did you not mention in your application letter that you worked for the Scorby family?" The blunt question caught Addy off guard. "Henry seemed rather shocked to discover you'd been hired straight out of the workhouse."

The overly bright tone didn't match the flinty glare in Charlotte's eyes, setting Addy on edge.

"One would assume that working for a family like the Scorbys would set you apart from other applicants."

"I did not obtain the job with your grandmother by subterfuge, Miss Glover," Addy said carefully.

Charlotte laughed lightly, waving off the implication. "Oh, I'm not worried about that. Granny is fierce enough to fight her own battles. But I am curious as to why you left the Scorby's in the first place."

"The time was right for me to leave," Addy replied, choosing her words with precision.

Charlotte's eyes sharpened with interest. The bubbly girl had vanished entirely, replaced by a determined young woman. In her place sat someone with a steely edge—qualities reminiscent of her future stepmother-in-law. "Some might consider that a trite response, Addy. Your grandmother always said you were too sharp for your own good," Charlotte regarded her thoughtfully. "Perhaps I should find out from them myself," she mused.

The words hung in the air like a challenge, but Addy treated them as rhetorical. Years of training in discretion served her well. She kept her expression blank, waiting for the next strike.

"You knew Henry when he was younger?"

"Yes, I did," Addy replied evenly. "His mother was a wonderful woman."

"And what of his father? His stepbrother certainly sounds like a man to behold—handsome as a devil, with a reputation to match."

"I'm afraid I had very little interaction with Mr Scorby. His work kept him away, and I was mostly in the kitchen or cleaning the fireplaces during my time there," Addy hedged.

Charlotte hummed as she turned to face the mirror. "Henry insists I shan't meet them until the wedding. He claims he runs one side of the business while his father manages the other. Yet, I'm intrigued by the family. They are wealthy and powerful, yes?"

"Yes, I believe so," Addy replied.

"Then I shall look forward to meeting them." Charlotte swivelled back to face her, spearing Addy with a look—a cheerful malevolence lighting her smile. "I'll be sure to mention their od scullery maid to them when I do."

Addy's mouth went dry, but she held her tongue. She wanted to believe Mrs Glover would not dismiss her on the whims of another woman, but she also knew how good Vanessa had been at twisting the truth.

"You're hiding something, Addy," Charlotte said, her voice silky with accusation. "I know it, deep down, and you should know by now—I always get my way."

∼

Addy was relieved when Mrs Glover was finally well enough to travel again.

The sense of impending doom as she'd waited for

Mrs Glover to discover her past employment history had felt like an axe hanging over her head. The train ride back north was a welcome reprieve from the tension that had plagued her. Yet even as London receded into the distance, that feeling only abated slightly.

She sat opposite Mrs Glover, who dozed lightly, rocked by the rhythmic *clickety-clack* of the train. The carriage was quiet, and Addy took a moment to study her employer's face. It seemed that this last illness had sapped more of her energy. Mrs Glover's complexion was still pale, her slack mouth bracketed by lines that appeared deeper than ever before.

October's heavy ground frost stretched across the land, glistening under the glow of the weak sunlight. The distant spire of Langmere's church came into view across the rolling countryside. The platform was distinctly less chaotic, and soon they were in the carriage on their way to Rose Villa.

Life in Langmere appeared to have ticked along merrily during Mrs Glover's absence. Harper and Mrs Thomas were still sniping at one another, while Gert chattered about the footman she'd met during an outing while they were away. Mrs Glover and Addy returned to their usual routine. Addy kept a close eye on her employer, concerned about her getting weaker, and Mrs Glover appeared eternally grateful.

When Addy wrote to Janie, telling her about who she had bumped into in London, Janie wasted no time suggesting they meet halfway again.

"You should tell the old lady," Janie urged. "It'll ease your conscience, at least. I can see the guilt eating you up."

"I can't," Addy shook her head, horror flitting across her face. "No one believed me back then."

"It seems your Henry does now," Janie said lightly.

Addy glanced nervously around the small tearoom, worried they might be overheard. "He isn't my Henry," Addy insisted. "And no one else knows the truth—not even Smale is there now to back up my story. It would be my word against Vanessa's." She sighed heavily. "I wish I could just let sleeping dogs lie."

Janie sipped her tea thoughtfully, considering Addy for a long moment.

"Knowing what I do about Mrs Glover, I doubt she'd give a fig about your past. Actions speak louder than words, and you've never let her down."

Addy travelled home that day, turning Janie's advice over in her mind. If she could explain her side to Mrs Glover—perhaps omitting the part about Henry's gift and their connection—Mrs Glover might side with her.

She walked into the dining room, intending to confess everything, only for Mrs Glover to announce that Charlotte had written and would be arriving at Rose Villa the very next day.

∼

LATER THAT NIGHT, Addy mused over the situation.

Charlotte and Henry would visit regularly. She would have to see them happy together again and again, endure Charlotte's snide remarks, and try keep her history with Henry secret from the other staff.

And what would happen when the time came for Vanessa to meet Mrs Glover? Charlotte would surely give her away.

The next morning, the house was in a flurry, with beds being changed and rooms warmed for their arrival.

It was barely eleven when the carriage pulled up outside Rose Villa.

The rolling fields beyond the house were still white with the morning's frost, and breath misted in the chilly air as Henry handed Charlotte down from the carriage. Addy was surprised to see Betty following them.

"You brought your maid?" Mrs Glover asked after warmly greeting her granddaughter.

"Oh, Granny," Charlotte said gaily, "Betty is now my lady's maid."

"I thought you were going to seek Addy's help in finding someone?" Mrs Glover paused in the hallway.

Charlotte's hand swished in the air. "Betty is highly skilled and well-versed in modern fashions. I'm afraid Addy's skills don't quite meet society's standards."

It was the first time Charlotte had openly insulted her in front of others.

Addy kept her head bowed, years of training carrying her through as she helped Harper and Gert with the luggage, ignoring Henry as best as she could.

Later, she carried the tea tray and set it on the sideboard. "Shall I serve, Mrs Glover?" she asked.

The three of them sat around the small dining room table. Henry's expectant gaze lingered on her with the faintest smile.

"The fire isn't quite warm enough, Addy. And my bags need unpacking. Do hurry—I'm famished," Charlotte remarked.

Addy did as instructed, working efficiently as murmurs of conversation carried on behind her. Then she dealt with Charlotte's belongings, ignoring Betty's complaints that she was interfering.

As dinnertime rolled around, Betty was nowhere to be seen. Charlotte had summoned Addy to her favourite guest room. She sat on the edge of the bed, scrutinising Addy.

"You've made yourself quite indispensable to Granny, haven't you? I imagine she'd be lost without you."

"I'm certain she wouldn't," Addy said truthfully. "She's more than capable of living independently. Though I do believe her to be the most pleasant company."

"Still," Charlotte sniffed disdainfully, "it must be rather lonely being tucked away here in the middle of nowhere. No grand parties or handsome suitors. But, I suppose, this is the life you've chosen."

Addy turned from the fireplace, keeping her head bowed deferentially. "Is there anything else I can help you with this evening, Miss?"

Charlotte watched her, her expression remote for a moment longer than was polite.

"No, I don't need anything from you. And I never will."

CHAPTER 48

The morning was sharp with frost, the sunlight casting a glittering sheen over the village square. Addy tugged up the edges of her shawl as she emerged from Mrs Drury's, stepping down carefully onto the ground frozen solid beneath her boots. She picked her way cautiously along the pavement until a pair of boots appeared in her line of sight.

She looked up into Henry's face, and her thoughts scattered in a thousand different directions.

"Beautiful morning," he said, his breath visible in the frigid air.

The subject, so tame and normal, drew a happy sigh from within. "Langmere always reminds me of Longhaven at this time of year," she replied.

"And Whitehurst?" he asked softly.

A smile graced her lips, touched that he would remember her childhood home. "I'm surprised you remember."

"I remember everything about you."

Her heart leapt with joy at his quiet admission. The

bustle of the square – carts and pedestrians fell away until only Henry filled her senses.

"Can I offer you a ride back?" He gestured across the square to a black and burgundy carriage.

She shook her head quickly. "No, that wouldn't be right."

Whatever he was about to say was cut off when Billy Baker hailed her from across the square. A jaunty wave accompanied his broad grin as he jogged towards them. She stifled a groan. The last thing she needed was Billy's teasing in front of Henry.

"Can I offer you a lift?" Billy asked, tipping his hat to her. "I'm heading to Rose Villa now."

Addy panicked and said the first thing that came to mind. "Actually, I'm going with Mr Scorby."

She sent Henry a pleading look and prayed that he wouldn't betray her.

Henry quirked a brow, amused, but said nothing.

Billy was undeterred, his attention on Addy. "I looked for you at the dance hall last weekend," he said. "I was hoping for another dance with you."

"We've been busy."

"That's okay then. As long as you haven't gone off me."

"No, nothing like that."

"Good," Billy leaned in, "Because you know I'll wait for you."

Addy laughed then because it was expected of her. "I've told you, Billy. I'm dedicated to my work."

"Can't blame a man for trying now, can you?" He winked at her, tipped his hat and sauntered off back towards his wagon, whistling tunelessly.

Henry's gaze followed him. "A friend of yours?"

"In a way," she replied quietly, reluctantly waving

back at Billy as his wagon rolled by them. "He's harmless enough."

"Shall we get back?" Henry swept a hand towards his carriage.

Addy allowed him to hand her into the carriage, her fingers tingling in a way that set her pulse fluttering wildly. The carriage bumped over the cobbled square as it made its way out of the village. Addy deliberately kept her gaze through the window, all too aware of Henry's attention on her.

"What happens at these dance halls?"

Her green eyes met his. She contemplated not answering him, though there wasn't any malice in his open gaze. "It's mostly local servants and farmhands," she murmured. "It's a social event that happens every month or so; dancing and a bit of music. There aren't many opportunities for servants and labourers to court. Harper usually lets Gertie go, but only if I am there to chaperone. Of course, he makes me go only so that he doesn't have to do it himself."

"I see," Henry teased. He waited a beat then said, "I never once pictured you as a baker's wife."

His words struck a nerve. Henry could tease, but he was never unkind. Until now. "Henry…"

"What? He asked, eyes wide in feigned innocence.

Inexplicably, she was annoyed by his reaction. "Billy is a hard worker. He might not wear fine clothes or have servants, but he's salt of the earth."

His jaw moved as he stared at her. "Do you love him?"

"No!"

His eyes hardened, the teasing vanishing from his face. "I once told you that I loved you and you never said it back to me."

"That was a long time ago," she reasoned. "You were still a boy really."

"A man knows love, Addy. Age doesn't come into it. Did you love me?"

They stared at each other across the confined space, tension pulsing between them.

"Why are you asking me this?" she whispered, her voice strained.

"I want to know," he sat forward, his eyes blazing.

"There is no point talking about what could have been," she said. "I am a maid – then and now."

"Addy," he growled, swapping to the bench she sat on. Awareness stole her breath as he closed the space between them. "Did you love me?"

Under his undivided attention, she could not deny him. "Y-yes," she husked.

His face was pained. "Why didn't you tell me so back then?"

"What difference would it have made?"

"I would have *known*," he said, agitatedly. "I would have known that something was wrong. Instead, I took the word of a woman who despises my mother because my father still loves her! I would have come looking for you."

"And then what? We would have married?" Irritation at his steadfast refusal to face the truth snapped in her blood. "I would have sat around that mahogany table in the dining room, with Vanessa and Isaac, making small talk over dinner?" Something between a laugh and a sob escaped her. "Your father would have disinherited you, Henry. You would have lost everything. Your status, your reputation."

"And I told you I didn't care about that!"

Addy met his anguish with some of her own. "But

you would have, Henry. I've lived a life where I've lost everything. Twice, in fact. I've fallen so far from society that I had to seek relief in the workhouse. It's horribly humiliating, and I wouldn't want that for you. If not for the kindness of others, I'd still be there."

His gaze roved her face, settling on her lips. He laid a hand on hers. "But we would have had each other. Things would have been so very different for you if I'd have been there."

"No, they wouldn't have, Henry," she murmured, her heart heavy as she pulled her hand from his. "You would have lost everything, and it would have been my fault."

The carriage rolled to a stop outside Rose Villa, the driver calling out to announce their arrival.

Neither moved.

"You're in love with Charlotte and Henry, she loves you, too," Addy whispered, eyes bright with tears that clogged her throat. "That is the way these things are meant to be. Please, just leave me alone."

Without waiting for him to say more, she reached for the door and stepped out. She hurried past the driver, not noticing Charlotte standing in the upstairs window, following her every step.

CHAPTER 49

The sitting room wasn't often used at Rose Villa.

Mrs Glover preferred the warmth of the drawing-room, where she was surrounded by memories and trinkets that had accumulated over her lifetime.

Charlotte sat in the high-backed armchair by the fire when Addy popped her head around the door. "You asked to see me?"

Charlotte didn't smile. "Come in and close the door."

Addy tried to quell the tremor running along her spine as she did as she was told.

"Henry has left?"

Addy clasped her hands in front of her dutifully. "I believe so, yes."

Of course, she knew. She felt his absence more keenly than she cared to admit. Henry had received a note summoning him back to the London office late last night, and he had left at first light.

Charlotte pursed her lips as she eyed Addy. "How long have you worked for my grandmother?"

Addy's brows drew together in confusion. "Just gone six years now, Miss."

"My mother and I have been speaking," Charlotte stated matter-of-factly. "My grandmother ails more and more with each passing week. Her needs are becoming greater, and Mother and I feel the time has come for her to have someone with a little more... experience, shall we say?"

Addy felt as if her heart had come into her throat. "I'm sorry?"

Charlotte gracefully rose and crossed to the large picture window. The grounds beyond were blanketed in the first snow of the season, blinding white in every direction. "Mother and I doubted your skills as it was, but now that we are aware of your past, neither of us is comfortable having you care for my grandmother. There are many valuables around this house, and—" Charlotte turned, spearing Addy with a cold look, "—considering your previous work history, we don't think it appropriate for someone of your low calibre to be in such a lofty position."

Addy took a step forward. "I haven't done anything wrong. Has Mrs Glover said she's unhappy with the standard of my work?"

"This isn't a question of ability, Addy," Charlotte folded her arms. "This is a question of trustworthiness."

Dread pooled in her stomach. "Please, Miss Glover, what have I done to make you question my honesty?"

Charlotte changed tack. "What was your relationship with Henry?"

Addy struggled to keep up with the abrupt shift in

subject. "I worked for his father; I've already explained this."

Charlotte arched a delicate brow. "You ought to mind your tone when talking to me."

"I beg your pardon, Miss. I meant nothing by it. It's just... has Mrs Glover said she's unhappy with my work?"

"Not in so many words, but her memory isn't what it used to be, is it?"

Addy could only shake her head. "Please, Miss Glover, I truly value this job. Your grandmother means a lot to me. I want to see it through."

"Out of the question," Charlotte said primly. "Mama has already placed an advert in *The Sketch* for your position. She was horrified when I told her of your connection to Henry and the Scorby family. Moreso when I explained about your... shady past."

Frustrated tears burned at the back of her eyes. "Please, miss... There is no connection between myself and the Scorby family, at least none that has existed for nearly ten years."

"And yet, I keep finding you and Henry in cohorts together. First in the outhouse in London, and just two days ago, he was seen dropping you off in his carriage outside. Do you deny this?"

Addy's mouth parted, but she hesitated in the denial. "No, I do not deny this. Mr Scorby was kind enough to offer me a lift back from the village."

"You will leave this place and find a new job with immediate effect."

Addy shook her head. "Mrs Glover hired me; I answer to her, not you."

"And you think my darling grandmother will deny

me what I want? You'll tell her you've found a job elsewhere."

Addy's face turned ashen. "I have to serve out a notice. She'll expect it."

"A week," Charlotte snapped. "No longer. And now that I've made sure Henry is out of the way, I can be sure you won't get your claws into him any further."

Addy longed to believe Mrs Glover would be loyal to her, but blood was always thicker than water.

"If you leave within the week, no more will be said on this matter. Your shameful, light-fingered past will remain a secret."

"And if I don't?"

"Then I'll ruin you. Mrs Scorby is most interested in hearing more details. Henry will choose me over you, and if he doesn't, I'll see to it that his life is in tatters. Mark my words."

"You've got it all wrong," Addy pleaded.

Charlotte held up a delicate hand. "Henry wouldn't be the first gentleman to have his head turned by a promiscuous maid," Addy gasped, but Charlotte continued, "and I won't have my mother's efforts to ensure that Henry fell in love with me go to waste."

Addy blinked. So much for the story of meeting at a dinner party and falling in love across the table.

"Granny keeps a tight hold of the purse strings, and after her death, I'm sure much of the finances will be tied up so that Mama and I will still have to come cap in hand to her board of directors. I need the Scorby money to secure my future, and I will not have Henry's head turned by a brazen hussy like you."

Humiliation and outrage stung, and she felt the crimson heat spread from her neck upwards. "I see."

"You'll pack your bags and be gone within the week."

"Just like that?"

"You can leave straightaway, without a reference, and you'll be back in the workhouse before you know it. Because, as I'm sure you're all too aware, not having a reference makes finding another job impossible."

Addy could only nod and fled the room, Charlotte's glorying chuckles ringing in her ears. She turned into the hall and almost collided with Betty. "Excuse me," Addy muttered, trying to rush past her, but Betty's hand shot out.

"I know who you are and what you did," Betty hissed as her hand bit into Addy's flesh, "Lady's maids talk, and it didn't take long for me to find someone from Longhaven. I know all about you, Adelaide Hill. This is what happens when women like you try to climb above their station. Trying to win over an engaged man. You deserve everything you get."

CHAPTER 50

The air in the drawing room was thick with tension. Addy stood before her employer, hands clasped tightly in front of her, as the widow's fury rained down upon her.

"Why, Addy? Why are you choosing now to hand in your resignation? Is it because I've been so ill?"

Addy kept her gaze on the floral rug at her feet. "I'm truly sorry, Mrs Glover."

"But not sorry enough to reconsider, are you?" She banged a hand against the arm of the chair. "Is my pay not satisfactory?"

"My salary is perfectly fine, Mrs Glover," Addy said quietly.

"Then explain yourself! Why would you leave now, when I need you the most?"

The plea in her tone nearly undid Addy. She struggled to maintain her silence. How could she tell Mrs Glover the truth—that Charlotte had threatened to ruin her if she didn't leave? That her beloved granddaughter was blackmailing her? Addy felt trapped, and the only clear way out, to save Henry and secure a reference, was to go peacefully.

"It's just time, Mrs Glover," Addy said, lifting her eyes to meet her employer's piercing glare.

Mrs Glover stared at her, and Addy's chest ached at the sight of the hurt written all over her face. She desperately wanted to explain, to tell her everything, but the words remained lodged in her throat.

"Very well," Mrs Glover relented when Addy kept her silence. "Your mind is clearly made up, though I know there is more you're not telling me. I shall write you a reference. How soon are you leaving?"

"The end of the week," Addy replied softly.

Mrs Glover nodded once, her mouth compressed into a thin line. "You may go."

Addy made a hasty retreat, her heart heavy as she made her way down to the kitchen.

Mrs Thomas and Gert fell silent as Addy entered. Betty sat near the fire; a garment spread across her lap. Addy saw the judgment written across their faces.

Gert was the first to speak. "Billy Baker's at the back door asking for you."

"Can't you tell him I'm busy?" Addy was in no mood for company, and the last thing she wanted was to fend off Billy's affections with everything else going on.

Gert simply levelled a look at her. "But you're not."

Betty snickered, and Addy didn't bother to conceal her sigh. This cold shoulder treatment from those she'd once considered friends would make the rest of the week feel endless.

She stepped out into the frozen morning air, frost nipping at her cheeks as she tugged her shawl tighter. She spotted Billy standing in the middle of the yard, dragging the toe of his boot through the snow. His collar was turned up against the chill.

She was about to send him away when he looked up. The usual playful grin was absent, replaced by an unusually serious expression.

"What is it, Billy?" she called from the doorway, crossing her arms against the cold.

He shifted from foot to foot, glancing toward the kitchen window. Addy followed his gaze and saw Betty standing there with Mrs Thomas, both watching. Irritation prickled through her.

How much of this would make its way to Charlotte's ears?

Addy crossed the yard, her boots sinking in the snow that packed the yard, and led Billy around the side of the building, out of sight of the prying eyes.

"All right, talk," she said curtly, her tone sharper than intended.

"I've got a message for you," he said quietly, low enough that she had to step closer to hear. "From your... friend. The one I saw you with in the village."

"Mr Scorby?"

Billy nodded.

"That's impossible. He left for London yesterday."

Billy shrugged. "All I know is he came to the bakery not an hour ago and asked me to fetch you. He's waiting there now."

"I don't understand..." Addy's mind raced. "Is this some sort of game? Because if it is, Billy, I don't think it's—"

Billy held up his hands to cut off her tirade. "He's desperate enough to pay me half a crown, Addy. He said I had to use discretion. I don't even know what that means, but I know what a week's wages are worth."

After everything she'd endured, Addy pinched the bridge of her nose, trying to gather her thoughts. Suspicion made her hesitate. Why would Henry be in Langmere but not stay at Rose Villa? Why would he send Billy instead of seeking her out himself?

"He said it was urgent," Billy prompted.

"I'm thinking," Addy replied, though none of it made sense.

Billy smirked faintly. "I'm no gentleman, but it's not in my nature to stand in the way of another man's affections. Anyone with eyes can see he's mad for you, and I reckon you're mad for him, too," he pressed a hand to his chest, "as much as it pains me to say it out loud."

Addy opened her mouth to deny it.

"I mean, if you like tall, dark, and handsome, rather than short, dumpy, and with a tendency to use bad words."

Addy laughed despite herself.

"It's half a crown, Addy. That alone tells me he wants to see you."

Caught between burning curiosity and sinking dread, she sighed. "Let me fetch my coat."

THE RIDE into the village was silent, save for the soft crunch of the horse's hooves muffled by the snow and the occasional creak of the wagon. Langmere was quiet, residents seeking refuge from the cold as fresh snow floated down. Billy pulled up in the yard behind the bakery. Addy was about to point out it was empty when Henry stepped out from under the eaves. He was wrapped in a dark wool coat, shoulders hunched against the chill as he waited for her.

"Told you," Billy said softly. Addy nodded mutely and climbed down; her attention fixed on Henry. By the time she looked back, Billy had disappeared, leaving the two of them alone.

The snow now fell steadily from the heavy clouds, catching in Henry's black curls and dusting his broad shoulders.

Yearning pulled at her. A dangerous warmth unfurled in her chest even as she knew it was dangerous for her to be standing before him. Yet, she drank her fill, wondering if this would be the last time she saw him.

Henry's piercing blue gaze locked onto hers. "Thank you for coming."

"What's this about, Henry? Why aren't you in London?"

His exhale was visible in front of his face. "I needed to see you."

"Henry…" she sighed, half-pleading, half-weary. "We shouldn't be doing this."

"I know," he admitted, stepping closer, eyes intense. "The same as I know you asked me to leave you alone. But I couldn't just leave things as they were. My man tells me you're leaving Rose Villa."

Addy broke the look, turning to look at the stone buildings that surrounded them. Of course, servants talked. They traded gossip like card players at the poker table. She couldn't be sure who it was who'd told Henry's valet the news. "It's time I moved on."

"Because of me?"

She couldn't look at him. He'd see the lie. "No."

"I don't believe you."

Addy closed her eyes, praying for the strength to see this through. She had taken enough risks just coming here. If Charlotte discovered this meeting, the consequences would be catastrophic. She steadied her breathing, drawing upon years of training to keep her expression neutral. When she looked up again, her face was composed. "This is wrong, Henry. You're engaged to be married. I'm a servant. Go back to Charlotte and leave me alone."

Two strides brought him to her, and before she could move, his hands gripped her shoulders, turning her back around to face him. His intensity left her breathless. "That letter summoning me to London? It was a forgery," he said sharply. "I have my suspicions about who sent it. I tried to…" He caught the words. "I don't know why, and frankly, I don't care."

Addy knew that Charlotte had sent the letter to get him away from Addy. He'd left on the same day Charlotte had told her to leave.

"Then I hear you've handed in your resignation. I got on the first train I could catch to bring me back here."

Addy could no longer feel her toes, and yet all she could think about was the manipulation that Charlotte was weaving them both into just to get her way and secure the Scorby money. Addy glanced nervously toward the edge of the yard. Beyond the low stone wall, the sounds of the village carried faintly. A cart rattled past, and distant voices greeted one another. "If someone sees us—"

"Do you think I care?"

"You should! Because I care, Henry! This –" She waved a hand between them. "This—whatever *this* is—

it's not right. It will only bring disaster for us both. I wish I could explain more but you simply must let it go. You have no idea what it's like to lose everything."

He grasped her by the shoulders and hauled her closer to him. "I spent years wondering what happened to you," he countered, his voice fierce. "Why you betrayed me. Why you disappeared. Only to discover that your hand was forced, and I wasn't there to help you." Her breath caught when he cupped her cheeks between his hands. His eyes searched her face, leaving her nowhere to hide. "Do you know what it's like to miss someone every single day?"

"Yes," she whispered.

Triumph flared in his eyes. His thumbs brushed her cheeks as he gave her a heavy-lidded smile. "Now that I've found you again, I can't stop thinking about you."

It would be so easy, just to stop fighting. To let go and see where the dice fell.

But then she thought about the long, echoing corridors of the workhouse. The clink of stone as those pitiful men spent hours pointlessly breaking rocks just to pay for their keep in the workhouse. The memory of Charlotte's threat, the spectre of the workhouse, loomed too large. Addy knew that she couldn't let Henry make this choice.

She pulled his hands from her face. Deliberately, she took a step back. "No, Henry. You're engaged. You have a life in London, and—"

"I'm going to call things off with Charlotte. I was working my way around to it when her maid handed me the note from London," he interrupted, his tone resolute. "That's why I'm here. This time, I won't be sidetracked."

Panic coursed through her, sending her eyes wide. "You can't do that!"

"I can, and I will," he stated. "I can't marry someone I don't love. I was just fooling myself that she'd be a good match, but she doesn't fill my heart the way you do."

Addy's breath hitched, her mind racing. If Charlotte discovered Henry's intentions, her wrath would be swift and merciless. She couldn't let this happen.

"I'm leaving Langmere," Addy said firmly, grasping at any way to defuse the situation. "I've already accepted another position far from here. If I go, then—"

"Then I'll follow you," Henry said simply. "You have my heart, Addy. You always have."

The raw emotion, the unyielding inevitability, scared her spitless. But she knew the stakes. Henry didn't understand what he was risking.

And so, she did the only thing she could to save them both.

"I don't love you, Henry," she said flatly.

The lie burned her throat. Her heart cracked as she saw the devastation in his eyes and watched as the light in them dimmed. She willed herself to stay strong as she forced the words out. "I'm not sure I ever did."

The words hung between them, heavy and final. She made herself watch the effect her words had on him, spreading like ripples on a still pond. The way his jaw tightened. The subtle shift in his posture as he stepped back.

When she couldn't bear it any longer, she hurried out of the yard, head bowed against the flurries. She didn't stop, wading through the snow drifts along the lanes. The freezing wind stung her cheeks, which were wet with her tears.

It was for the best, she told herself, over and over.

By the time she reached Rose Villa, she was frozen to the bone. She struggled with the door handle, her fingers numb with cold. She stumbled inside, the warmth enveloping her like a welcoming friend. She leaned against the door as she tried to steady her ragged breathing.

Downstairs was silent save for the faint crackle of the kitchen hearth and the hum of the low fire in the stove. It was that time of day when there was always a natural lull between lunch and supper. The others were most likely taking advantage and having a rest. Addy hung up her soggy coat and pinned her mob cap into place. She would check on Mrs Glover. She tended to doze in her armchair when she needed a more restorative sleep in her bed.

The house felt eerily quiet as she climbed the narrow stairs and turned for the drawing room. When she opened the door, she frowned at the empty armchair.

Wondering if perhaps Betty had helped Mrs Glover to bed, she turned for the main staircase and froze.

She had seen death.

She'd seen it take many forms

Mrs Glover lay in a crumpled heap at the bottom of the stairs, her small frame still. The lavender perfume she favoured lingered in the air.

Addy exhaled shakily as she approached the lifeless form, leaning down to touch the still-warm cheek of the woman who had shown her so much kindness. "I'm so sorry," she whispered.

A sharp click of footsteps sounded behind her, and

Addy turned in time to see Charlotte stop dead in the hallway. Her surprise flickered to one of sheer horror. Her pretty eyes darted between Addy and her grandmother, her mouth falling open.

Mrs Thomas appeared behind Addy, gasping at the sight before her. But it was Betty, standing at the top of the stairs, who broke the silence.

"Call the constable!" Betty shrieked, her finger trembling as she pointed accusingly downwards. "I saw her! I saw her push Mrs Glover! Addy Hill is a murderer!"

CHAPTER 51

The last few hours had been like a terrible blurry nightmare that Addy couldn't wake from. It had all happened so fast. One moment, she had been crouching over Mrs Glover, mourning her. The next, the constable was hauling her away.

Accusations had been laid at her feet. Terrible, vile allegations. No matter how much Addy had sobbed, begged and pleaded her innocence, none of it mattered. Betty's damning statement that she had seen Addy push poor Mrs Glover from the top of the stairs had sealed her fate.

She felt like she was on a slippery downhill slide with no way of stopping.

Langmere didn't have a police station, so she was taken in a black police cab to the next town over. Iron shackles bit into her wrists as she was pulled into the building.

The police station was housed in a squat building with barred windows. Inside, the air was redolent with dampness and the lingering stench of tobacco smoke.

Several men turned to watch her. Her heart pounded in her chest, humiliation under the weight of their stares crushing her. She was led through the main room and out along a dimly lit corridor to a room with stained, bare walls. The room was empty save for a table and two wooden chairs. Addy was shoved roughly into one chair; the constable was unrelenting and unfriendly as the winter's day beyond the dirty window.

He sat with a grunt. He had very little hair left and wore a permanent scowl. She couldn't recall his name for the life of her. She couldn't remember much except for those lifeless eyes that stared up at her from the floor.

"Miss Hill," he began, his voice flat and unforgiving. "Let's look at the facts as I see them. A noteworthy member of Langmere is dead. Murdered, it appears. You were found standing over the body of Mrs Glover. We have a witness who saw you pushing her down the stairs."

Addy kept her head bowed, silent tears tracking down her cheeks.

"The staff say you were planning on leaving. That this decision had come out of the blue, and you were leaving at the end of this week."

The last time Addy spoke with Mrs Glover, the woman had been deeply hurt, believing that Addy had betrayed her. What hurt Addy the most was that her beloved employer, someone who'd become a good friend, had gone to her grave thinking Addy *wanted* to go.

"Both Mrs Thomas and the young maid said that you had quarrelled with Mrs Glover this morning. What about?"

"My resignation," Addy said slowly.

"You'd already packed your bags, though," he said.

Addy frowned then and finally looked up.

She hadn't packed a thing.

"You'd also helped yourself to some of Mrs Glover's items," he paused to check his book, but Addy was already shaking her head, even as icy terror filled her.

"I hadn't packed," she said. "Not a thing."

"You own a dark brown carpet bag, yes?"

Throat dry, she was overwhelmed by the all-too-familiar sensation of losing control over her life, a helplessness born of being manipulated. "Yes."

The constable regarded her steadily, his expression unmoved.

"The last time I saw Mrs Glover was in the drawing room earlier today. She was alive and well. She is – *was* a wonderful employer. A good friend."

"Then why did you push her down the stairs?"

Addy choked on a sob. "I didn't do it."

He leaned back in his chair, folding his hands over his corpulent stomach. "It's not up to me to decide your guilt, Miss Hill. That will be up to a judge but a maid with her bags packed and one foot out of the door, whilst standing over the dead body of an upstanding member of society doesn't look good for you, does it?" He slapped a hand against the tabletop, making her jolt. "You'll be taken to Kirkdale where you'll await trial." The chair scraped against the stone floor as he pushed back from the table. He stood and leaned towards her. "But with the evidence I have before me, I predict the hangman's noose for you."

THE CLANG of the iron prison gates echoed along the long, dank corridor. Addy stumbled forward when the prison guard gave her a shove in the middle of her back.

She was being held on remand, trapped in a grim limbo between life and death. Isolated from other prisoners and convicts, she was confined to a rudimentary cube equipped with only a slatted bed, a straw-stuffed mattress, and a wooden pail for her slops, which she was expected to empty each morning. The process had been eerily reminiscent of her admission to the workhouse: a tepid bath awaited her after she had exited the rattling confines of the 'Black Maria' prison van. She wore her own clothes for now, though the dress she had on was fit for nothing more than the fire, stained and filthy from her ordeal.

She had lost count of the days she'd been here, though she hadn't slept a wink. How could she? With the desperate wails of despair from the other inmates and the ceaseless squeal of rats as they skittered across her legs in her prison cell, she hadn't dared shut her eyes for even a second. Her stomach was hollow, but she hardly noticed. Her mind was too full of how she had ended up in this bleak place.

When the guard had banged her door, she'd been curled up in a small ball on a straw mattress that was marked with mildew spots. "Up! You have a visitor!"

A visitor! She almost laughed at him. Who was going to come for her here?

She shuffled along as best she could, the movements limited by the cold shackles around her ankles and wrists. The guard stopped by a painted black door that swung open with a squeak. It looked similar to the room where that wretched constable had interviewed her. Stark whitewashed walls. The wide, barred window on the back wall framed a crisp winter's day; the frame was edged with the fresh powdery snow that she could see on the rooftops beyond the prison walls. Addy squinted at the brilliance until her vision had adjusted.

A man she'd never seen before sat at the only table. "Sit." He gestured at the chair on the other side of the table. The guard shoved at Addy, and once seated, he left, locking the door behind him.

Addy adjusted her position, the iron bracelets clattering on the badly scarred tabletop that was in dire need of a wipe.

The man had an immaculate appearance. He wore a good quality dark suit. His salt-and-pepper hair was neatly combed back from a wide forehead. He shuffled a sheaf of papers in front of him, the cream-coloured sheets filled with flowing script.

"My name is Detective Samuel Atwood," he said. "I'm with the Liverpool Borough Station, North division. I've been assigned to handle the investigation. How are you, Adelaide?"

She looked at him but said nothing. What was the point? No one here cared how she was. She was tired, her hope dwindling with each passing hour.

She had no fight left in her.

Atwood studied her for a moment. She doubted his dark brown eyes missed a trick. He reached inside his coat pocket to pull a small black notebook out and laid it alongside the papers. He then took out a pencil and flipped his notebook open to a blank page.

"I have reviewed the statement you gave to the constable at the time of your arrest, but I would like to hear your version of what happened," his pencil was poised in the air.

"I've already said everything there is to say," she rasped, her voice rusty from lack of use. "Over and over, though it didn't do much good, seeing how I ended up in here."

"And now you'll explain it to me," Atwood said, levelling a steady gaze at her.

"You have your report," she jerked her chin at the papers by his hand. "Can I go back to my cell now?"

His expression didn't change, though his tone did. "Miss Hill, you're being charged with the most heinous crime. We have an eyewitness who says you pushed your employer down the stairs, leading to her untimely death. Your bag was packed in your room. You were suddenly leaving a steady position."

Addy's eyes drifted closed as she listened to the facts, her head drooping under their gravity.

"Several valuable items were inside the bag, small items that could easily be sold for a tidy sum", he continued, "all belonging to the victim, Mrs..." he paused to consult his papers.

"Glover," Addy said forlornly. "Mrs Prudence Glover. And I didn't kill her."

Atwood sat forward, forearms on the tabletop. "That's not what Betty Owens said."

Addy didn't flinch as she glared at him. "Betty is lying."

He exhaled slowly, then wrote something in his notebook. He flicked over two sheets of cream paper and looked up. "According to the constable who arrested you, you claimed you'd been in Langmere and had just returned home."

"That's right."

"He notes here that the weather that day was blizzard-like. Are you prone to going out alone in inclement weather?"

Addy blinked at him.

He leaned on one elbow, long fingers looping in front of him. "Where were you?"

Addy's firmed her lips. How could she possibly answer that? If she told the truth and implicated Henry, what would follow? Would Charlotte turn her wrath on him, tearing apart his life as she had done to hers? Charlotte had already proven just how far she was willing to go to destroy her.

And then there was the nagging doubt that Mrs Glover had not fallen like she'd first assumed but had indeed been pushed by someone else in the house that day. That there really could be a murderer in Rose Villa.

The idea that such a vital woman had been snuffed out was too horrible to comprehend.

She tried to knuckle away her abrupt tears, but her shackled wrists prevented her, and she let them clatter back to the scarred surface.

"You know," Atwood began as he set his pencil down, "I've been doing this job for twelve years. Every case starts the same way for me. At nine o'clock sharp, my superintendent assigns an officer to a case. He chooses one with the most relevant experience. I like it because each day is different." He folded his arms, his nose twitching until he rubbed it. "We conduct interviews and I note down anything relevant in my notebook. At the end of each day, I have to go back to the station and write everything up in a logbook. There's a logbook for specific crimes – robbery and such."

Even though she didn't want to be, Addy was interested enough to listen closely to him.

He continued as though they were friends enjoying afternoon tea, not in a room in a prison. "Detectives take on everything. Burglary, thefts, arson investigations, murder." His sharp eyes returned from meandering around the room and settled on her. "Tracking down prostitutes. We protect warehouses and conduct racecourse surveillance. Handle royal visits. It's a varied line of work."

He tapped a blunt fingernail on the sheath of papers. "The report I read on you this morning is fairly damning. Betty Owens claims she saw you shove Mrs Glover from behind. The victim's valuables were packed in your bag. You say that the younger Mrs Glover had placed an advert, but she denies this. Your colleagues say that your resignation was most unexpected. You were heard quarrelling with the victim on the morning of her death. No one to corroborate your story that you were in Langmere after William Evans, the baker's son, had dropped you off."

Addy linked her hands as best she could, her knuckles turning white. "I didn't do it. I respected Mrs Glover very much. She was a wonderful employer."

"Then why were you leaving her employ? The other servants claim that she relied heavily on you for her care. That you'd been very attentive during several recent bouts of illness."

"As I told the other policeman, it's entirely possible that Mrs Glover had another dizzy spell and lost her balance. I just happened to come in at the wrong time."

"Betty Owens says you pushed her."

Temper burned inside her. "And I keep telling you

that she's lying," she gritted out between clenched teeth.

Atwood patted his lips thoughtfully. "Why would she lie about such a thing?"

Because Charlotte made her. The words echoed in her mind like a scream. She narrowed her eyes instead.

"And just this morning, more critical evidence has come to light," he said conversationally.

Addy held her breath, fear thrumming in her blood as she waited for the next nail in her coffin.

"Mrs Glover has named you in her will."

Shock forced the gasp out of her. "What?"

Atwood didn't seem moved by her reaction. "Her solicitor has confirmed yesterday that you are named as a beneficiary in the event of her death. A significant sum, as it goes."

Addy had known Mrs Glover to be kind and generous, but this... this was profound. "I don't... I had no idea..." Emotion strangled her voice, and Addy subsided into tears once more. She tried to compose herself, but his immutable expression and scepticism only made it worse.

"No one witnessed you returning to the house, though both the cook and Miss Owens saw you leave. Eyewitness reports place the baker's son back in the shop shortly after dropping you in Langmere. That leaves a substantial window during which your whereabouts are unaccounted for."

Addy's pulsed roared in her ears, panic clawing at her frozen mind, grief for the poor woman who'd tried to do her best for people and had ended up dead at the foot of the stairs.

Atwood leaned in; his brown eyes lit with victory. "Ample time for you to sneak in the house and push the old lady down the stairs to hurry your inheritance along."

His blunt words landed with the precision they were intended. An idea struck her through the tangle of outrage, and the words were out of her mouth before she could stop them. "Who else was named in the will?"

The detective gave a start, momentarily thrown off. He flipped his little book shut, his fingertips drumming against the worn cover. "That's an unusual question."

She swallowed hard, realising that the question showed she really did know more than she was letting on. That Charlotte had told her she didn't want to have to ask permission from the board of directors for access to money.

Addy clamped her lips shut, unspoken words hanging between them.

"I don't know all the details," he admitted slowly, studying her, "but I can check. I do know the granddaughter was less than pleased when she learned you were a named beneficiary."

Addy's brow flickered and she sat back. She could easily picture the fit of fury that Charlotte would have pitched. The thought of the venom that would have been unleashed turned her anxiety up to a rolling boil inside.

Atwood placed his elbows on the table and pressed his palms together. "You know, I can usually tell when someone is lying," he wiggled the fingers of his left hand behind his ear. "I get this little itching right here. There's something amiss in this case," his brow furrowed as he flipped through his notebook and scanned the contents again. "You previously worked with the Scorby's, correct?"

Addy's heart stuttered in her chest. "Yes," she husked.

Atwood looked up. "The same Scorby as Miss Glover's fiancé?"

Dread pooled deep in her belly. "Y-yes," her voice was wispy, and she prayed that he wouldn't connect the dots any further. Henry's life would certainly be ruined if he was named in a murder scandal and linked to her.

Atwood closed the book with a snap. He gathered the papers up and folded them along the creases before standing. "Thank you for your time, Miss Hill. You'll be taken back to your cell."

"Is that it?" she blurted.

He rapped twice on the door and gave her an unreadable look as it opened inwards. "For now, yes. But I will be back to see you soon."

CHAPTER 52

*R*outine.
She knew routine.

Each morning, the bell tolled early to wake up prisoners and convicts. Half an hour of exercise a day. A visit to the bathhouse once a week. The time in between meals was hers alone. Though she couldn't bring herself to read.

Where she used to find joy and solace, it only reminded her of all she had lost. Instead, her mind drifted. She heard her father's voice weaving vivid images of a world where terrible monsters roamed, where gods ruled with power and fury. His face danced in her memory, and she lost herself in those stories once again.

Addy was trapped in Tartarus, the deepest and darkest pit of the Underworld. Shrouded in eternal mist and surrounded by impenetrable bronzed gates, Tartarus was a wicked place for the most loathsome and irredeemable souls condemned to eternal suffering. Tormented cries of fellow inmates echoed off the walls where despair reigned supreme.

In her realm of endless torment, it was as though time stood still.

The sour-faced guard's gruff announcement that she had another visitor shattered the monotony of the bleak routine. She shuffled along behind him through a series of gates, though this time was different.

The absence of the shackles filled her with unease.

A different route through the maze of halls.

She wrapped her arms around herself, chilled by the damp air that filled the long, stone corridors. The gloom lifted slightly, and she realised that she was being taken away from the suffocating heart of the building and closer to the outer parts of the prison. Curiosity stirred within her. The walls seemed brighter, the air fresher. Soon there were no iron gates left to be taken through.

Instead, she was prodded into a room that was grand by most standards. A stove filled the room with a warmth that she had forgotten. A walnut desk with a fine leather chair. The surface of the polished table gleamed in the daylight. Six more chairs tucked under it. Sunny yellow walls and a plant on the windowsill.

Left alone and uncertain, she lowered herself onto the hard bench along the far wall. There were no bars on the wide window in here. Beyond it, snow covered the land. Unable to help herself, she crossed to the window and looked out. Smoke curled from several chimney pots. She could make out the tops of carriages as they made their way along the street past the high walls. Faint voices carried on the light wind, distant sounds of people moving about their lives.

Life has continued whilst she'd been in the

desperate abyss of misery. Her breath fogged against the glass as she leaned in, drawn to it all, until the sound of approaching footsteps made her turn to face the door.

Moments later, the door swung inwards. Detective Atwood strolled in, his expression neutral, though it was the man whom he held the door for that made her heart stall in her chest.

"H-Henry?"

Jet-black curls tumbled in disarray across his forehead, the way they did when he'd been hard at work. Shadows under his eyes didn't diminish the flare in his eyes as they met hers. Astonishment gave way to pleasure, followed by a rush of sorrow.

"Let's make this as quick as possible, shall we?" Detective Atwood set his leather satchel on the desk and then held a chair out for Addy. "Why don't we all take a seat?"

Addy dragged her eyes away from Henry, a whirlwind of emotions battering her. "What's going on?" Her legs gave way into the chair proffered. "Henry, why are you… what are you doing here?"

Detective Atwood, either oblivious to or ignoring the undercurrents between the other occupants of the room, sat in the leather desk chair. His attention was on the papers he was smoothing out on the desktop. "Ah, Miss Hill. I ought to thank you."

Addy tucked her hands into her lap, trying to gather her errant thoughts. All too aware as Henry drew out the chair next to hers and sat down. "For what?"

Atwood looked up, a faint smile on her blank face. "You reminded me of one of the golden rules of crime," his extended index finger wagged at her. "Follow the money."

Addy nervously exchanged a look with Henry, who was yet to take his eyes off her.

Atwood leaned back in his seat, those dark eyes shining with the thrill of victory once again. "Your question about who else was named in the will caught me off guard," he began. "It made me dig a little deeper. As expected, Charlotte Glover was listed as a beneficiary of the late Mrs Glover's estate. She's entitled to an annual sum, but here's where it gets peculiar—there's a stipulation that she must go through the trustee for any additional funds during the year. It's an unusual clause, don't you think? Why not simply grant her the estate outright, as a lump sum?"

Atwood, comfortable in his storytelling mode once more, crossed his ankles. He didn't wait for either of them to reply. "The trustee was one of the financial directors. An eccentric type who was difficult to pin down to a meeting. When I eventually spoke to him, he explained that the clause was because Mrs Glover felt her daughter-in-law, and by that nature, her granddaughter, didn't truly appreciate the value of money.

"Their spending was frivolous, and I'm paraphrasing a little here, but Prudence Glover didn't trust that her family wouldn't blow the money as soon as they had it and waste all of her life effort."

Addy's lips twitched. That sounded just like Mrs Glover, astute in even death.

"So, I look a little harder at the Glover women. Which was... enlightening, shall we say?"

Atwood appeared to be thoroughly enjoying himself. Addy just wished he'd get to the point.

"They're broke," the detective paused, and Addy calmly held his look, "And I can see by the look on your face that this isn't news to you."

"No, I can't say that it is," Addy said quietly.

"Why didn't you say tell me this?"

"It seemed like anything I said was dismissed," she replied honestly. "What would have been the point?"

He grimaced. Sat up. "Is that why you also neglected to tell me that you were with Mr Scorby that morning?"

Addy's gaze shot to Henry. "You told him?"

"Addy," Henry said softly and for a second, her world narrowed until it was only him. "Of course, I told him. The minute I'd heard what had happened, though, that wretched constable from Langmere gave me the run-around. Took my statement, which was conveniently lost. By the time I managed to get to speak to anyone who was not under Charlotte's influence, it was already too late, and you were in here."

"But," she blinked as the tears filled her eyes, "people will know that you were alone with a maid. The shame..."

"Oh, to hell with shame, Addy!" Henry threw his hands wide. "You did not kill Mrs Glover. You never would have!"

The conviction in his voice broke the dam of tears. Through the watery smile, she held the belief she could see in his face close to her heart.

Henry believed her.

"Everyone will know, Henry. You were alone with a *maid*. If your father knows, he will disown you. You won't have a job!"

Henry leaned in, wrapping her hands in his. "How many more times must I tell you that I don't care?" he whispered fiercely, bringing her hand to his mouth. He kissed her fingers. "I promised you that I would save you, didn't I?"

Atwood coughed, and Henry lowered their joined hands, though he didn't let her go. Addy clung to his touch like a lifeline. "With Mr Scorby's statement and the news that the engagement had been broken, I went to see the young Miss Glover." He passed a hand across his face as if trying to erase the memory. "I've seen liars in my line of work. Plenty of them. My mother always said that if you give a liar enough rope, eventually, they will hang themselves. They get tripped up… caught out. Pull on a thread in a web of lies, and it will quickly come undone.

"I can't say for certain yet which of them it was – Owens or Miss Glover – who pushed the late Mrs Glover, or even if the poor woman just fell and, as you said, it was bad timing… perhaps we'll never know. I am also looking at the constable who arrested you. It seems several key pieces of evidence, such as Mr Scorby's statement given at the time of your arrest that he was with you in Langmere, were missing." Atwood picked up the papers on the desk and carried them across the room. She took the pen he handed to her. "The wheels of justice move slowly, but this shows that all charges against you are dismissed."

Addy looked to Henry, unsure that she'd heard the detective correctly. "It's over?"

Henry nodded and smiled with satisfaction.

"Sign this, and you're free to go," Atwood confirmed.

Disbelief washed over her. Was she lost in a dream? In a trance-like state, Addy dipped the nib into the small pot the detective had placed before her. The faint scratching noise it made against the paper grounded her somewhat. Addy watched as Atwood packed up his belongings; she listened as he murmured an apology for the inconvenience she'd suffered. He tipped his hat respectfully and strolled from the room, his measured steps on the stone floor fading along the corridor.

"I want to say so much to you, Addy," Henry drew her to her feet, "but you are not staying in the dreadful place a moment longer. Here," he held out her coat. She didn't question how he'd come to possess it but stepped into it without hesitation. "It's cold out." Henry buttoned it deftly, his finger brushing her cheek as he smiled. "Let's go."

He led her out past the guards, their demeanour a stark contrast to when she'd arrived. Polite words and friendly nods followed her and then she passed beyond the heavy wood and iron doors.

Her boots sank into the soft fresh snow with a delicate crunch. Sunlight brushed her cheeks, and she tipped her face up to its blissful warmth. She inhaled deeply, delighting in the delicious air that filled her lungs.

"I am certain I've never smelled anything quite amazing as this."

"Come on," Henry chuckled, taking her hand once more, his touch steady as he led her to the sleek black carriage on the opposite side of the road. The driver hopped down and waited whilst Henry handed her into the carriage. Once inside, Henry gently tucked a thick woollen blanket around her and then sat next to her. He smiled. "Better?"

Addy looked up into his handsome face. The face that had lingered on the periphery of her mind. The man that she had loved without question for more than a decade. The one she had been prepared to give up everything for, just to protect him.

Her bottom lip wobbled, and the fragile hold she had on her emotions finally broke. Without hesitation, he laid an arm around her shoulders and drew her to him, securing her tightly as she cried. He laid a cheek on her crown. He said nothing as sobs, wracking, wrenching sobs, filled the cab's interior.

Like the tide ebbing away, slowly, her tears slowed. Until finally she just rested against him.

She slept.

CHAPTER 53

"It's just temporary," Henry set the taper to a second oil lamp. "A shorthold tenancy was all I could find on such short notice."

Addy watched as the gentle glow filled the cosy sitting room.

The modest townhouse sat at the edge of Chester, nestled between similar red brick-fronted homes with white-painted windowsills. When Addy had finally woken in Henry's arms, the soft light of the waning day cast golden hues through the carriage window across the snow-dusted rooftops of the city. Henry hadn't let her go, and they'd rode in silence for the last part of their journey as darkness settled over the lands.

The house was unassuming yet welcoming, with practical furnishings suited to a gentleman of humble means.

Henry shrugged off his coat and dropped it on the back of the chair. He drew the curtains on the night, closing them into the comfy space. "It's not much to look at," he said, following her gaze about the room.

"Just the housekeeper and a maid to keep things running for now, though my valet has graciously agreed to stay on as a sort of butler for the time being."

The wooden floor held a faded rug. Pale green wallpaper was decorated with golden vines. Two armchairs, upholstered in a muted red velvet, bordered the stone hearth where a small fire crackled softly. In the centre of the sturdy oak table was an arrangement of evergreen branches, the red berries and gilded oranges giving a pop of colour. Twin candlesticks with tapered candles edged the display. Around the plain mantlepiece, a holly and ivy garland was threaded with red ribbon. Sprigs of holly poked out of the picture frames on the walls. The fluffy spruce tree in the corner boasted baubles and trinkets.

"Are you warm enough? Let me sort the fire–"

"Henry," she breathed, her eyes misted with tears. She indicated the decorations about the room. "What... what is all this?"

Delight lit up his face and he tilted his head as he walked towards her. "Addy, today is Christmas Eve."

Her brow moved. "It is?" It had been November when she'd been arrested. *A month.* More than a month of her life was lost. "I... I lost track of everything."

He stood before her, those incisive eyes searching her face. "I tried so hard to get to you sooner. I would have pulled that place apart brick by brick, if I could have."

Addy shook her head, her heart aching as she thought of him fighting. Of everything he had given up. "Your father–"

"You were right," he interrupted her, a wry smile touching his lips. "He was furious. He cut me off instantly, especially when I told him the real reason for Isaac framing you."

Her lips parted with a regretful sigh. "It's too much."

His mouth twisted. "It's a choice I was happy to make. It's up to my father whether he chooses to bridge the divide between us. I made it clear that we will never visit him whilst Isaac remains under his roof."

She opened her mouth, and he laid a finger across her lips, silencing her. "Enough, Addy. No more. It's done, and I'm all the happier for it. You are all I've ever wanted, and when I think about what Charlotte did, packing your things and hiding the jewellery in there. I suspect she got that idea from my despicable step-brother."

His hands settled around her waist to gently tug her closer. "We will be fine because we are together. I will find a job. I already have people I can go to. I have a wealth of experience, and I have the shipping contacts for the business," he smoothed the pads of his thumbs over her puckered brows. "I don't want you to worry. I will work so hard to give you the best life I can."

She drifted along on his words, buoyed by the dreams that flitted through her mind. Dare she begin to hope that he was here to offer everything she could want?

"I have some savings to tide us over. We won't live like kings, of course. But we can live a modest life."

He framed her face between his hands, fanning his thumbs over her cheeks, then the edge of her mouth that turned her insides molten. Her stomach did a slow roll when his gaze settled on her mouth.

"I love you, Adelaide Hill."

"Oh, Henry," his name broke from her lips. "I love you, too. So very much."

He shook when she stood on tiptoe to kiss him again.

"I want you to be my wife, Addy. I want to share everything with you – the good and the bad. I want to hold you until I'm too old to stand. I want to love you until I draw my last breath," he leaned down and touched his lips to the side of her mouth. To the other side. "Marry me, Addy. Be mine."

Her breath shuddered out as her eyes drifted closed. Her answer slid out on a sigh of acquiescence. It was the easiest yes to her, because she'd always been his.

His lips explored along her jaw. Her eyelids. And once more, he claimed her mouth as his.

Somewhere beyond the cocoon of the sitting room, a clock struck midnight.

Henry drew back, his eyes blazing with a passion that matched hers in intensity. "Merry Christmas, my love."

"Merry Christmas, Henry."

EPILOGUE

"And the sea raged, tossing the ship about in the inky black waves," Henry sat cross-legged on the floor, the book propped open on his knees. He cupped his hands around his mouth, deepening his voice. "*'Hold fast, lads!'* Captain West yelled, *'the storm will not best us tonight!'*"

Sitting across from him, the raven-haired little girl with eyes as green as the summer meadow was held enraptured by her father. Addy watched from the doorway, her heart swelling with love for them both. She stepped into the room, a smile playing about her mouth.

"Maggie, please tell me Papa isn't reading your new book. You only had that this morning."

"You told me I had to sit still until our guest arrives, Mama," Maggie explained reasonably, making Addy shake her head wryly.

"You're right, I did."

"It's my fault," Henry unfolded his long frame, standing stiffly. "I'm getting too old to sit like that," he grimaced as he hobbled, and Addy's smile rolled into laughter.

Behind them, a throat cleared. Charlie, once a footman at Longhaven, now wearing the livery of a butler, announced, "Pardon me. Mr Scorby is here."

Addy exchanged a quiet look with her husband, though they didn't have time for any further conversation as Maggie squealed and erupted from the room.

"Grandpapa!"

Addy turned into the hallway to see Reginald catch Maggie mid-leap. His face was wreathed in smiles as he spun her. "There's my favourite girl in the whole world. Merry Christmas, my darling!"

"Merry Christmas, Pop-pop," Maggie hugged him back tightly.

Henry silently slipped a hand into hers and squeezed, bumping his shoulder to hers. Addy was still wary of the man standing in the unadorned hallway of their house, but somehow, in the last four years, they'd reached a sort of truce.

It was largely down to the little girl currently enthusing ecstatically about her new book. Reginald had been smitten with her from the moment he'd looked upon her angelic face. With her wild black curls and sable lashes, Margaret Prudence Scorby looked very much like her namesake. The little girl's presence had been a balm to the old wounds.

"Aren't you meant to wait until bedtime for a story?" Reginald asked her.

Maggie wrinkled her nose, confident in her reply. "That's what Mama said."

"But your father read it to you anyway," Reginald's dark eyes gleamed in mirth at his son as he set Maggie on her feet. "I shall have to have a word with him, won't I?"

"No arguing," Maggie told him succinctly. "You both promised me. Come on, Mrs Thomas has made your favourite – plum pudding and brandy sauce. I tasted the sauce, though. I didn't like it," she explained as she led a compliant Reginald past her parents and down the hall to the dining room.

Reginald grinned as he passed them by. "Then that means Mrs Thomas followed my advice on the amount of brandy she uses in her sauce." Their voices faded away as the dining room closed on them.

Addy exhaled shakily.

Henry caught her hands, his earnest gaze searching her face. "Are you alright? I can tell him you're unwell if you'd prefer. I know that you're not the most comfortable when he's here."

"No. Besides, Maggie loves it when he's here."

Henry wagged a finger at her, mimicking their daughter, "No arguing."

Addy laughed softly. "As long as neither of you brings up anything to do with work, I think you'll do fine."

Reginald didn't care for Henry's firm embracing the vision of faster, more modern ships to cross the Atlantic. Perhaps it was because his son was blazing a new path ahead of the Scorby company, or because Henry had turned down his father's demand that he return to the family business. Not even the news that Isaac had been caught embezzling funds was enough to coax Henry back.

Henry put his fingers to his lips and made a motion like a key turning in a lock. "Not a word."

Addy smiled up at her husband. "It's easier now

that I know Vanessa is definitely out of his life, though why he won't divorce her, I don't know."

"He is still old-fashioned. He made a promise. Installing his wife into a place in London and making sure she has an income is as good as a divorce in my father's eyes."

"Even though they seem to despise each other," Addy said.

"Dinner is ready, madam," Charlie said from down the hallway.

"Thank you, Charlie," Henry called. "We'll be along shortly."

Hiring a man they trusted to manage their modest home had been an easy choice in Addy's eyes.

Early married life had been a whirlwind of challenges, though as newlyweds, they had scarcely noticed the strain. A determined Henry had taken his contacts and knocked on countless doors, eventually deciding to take matters into his own hands by founding his own small shipping company. Addy, resilient as ever, worked tirelessly, cleaning houses and taking in washing to help make ends meet.

Their efforts, combined with the money bequeathed to her by Mrs Glover, paid off when they purchased a modest townhouse in Chester just after their second wedding anniversary. Tucked along a row of similar homes occupied by other working families, the house was simple but welcoming. Inside, the small rooms were practical.

Their lives felt truly complete when Addy discovered she was pregnant. It was shortly after their momentous news that a letter arrived from Reginald, asking to meet with them both. Henry had been steadfast at her side, defending her fiercely during that reunion, his loyalty to her unwavering.

And they'd been slowly tiptoeing around each other ever since.

Later that day, with their bellies full and Maggie occupied by the new dolly that Reginald had given her to unwrap, they sat in the parlour on the sofas. The crackling fire cast a warm glow around the room.

Addy was staring into the fire. The news of Charlotte's imprisonment—alongside Betty, who had been implicated in the poisoning of Charlotte's new husband—had stirred complicated feelings in Addy.

"They're not worth your thoughts, my angel," Henry said quietly, his touch drawing her gaze from the dancing flames.

Addy inhaled sharply, shaking her head slightly to shake off the melancholy. "Sorry. I can't help it, though."

"What's this?" Reginald asked.

Henry's sigh carried more than a hint of frustration. "My wife is too soft for her own good."

Reginald nodded with understanding. He checked that Maggie was still occupied and sat forward. "Henry is right, Adelaide. Neither Charlotte nor Betty deserves your compassion."

Addy's smile was sad. "I know that you're right, but those places are so dreadful, especially at this time of year. Their first Christmas in a prison cell. It's hard not to feel sorry for them, no matter their crimes."

Henry patted her hand as Reginald said, "They've been found guilty. There was never any proof over Mrs Glover, but the evidence was solid when it came to what they did to that poor man. From securing enough rat poison to fell an elephant, to putting it in a figgy pie. All to get their grubby hands on his money," Reginald's face darkened. "That could have been my son, Addy. I wouldn't spare them not even a single second of your time."

Addy looked to Henry. He nodded in agreement.

Reginald waved a hand. "Enough of this talk. It's Christmas day. Let's not ruin it with dark thoughts."

"For once, I agree with my father," Henry said, squeezing her hand.

"Ha!" Reginald clapped. "Then it truly is a magical day."

Laughter rolled around the room. Addy watched the two men, adversaries for such a long time, exchange a look of affection. Somehow, they seemed to be finding common ground. They clashed over several issues, but there was a foundation of mutual respect that was growing between them. She liked to believe that Margaret was watching them both in approval.

She wondered what the future might hold when she felt it. Her hand went to her stomach with a small gasp. It was there again, a fluttering deep within.

Just as it had done with Maggie.

She caught Henry's eyes, and they shared a look. Of gratitude. Of hope as they continued to build a life on their terms.

Speculation shone in Reginald's eyes. "Are you quite alright?"

Henry questioned his wife with just a look, and she nodded. "Well, Father, we have some news…"

Addy watched the delight spread on her father-in-law's face. Another grandchild for him to love unconditionally. Her hand rested on the slight swelling of her belly as they started to debate whether or not the time was right for them all to move back to Longhaven. Addy interrupted them both, asking for ideas for suitable names. It worked, and the debate swung in a different direction.

Tomorrow, Addy would write to Janey to tell her about the news of the new arrival expected next summer.

The past, with all its heartache and trials, had led them to this moment. A quiet family Christmas filled with love, laughter and the promise of new beginnings.

ALSO BY ANNIE SHIELDS

The Dockyard Darling

In the haunting aftermath of her father's sudden death, Ella Tomlinson finds herself at the mercy of her cruel stepmother, Clara. Left destitute, Clara devises a sinister plan to regain her fortune by marrying the very doctor who tended to Ella's late father. As Ella uncovers Clara's dark secret, unsettling questions about her father's demise surface.

Desperate to escape a forced marriage, Ella seeks refuge with her estranged uncle in his lively tavern, hidden in the heart of London's bustling Docklands. Here, she is plunged into a dangerous world filled with sailors, boatmen, and shadowy traders.

Ghosts of the Mill

As Hawks Mill teeters on the brink of collapse, Lena Pemberton stands at the helm of a revolution, challenging every norm Victorian society has set.

Alone, she must navigate the treacherous waters where others believe a woman has no place at the helm. Her only hope lies with the millworkers, who urge her to seek the aid of an enigmatic engineer, Henry Wickham. He is a man of guarded emotions and a mysterious past. Lena needs his expertise to rescue the struggling mill, but Henry has encountered her kind before - profit first, safety last.

The Queen of Thieves

Abandoned by their family, sisters Trixie & Lily White were starving & destitute. Until Stella came looking for their errant older sister, and took both children as payment for her debt.

They joined a gang of girls who made their living for Stella by stealing, pickpocketing & thieving whatever they could. But Trixie was good at it, better than all the rest. She soon became known for her ability to dupe people and crack open even the most complicated safe.

Felix Huxley was the best diamond dealer in the business despite being raised an orphan. When Felix arrived in London with a horde of stones, Trixie is sent to break open the safe.

She doesn't expect to fall in love with the enigmatic man.

How can she take from the only man who might just love her in spite of her past? When Stella realises that Trixie is about to let the stones go, she takes desperate measures.

Will Trixie choose the man she loves, or try to save her little sister?

ABOUT THE AUTHOR

Annie Shields lives in Shropshire with her husband and two daughters.

When she doesn't have her nose in a book, you'll find her exploring old buildings and following historical trails, dragging her ever-patient husband along with his trusty map.

If you would like to be amongst the first to hear when she releases a new book and free books by similar authors, you can join her mailing list HERE

As a thank you for joining, you will receive a **FREE** copy of her eBook The Barefoot Workhouse Orphan

It is the prequel to the book In the Shadows of the Workhouse, where we meet William Finnegan and Connie for the first time.

Your details won't be passed along to anyone else and you can unsubscribe at any time.

The book is yours to keep.

Printed in Great Britain
by Amazon